SBA

SHERBORNE LIBRARY

Tel: 01935 812683   10 MAR 2002

21. DEC. 2001   04. APR 2002
26. APR 2002

09. JUL 2002
09. JUL 2002

31. DEC 2001   20. MAY 2002   23. JUL 2002
18. JAN 2002

28. MAY 2002

05. AUG. 2002
12. AUG 2002

02. FEB 2002   11. JUN. 2002   05. SEP 2002
04. MAR 2002   27. JUN. 2002   12. SEP 2002
19. SEP 2002

DORSET COUNTY COUNCIL

- Stock must be returned on or before closing time on the last date stamped above.
- Charges are levied on overdue stock.
- Renewals are often possible, please contact your library.
- Stock can be returned to any Dorset County Library.

PLEASE LOOK AFTE
RETURN ON TIME T

Dorset County Library HQ, Co
Dorchester, Dorset DT1 1XJ
DL/M/2372

GW00505090

Withdrawn Stock
Dorset County Council

DORSET COUNTY LIBRARY

203862839 +

THE BLACKBIRD'S SONG

THE BLACKBIRD'S SONG

Nicola Thorne

Dorset County Library	
203862839 ✝	severn House
Askews	
	£17.99

This first world edition published in Great Britain 2001 by
SEVERN HOUSE PUBLISHERS LTD of
9-15 High Street, Sutton, Surrey SM1 1DF.
This first world edition published in the USA 2002 by
SEVERN HOUSE PUBLISHERS INC of
595 Madison Avenue, New York, N.Y. 10022.

Copyright © 2001 by Nicola Thorne.

All rights reserved.
The moral right of the author has been asserted.

British Library Cataloguing in Publication Data

Thorne,   Nicola
   The blackbird's song
   1. Women journalists – England – London – Fiction
   2. London (England) – Social life and customs – 20th century – Fiction
   I.   Title
   823. 9'14 [F]

ISBN 0-7278-5777-0

Except where actual historical events and characters are being
described for the storyline of this novel, all situations in this
publication are fictitious and any resemblance to living persons
is purely coincidental.

Typeset by Hewer Text Ltd.,
Edinburgh, Scotland.
Printed and bound in Great Britain by
MPG Books Ltd., Bodmin, Cornwall.

One

From her perch on Blackfriars Bridge, high above the brown swirling waters of the river, Peg Hallam gazed at the barge passing underneath. Suddenly one of the crew members standing by the tiller looked up and smiled at her, raising his hand in greeting. Impulsively she waved back.

Rather wistfully she followed the progress of the barge as it moved towards Tower Bridge, the crew member looking back at her, smiling and waving until the barge passed out of sight.

Peg wrapped her coat tightly about her against the keen wind blowing upriver and thought of faraway places, even though the barge's destination would only be to Tilbury. From there, however, the great ocean-going liners sailed, and maybe one day she would be on one of them.

Peg was a dreamer with a wanderlust which coming to London had only partly fulfilled. The wind stung her face and, as the hour of two boomed from the clock on one of the great towers of St Paul's Cathedral, she turned away and hurried back to her office tucked away in a narrow alleyway that ran towards the river from Fleet Street.

Every day during her lunch hour Peg went to the river, sometimes walking along Lower Thames Street towards the Tower, exploring the narrow lanes and byways of that great city which she now called home.

And yet it was a far cry from home, the little village near the

1

Dorset town of Sherborne where she had been raised, the daughter of a butcher who had died soon after she was born. Her mother had married again and the family had moved to Sherborne, where her stepfather was head gardener to Lord Ryland.

Hers had been a largely contented, almost privileged childhood, until the war came when she was eleven. Then the family seemed to fragment: her stepfather was called up, her elder sister Verity took a job as a nurse in London and her middle sister Addie had a baby by a man to whom she wasn't married, a scandal that had been hushed up.

Always imaginative, a writer of short stories, Peg had noted everything down or stored the events in the back of her mind for use as material in the future.

Mother had wanted her to be a teacher, as Addie had now become. To Mother teaching was the height of respectability, but Peg longed for the lights of the big city, the freedom this would bring, and the smell of newsprint, which she hoped would turn her into a journalist.

Peg climbed the dark narrow stairs towards her office on the first floor of an old building which had a noisy press clattering away on the ground floor. At first after the quiet of the country she had thought she would never get used to the racket the heavy machines caused, but somehow she had. The noise, the bustle in the streets outside, the smell of oil from the press and of the spices coming from the warehouses ranged alongside the river were all very exciting. She loved to wander through the London streets and often she walked half the way home to Hampstead, where she shared a flat with Verity. Then things quietened down, because Verity kept a very strict eye on her pretty younger sister. In many ways it was like being a child in Mother's care all over again.

Peg looked guiltily across at her boss, who sat at his desk correcting copy, his eyes shaded from the bright light over his desk. This was her third month working for the news agency, which gathered information from all parts of England to be sent all over the world. From nine in the morning until five thirty in the late afternoon it was Peg's job to type the copy, which went down to the press to be set or was telegraphed to overseas agencies from America to China.

Reg Overbridge was a choleric, red-faced ex-Fleet Street hack of fifty or so who had started the news agency because he found it almost impossible to keep down a job owing to the amount of liquor he ingested in the course of a day. He had a deputy, Alan, who took over when Reg was otherwise indisposed – which was quite often – or failed to return from a liquid lunch, which happened even more frequently. But today Reg was at his desk, his habitual scowl on his face, a stale, stained cigarette clamped between his lips, cursing at the inaccuracy of the copy on the proof he held in his hand.

'You're late,' he growled at Peg without looking up, as she slid into her place at her desk.

'I only went out at quarter past one, Mr Overbridge,' Peg said glancing at the clock on the wall. 'You wanted me to finish what I was doing.'

'Don't answer back,' Reg snapped. 'There are plenty more where you came from.'

It was true. Having at last reached the proximity of Fleet Street, Peg dreaded losing her job. She blushed and looked angrily at Alan, who smiled at her sympathetically and pointed knowingly at the clock. Any minute Reg would exit, probably for the rest of the day, and the atmosphere in the office would immediately improve.

Apart from Reg and Alan there was another typist called Mabel, who only worked part time as she had a family, and Arthur, who came in twice weekly to do the accounts. It was a small office with two tall, always grimy windows looking out on to the narrow street, and Peg imagined it would be breathlessly hot in summertime.

A flight of wooden steps led up from the ground floor and just outside the door was a lavatory that didn't always flush, with a stained, cracked washbasin, a very dirty hand towel that was seldom changed and a cupboard where the occasional cleaner kept her materials.

It was not the glamorous sort of environment that Peg had envisaged when she had first planned her career in Fleet Street, that Mecca of aspiring journalists; but it had been a start. After secretarial college she had worked in a bank and then for a trading company until she answered the ad for the agency. She planned to spend the minimum amount of time there in order to gain experience before she looked around, hopefully for an opening on a real newspaper.

After Peg began assiduously typing the scrawled copy Reg had placed beside her typewriter she saw him yawn, sit back, scratch his chest and stretch his arms.

'Time for a bite, I think,' he said. 'Take over, Alan.' He got up, shrugged on his jacket, took his hat from a filing cabinet by the side of his desk and left without another word.

Peg immediately stopped typing. Alan raised his arms above his head and carefully cracked his fingers.

'One day I hope he goes out and doesn't come back,' Alan said. 'I hope he gets run over by a bus.'

'Oh, don't say *that*,' Peg protested.

'Seriously, I do.'

'Why don't you get another job if you dislike him so much?'

'Don't you think I'm trying?' Alan angrily snatched up the paper on his desk and pointed a finger at a column of advertisements, some heavily scored with a pencil. 'For every vacancy there are ten applicants, twenty or more in some cases. Many men coming back from the war have been unable to find work.'

'I know.' Peg bit her lip, thinking of all the ex-army men in the street pathetically trying to sell boxes of shoelaces or matches. Some were blind and many were crippled. All looked undernourished. 'EX-SOLDIER BLINDED IN THE WAR' was a familiar legend fastened to trays held by these unfortunates. It seemed a scandal that these heroes of the war whom the country

4

had promised to look after should have become victims of an uncaring society.

Alan was too young to have been in the war. He was twenty-two, two years older than Peg and as ambitious as she was. This too for him was just a stepping stone to a national newspaper. He came from the north of England, where he had worked on a provincial paper as a reporter. He had good shorthand and typing but he had little chance to deploy his journalistic skills as all the copy came in either by wire, messenger or post. He followed up on routine crime stories and spent a lot of time watching bodies being fished out of the Thames.

He was rather unprepossessing: a thin, tall, untidy young man with lank hair who cared little about his appearance. Peg knew that he liked a drink too – not yet as much as Reg, though she thought that in time this would come. He lived alone in lodgings on the Clerkenwell Road and his hobby was attending political meetings. He was an ardent socialist.

It was impossible not to like Alan, despite his lack of good looks. He was good-natured and kind, unfailingly polite and helpful, almost like a brother. He brooded continuously on his dislike of and contempt for Reg, on the poor wages he paid and the long hours of work he extracted. Alan would mutter darkly about trade unions and the inevitability of socialism overthrowing the government, currently led by Baldwin and the Conservatives. He offered to take Peg to meetings, but she always said she had to get home. She didn't think Verity would approve of Alan and his far-left views, his lack of personal appeal or his dishevelled appearance. His shirt collars were usually a little frayed, his suits slightly shabby and most of his ties had seen far better days.

He was not poor. He was an idealist, and ideals were what mattered. Peg had never known anyone remotely like him and she rather admired him.

Peg always proffered the excuse that she looked after her sister, who was a busy nurse at the Royal Free Hospital. This was only partly true: in many ways it was Verity who looked after Peg, cooking the evening meal if she was at home and making sure she went early to bed.

Peg admired her sister but she was also in awe of her. Verity had always been an example to her younger siblings, perhaps because they had not grown up together, and there had been an intangible, slightly intimidating quality about Verity, who had dispensed advice on her rare visits home. Verity had been adopted as a child by an aunt and uncle because her mother had not been able to look after all her children after the death of her husband. Peg had been a baby and had stayed at home with her sister Addie until their mother remarried. She had quickly had two more children, Stella and Edgar, always known as Ed.

Verity had nursed in the war and had a tragic romance with a doctor who jilted her on the eve of their wedding. This had inspired a short story which Peg had never dared show to anyone, certainly not Verity, who had persuaded their mother to let Peg come to London and share a flat with her while she trained as a stenographer.

At that time both were studying: Peg at a secretarial college and Verity in midwifery at the Royal Free Hospital on the Gray's Inn Road.

In the course of the afternoon Peg and Alan worked assiduously at their desks and, as expected, Reg did not return from lunch. Alan was quite used to locking up, and at five thirty he glanced at the clock.

'Time to go,' he said, looking across at Peg, who finished what she was doing and then covered her typewriter. She rose, got her hat and coat from a stand by the door, and was fixing her hat with the help of a wall mirror when she saw Alan peering at her.

'Are you walking home tonight?'

'Probably.' Peg turned. 'Part way. Why?'

'I can walk with you. I'm going to a meeting at Conway Hall in Red Lion Square. You wouldn't like to come with me, would you?'

6

'I'm afraid I can't.' Peg put her hat squarely on her head. 'My sister . . .'

'It seems to me you're dominated by your sister,' Alan said as he stood aside to let her pass before putting out the light and locking the door behind him.

'That's a very unfair thing to say.' Indignantly Peg turned to face him on the narrow landing. 'It's just that she's a very busy nursing sister and—'

'I know you have to cook for her. It doesn't sound very liberated to me. You need to break out from the ties that bind you.'

'Oh, do I?' Peg stamped her foot. 'Well, thank you very much. I can find my own way back.' She sped down the stairs, aware that Alan's steps were close behind her. Once outside she turned towards Fleet Street, but had to stop in order to cross the busy road, by which time he had caught up with her.

'Sorry,' he said humbly, touching her elbow.

'I should think so. My sister is a very good, very noble person. She served all during the war in a hospital theatre where she saw the most appalling sights.'

'I realise that. I'm sorry I spoke as I did. But you must have a life of your own.'

'I do.'

'You never seem to go out.'

'How do you know?'

They crossed the road and walked towards Ludgate Circus where Peg decided she would forgo her stroll and get on a bus.

'You never talk about it.'

'I don't have to tell you what I do.'

'I know. I've been clumsy.' Alan stopped and Peg stopped too. His expression was contrite, his pale face lit by a shy smile. 'I didn't mean to offend you. I just thought as you're such an intelligent girl – I mean young lady – you might enjoy attending a lecture on politics, especially as we hope to bring to power a Labour government.'

'My sister says that's impossible.' Peg looked shocked.

'No, it *is* possible. Ramsay Macdonald, the new Labour leader, is a fine man. There is so much unrest in the country and abroad. You mustn't listen to what your sister says *all* the time, you know. You should have a mind of your own.'

'I don't . . . and I do. I do have a mind of my own.' Peg looked out anxiously for a bus. 'You're starting to be unpleasant again, Alan. Anyway, I can't come tonight, even if I wanted to, which I don't.' She looked at his earnest face and seemed to relent. 'But another night, maybe. Look, I'll ask my sister.' And she jumped on the bus, which sped up the road.

Once on the bus Peg turned and caught a glimpse of Alan looking dejectedly after her. Maybe she'd been too harsh on him. He wasn't bad really, and he *was* an idealist. Some of his ideas seemed to be unrealistic, but then she knew she was very ignorant about politics, as she was about most things. She was a country girl. Maybe Alan could teach her something.

Verity, masked and gowned, stood beside the doctor, watching his skilful manipulation of the forceps as he probed inside the woman's body, trying as gently as he could to extract the baby that was reluctant to leave her womb. It had been a long and protracted labour and, occasionally, the doctor turned his forehead towards her, and she would gently wipe away the perspiration. The semi-conscious mother was watched anxiously by two nurses standing by her head.

Dr Beaumaurice was the senior registrar and a skilled obstetrician. If she was in charge of the labour ward, during an emergency, Verity always sent for him, rather than the consultant. Dr Beaumarice was not going to fail her.

Very gently and carefully he finally succeeded in drawing the baby's head out of the mother's body with his giant forceps. Verity simultaneously leaned forward to assist by grasping the baby's shoulders.

'Gently, sister,' he murmured, 'not too fast.'

He put aside his forceps and, his hands still around the baby's head, continued to ease it away until, finally, it lay between its mother's legs. For a moment Verity thought they had been too late. Mother and child were exhausted. A nurse came forward with a towel. Dr Beaumaurice took the baby and, holding it upside down, administered a sharp tap to its buttocks. For an agonising moment it hung there and then it uttered a lusty cry. Verity felt the tears spring to her eyes as they invariably did at moments like this. However long you worked in the maternity unit, the miracle of birth never ceased to move and amaze.

Later, as usual, she and Dr Beaumaurice enjoyed a cup of tea in Sister's office, while the doctor wrote up the case.

'Another cup, doctor?' Verity enquired solicitously and the doctor looked up and smiled.

'Have you ever known me say "no", sister?'

Verity smiled back and turned to the teapot, relishing the intimacy of their shared moments together. They were close; they shared a rapport and were both very good at their jobs. Verity had been deputy sister in charge of the maternity ward since completing her midwifery course the previous year. The current incumbent, Sister Atkinson, was near retirement, never in very good health, and Verity hoped she might succeed her. She loved her work and she loved the Royal Free, among whose former distinguished students had been Elizabeth Garrett Anderson, one of the first female doctors, a pioneer who had undergone many vicissitudes and much male prejudice in order to succeed.

This was a very happy time in Verity's life. She felt fulfilled, and memories of her failed romance scarcely ever troubled her. She enjoyed living with her young sister, watching her blossom into a beautiful, talented young woman, knowing that she was dedicated to her profession in the same way that she, Verity, was to hers.

In many ways they were branches of the same tree, their mother a shining example to them, as to the whole family, of perseverance and fortitude.

Dr Beaumaurice finished making his notes, sat back and folded his arms.

'My wife and I wondered if you'd like to come to tea? She would very much enjoy meeting you.'

Verity was conscious of a sudden surge of blood to her cheeks.

'Why . . . how *very*, very kind. I would like nothing better.'

'I'll ask my wife to write to you,' Dr Beaumaurice said, getting up. 'Now I think it's time for our rounds, Sister Carter-Barnes.'

There was a certain formality between them, in itself a source of fascination and almost, though she did not realise it, titillation.

Dr Philip Beaumaurice was about thirty-seven, tall, dark-haired and good-looking. He already had the air of gravitas required of a senior medical practitioner. Verity felt the sort of veneration for him that she had towards some doctors she had worked with in the past. It wasn't love or physical attraction, most certainly not, she was sure of that, but a feeling more of respect and admiration for their skills.

Verity was devoted to medicine, to her work as a ward sister, a midwife.

That evening she got off the bus that took her to the top of Haverstock Hill and walked the few hundred yards to the large old Victorian house that had been divided into flats, one of which she shared with Peg. A light was on in the top room and with an air of pleasant anticipation she let herself in and went through the hall and up the stairs to their flat on the top floor. As soon as she put the key in the lock the door flew open and Peg stood there to greet her.

'I was getting worried,' she cried solicitously, taking her sister's coat and bag.

'We had a late delivery. Dr Beaumaurice—' Verity began.

Peg interrupted her excitedly, waving a letter in her sister's face.

'Such good news, Ver. I'm to be bridesmaid to Addie and

Harold; *chief* bridesmaid,' she said breathlessly. 'The others are Stella and Jenny. Ed is to read the lesson. It's to be in August—'

'Steady on.' Verity smiled at her excited sister and looked anxiously towards the kitchen. 'Can I smell burning?'

'Oh, *dear*.' Peg flew to the oven door, opened it and extracted a pie with a very brown crust which she looked at with dismay.

'I like it well done,' Verity said loyally. 'It's wonderful news about the wedding. They've had quite a long engagement.'

'That's because Harold's hopes for a headship last year were postponed. Now it's confirmed and the date is set.'

Peg put the pie carefully on the table by the window, put the vegetables into dishes and brought them over.

'Hot,' she said.

'I've some good news, too,' Verity flushed. 'Dr Beaumaurice has invited me to tea.' She sighed as she sat down. 'I like him *so* much.'

'Oh?' Peg looked at her archly.

'He's married, of course,' Verity said quickly.

'Oh!' Peg's intonation this time was different.

'Don't misunderstand me.' Verity looked at her sternly. 'I always *knew* he was married. I like him professionally, nothing more. I admire him, and I'm very much looking forward to meeting his wife.'

'Has he children?'

'Two, I think.' Verity's expression was vague as Peg helped her to pie and vegetables. 'I don't know much about his private life. It's something we never discuss, but I consider it an honour to be invited to his home.'

'*I* have an invitation, too,' Peg said, glancing at her sister.

'Really? Excellent pie.' Verity looked up approvingly. 'You are quite an accomplished cook, Peg. Much better than me. What is your invitation – or rather, who is it from?'

'Alan at work. You know, the man in my office? I've mentioned him. He wants me to go to a political meeting with him. I keep on turning him down, but I do like him – though not in any

11

special way,' she added quickly. 'I mean, I don't find him the least bit attractive, but he *is* interesting. He's a socialist.'

'Well, I hope he doesn't influence you with his socialist views.' Verity pursed her lips disapprovingly. 'Also, I don't altogether think it a good idea to go with him alone to one of these affairs. He might get the wrong idea. Is there no female friend you could ask to go with you?'

'Oh *Ver*,' Peg cried, sitting back, 'don't be so old-fashioned. Nothing's going to *happen*. Alan's not a bit handsome; but I *do* like him and I don't want to hurt him. Besides, he may be leaving soon.'

'Oh?'

'Yes. He applied for a job on a newspaper. I shall miss him if he goes, I shall just have that awful Reg. Alan isn't a bit like *him*.'

'Well . . . you're not yet twenty-one, and Mum did ask me to look after you. I hope he'll see you home.'

'I'm sure he'll put me on the bus.'

'It's not quite the same.' Verity paused. 'How old is he?'

'Twenty-two. As I say, he is *not* good-looking, he does *not* dress well and he *is* a socialist. Now you know all about him there is to know.'

'Well, I don't know why you want to go out with him in that case. Men usually don't ask young women out for no reason, especially pretty girls like you.'

'Alan doesn't *see* me as a girl, I'm sure. He's only interested in politics. I think he wants to convert me to the cause.' Peg giggled. 'Of course I shan't be converted. Don't worry about that. But I would like to know more about politics. He thinks Mr Macdonald may be the next prime minister.'

Verity snorted. 'Well, then, he doesn't know much if he thinks that. This country will never, ever have a Labour government. English people are much too sensible.'

The speaker, though calling himself a socialist, didn't consider that Ramsay Macdonald was nearly radical enough. He was really, it seemed, part of the establishment. Instead the speaker enthused about the Soviet Union and the wonderful things that were happening there under Comrade Lenin, the benefits brought to the country by the revolution. In Russia all people were truly equal, whereas in England there was an enormous barrier of class, of haves and have-nots. The war had done nothing to change this; the only difference was that, because of the universal discontent in the aftermath of war, there was more hope now of world revolution on the Soviet scale.

The speaker had been twice to the Soviet Union, which he considered a real socialist country ruled by the people for the people. He spoke for an hour and his audience grew restless towards the end. Was there nothing good to be said about the great strides the English Labour Party had made since the war?

Alan was the first to jump up when at last the lecturer sat down and pointed to the good things that could be expected in England from a Labour administration. He thought communism was totalitarian and gave as an example hardships suffered by the peasants in the terrible Russian winters. The speaker didn't agree. At least they had got rid of the aristocrats; the ruling classes had been sent packing. The two men got into a fierce argument that was interrupted by the chairman asking Alan to sit down and make way for another question. 'We must all have our turn,' he said politely and waved at a woman who had her hand raised.

Alan, red-faced, scowled at Peg who was both amused and impressed by his outburst. She felt rather proud of him and as the crowd streamed out of the hall at the meeting's end she tucked her arm through his.

'I think you did *very* well.'

'I'd like to knock his block off,' Alan said savagely.

'I thought you were going to.' Peg smiled and they stood outside, huddled against the biting March wind. 'Well, thank you very much,' Peg began. 'I did enjoy it. I really did. I learned a lot.'

'I thought you would. You'll be able to tell your sister—'

'Oh, my sister would *never* agree with socialism. We're country people, you know, and country people are utterly conventional.'

'You're not conventional.' Alan turned and looked at her, his eyes smarting from the cold. 'Shall we try to get a cup of tea? It's only eight o'clock.'

'I'd like that,' Peg said. 'Though I promised Verity—'

'You wouldn't be late home,' Alan finished for her. 'I'd like to meet this sister of yours. She sounds formidable.'

'She is. At one time I didn't think she'd like you, but now I think she might.'

They made their way along Southampton Row towards Russell Square looking for a cafe.

'I expect you're hungry?' Alan said.

'Yes. Verity will probably have supper waiting for me. A cup of tea, though, would be nice.'

They walked almost as far as Euston station before finding a cafe, its windows clouded with condensation. Inside was a party of workmen, who probably worked at the station, attacking plates of food.

'Sure you won't have anything to eat?'

'Sure.' Peg smiled at Alan and looked about her with interest. Apart from the noisy group of workmen, an elderly man with a dejected looking dog at his feet sat at one of the tables gloomily reading a newspaper, and in a corner a lone, well-dressed woman sat staring in front of her, her tea untouched. What sad memories was she harbouring? Peg wondered. She raised her eyes, as if aware that Peg was looking at her, but there was no spark of light in them. Dead.

Peg shivered for no reason. Who, after all, knew what fate lay in store for them?

She smiled gratefully at Alan as he brought over a tray on which were two cups of tea and a packet of biscuits.

Peg sipped at the hot tea. 'Well, thanks for the evening. I

enjoyed it. I thought you were very good. Did you ever think of going into politics?'

'Not yet.' Alan pushed his lank hair back from his face, which was unusually flushed, and sipped his tea. 'But I do have something to tell you.'

'Oh?'

'I got the job on the paper. I had a letter this morning. I start the first of April.'

'Oh!' Peg's initial reaction was one of dismay. 'I'm terribly pleased for you, Alan, but I shall miss you.'

Alan's expression was mysterious.

'Maybe not for long. Once I'm installed I'll see if there is anything for you. They're sure to need stenographers and secretaries. They have a pool.'

'But I don't want to *be* a secretary,' Peg wailed. 'Don't you see? I want to be a journalist, a reporter like you. You talk about equality, but women don't have the same rights as men, you know they don't. There's no equality there.'

Alan put a hand on her arm and gazed at her earnestly. 'I know they don't, not at the moment. But it will come. When Labour gets in everything will change. Meanwhile on a big paper you have a chance. You have to get your foot in the door first.'

Two

The Beaumaurices lived in a large house in a leafy lane at the top of Highgate Hill. Verity had walked through Waterlow Park with Peg and Alan, to whom she had been introduced a few weeks previously. Verity did, after all, approve of Alan. He was working class, but then so were they. Her father had been a butcher and after his death their mother was so hard up she had been forced to take in washing.

Though Verity had been brought up by a wealthy uncle and aunt, who were clearly middle class, she did not forget or forsake her origins. What mattered to her was the fact that Alan was intelligent, hard-working and kind. No matter that he was a socialist. He was young and that phase would pass. As for the long term, it was clear that Alan had not swept Peg off her feet. He was indeed very plain, even for a man, and that made him comforting to Verity who was sure his main intention towards her sister was not to despoil her virtue but to convert her to socialism. It was political rather than physical.

Verity arrived at the door of the tall red-brick house slightly out of breath after her long walk, during the latter part of which she had hurried in case she was late. She had worn a pair of good stout brown brogues for her walk and her overcoat was done up to her chin, her gabardine hat set squarely on the crown of her head, and in her hand she carried a bag in which was her purse and her indoor shoes.

Verity had never been a beauty but she was a tall, slim, good-looking woman whose facial expression had been sombre and composed from her youth. She had not wanted to be adopted and leave home but had done so out of a sense of duty, and duty had dominated her life ever since. She had brown hair with a slight wave and large, rather melancholy brown eyes but when she smiled her face assumed a radiance that completely transformed her, surprising the onlooker. Her strong features made it difficult to determine her exact age. She was in fact now twenty-nine but she looked older.

Verity paused for a few moments to compose herself and then rang the bell, which in a short while was answered by a maid in a uniform of black dress, white frilly apron and cap.

'Miss Carter-Barnes,' she said politely, and Verity smiled and stepped inside just as Dr Beaumaurice appeared from a room off the hall and came towards her, arms outstretched.

'Sister Carter-Barnes, how nice to see you! I feel I should have offered to collect you in my car.'

'That's perfectly all right, doctor.' Verity took off her coat and handed it to the maid, shaking out her hair as she did the same with her hat. 'I enjoyed the walk. I came with my sister and a young colleague of hers.'

'And what did you do with them?'

'Oh, I left them in the park. They will walk back home. It's such a nice day, for a change.'

It was odd seeing Dr Beaumaurice away from their natural environment – he white-coated, she in uniform, hair tucked out of sight. She felt both awkward and a little foolish standing in her stout brogues when she had taken more care than usual with her appearance. She wore a neat blue belted dress with a white collar and had put on a little lipstick, just the merest trace. Her fine brown hair had been well brushed and she had done her best to banish her rather stern nursing-sister image.

Behind Dr Beaumaurice there now appeared a tall, regal-looking woman who was smiling pleasantly at Verity.

'My dear, may I introduce Miss Carter-Barnes. Miss Carter-Barnes, my wife.'

'How do you do, Mrs Beaumaurice?' Verity shook hands, realising her nerves had made them a little clammy and wishing she had had the sense to change her shoes before she rang the doorbell.

Mrs Beaumaurice looked charming. She was also beautiful and seemed immediately to size up Verity's dilemma over her shoes. She pointed to a door to one side. 'I'm sure you'd like to freshen up after your long walk. Elsie will show you into the drawing room when you're ready.' She had a well modulated voice that went with her warm, gentle smile.

She took her husband's arm and tactfully they turned their backs on Verity while the maid who had been hovering showed her into a small cloakroom with a mirror, toilet and washbasin where Verity changed her shoes, checked her hair and straightened her dress. She then followed the maid to the drawing room, which was large and gracious and overlooked a garden where the trees were already in leaf.

Dr Beaumaurice stood in front of a fire while his wife fussed over a table on which tea had been laid. She looked up as Verity entered.

'I am so happy to meet you at last, Miss Carter-Barnes. Philip talks about you such a lot. He is a great admirer of yours.'

'And I of Dr Beaumaurice,' Verity said, also smiling.

'We're a good team.' The doctor spoke gruffly. 'Miss Carter-Barnes was theatre sister at Charing Cross Hospital throughout the war, Geraldine.'

'Oh!' Mrs Beaumaurice's fine forehead creased momentarily. 'It must have been *dreadful* for you.'

'It's surprising how one got used to it,' Verity said calmly. 'Terrible, but necessary too. We saved many lives, or rather our skilled surgeons did.'

'Philip was also in France.' Mrs Beaumaurice turned to her husband. 'In the thick of it, weren't you, dear?'

Dr Beaumaurice nodded. 'It is a time best forgotten.'

'Oh, I don't think we must forget,' Verity said sharply.

'I don't mean forget the brave men who died and the wounded who survived, but the horror. I'm sure you agree with that, Miss Carter-Barnes? One can't dwell on it.'

'Milk and sugar, Miss Carter-Barnes?' Mrs Beaumaurice's smile was a little forced, as if anxious to bring the conversation to an end.

'Please,' Verity said. 'Just very little sugar.'

Verity took her cup and saucer and placed it on a table by her side. The maid hovered with a plate of sandwiches. Verity selected two. They were filled with tomato and cucumber, were wafer thin and melted in the mouth.

Dr Beaumaurice leaned forward and helped himself, and Mrs Beaumaurice took her tea to the side of the fireplace and sat down opposite Verity. Verity noticed that she ate nothing, perhaps to preserve the lines of her slender figure.

Her appearance was most striking. She wore a grey chiffon tea gown which reached almost to her ankles and an overgarment made of the same material which billowed about her as she walked. A cerise scarf was draped loosely round her throat, its folds falling against her breasts. Her eyes were blue, large and luminous, and her mouth curved so that she appeared to have a slight air of disdain, of remoteness, which may have been unintentional. Her voice was low and melodious. She was detached, elegant, gracious, her most notable feature being her elaborate coiffeur of snow-white hair which was plaited and coiled about her head and fastened to one side with a large ornamental tortoiseshell comb. Yet her skin was that of a young woman, not much over thirty and, belying her demeanour, her manner appeared warm and gracious.

She turned as the door opened and two small girls were led in by a woman who was obviously their nursemaid, wearing a green dress over which was a long starched white apron. Mrs Beaumaurice put her cup down with a small cry of pleasure.

'Darlings,' she cried, rising to greet them. 'Come and say hello to Miss Carter-Barnes, who works with Daddy.'

The children were about six and eight, fair-haired, blue-eyed, their expressions angelic. The elder one wore a pink muslin dress with a white collar and cuffs on her short sleeves; the younger white cotton with a scattering of flowers, a scalloped collar and tiny red bow at her neck. They wore long white socks and black patent leather shoes. They were obviously well brought up and beautifully behaved.

'This is Caroline,' Mrs Beaumaurice said, bringing forward the elder.

'How do you do?' Caroline asked politely.

'How do you do, Caroline?' Verity replied as they gravely shook hands.

'And this is Ruth.'

Ruth was more shy and kept her eyes on the floor.

'And where do you go to school?' Verity asked Caroline.

'At Miss Mossley's, but I am leaving soon to go to a big school.'

'Miss Mossley's is a little private school round the corner. Both girls have done well there, particularly Caroline. Ruth is a little slower.'

Her mother's remark made Ruth blush and she kept her eyes firmly on the floor.

'I'm sure Ruth will catch up,' Verity said kindly, reaching for her hand. 'Won't you, Ruth?'

Ruth appeared unsure and looked appealingly at her mother.

'Time for nursery tea, I think.' Mrs Beaumaurice glanced at the clock on the mantelpiece then towards the nursemaid. 'Miss Carter-Barnes, this is Nanny Brown. We have had her since Caroline was a baby.'

Nanny Brown, who seemed an amiable sort of young woman, gave Verity a brisk smile.

'Off you go now, children.' Mrs Beaumaurice shooed them away. 'Say goodbye to Miss Carter-Barnes.'

'Goodbye, Miss Carter-Barnes,' they chorused dutifully then, each taking one of Nanny's hands, they left the room.

'So lucky.' Mrs Beaumaurice rose to help herself to more tea. 'I don't know what we'd do without Nanny. She's a treasure, isn't she, Philip?' Dr Beaumaurice nodded.

Verity sensed a curious subterranean tension between the two which had become more apparent as the afternoon progressed, as though they were continually at cross purposes. This rather surprised her. To all appearances they had everything: a lovely house, two beautiful children. They were both good looking, attractive people and Dr Beaumaurice was so very clever and destined for rooms in Harley Street in the near future.

Maybe Mrs Beaumaurice, who was obviously an intelligent woman, did not have enough to do? Maybe she was a nag, which would not show in public. She had a nanny, obviously a full complement of servants. For a woman who had worked hard all her life idleness bewildered Verity, even though she knew it was the norm among leisured, middle-class women.

'Do you paint?' she enquired suddenly, observing the number of pictures on the walls of rural scenes, some quite accomplished.

'Oh, you noticed?' Mrs Beaumaurice seemed pleased.

'Geraldine is a *most* gifted artist.' Dr Beaumaurice gazed fixedly at one of the pictures. 'Of a professional standard, we have been told.'

'Do you like to paint, Miss Carter-Barnes?' Mrs Beaumaurice looked across at her guest with interest.

'A little,' Verity acknowledged. 'The uncle I was brought up by was an entomologist and I used to help him draw his specimens. I think I developed a meagre talent,' she finished modestly.

'Oh, but you must show me some of your drawings.' Mrs Beaumaurice suddenly seemed to have come to life. 'Maybe next time you come?'

'No, you must come and have tea with me, and meet my sister Peg. She is not much of an artist but a very accomplished writer. I have read some of her short stories. I suppose I am a little prejudiced, but I found them remarkable.'

'And what does Peg do now?'

Verity leaned forward, thoughtfully joining her hands.

'Peg would like to be a journalist and is working as a steno-grapher for a Fleet Street news agency. She has not yet had a chance to show her talents, however, in that direction. Being a woman in a profession such as journalism is not easy.'

'It seems to me a strange profession for a woman,' Dr Beaumaurice said loftily, helping himself to a small iced cake and examining it carefully as he sat down as if looking for sources of infection.

'Oh, why so, dear?' His wife's tone was a little cutting, as if she already knew the answer. The tension was more apparent now.

'I suppose it seems all right to you?' There was an edge to Dr Beaumaurice's tone as he turned to look meaningfully at Verity. 'My wife is rather radical in her political views,' he said, em-phasising the word 'radical'. 'Besides, her brother owns a news-paper.'

'I would have liked to be a journalist myself.' Mrs Beaumaur-ice's tone bore a trace of bitterness. 'But it was not to be. I will not say I am "radical" in politics, but I welcome the emergence of a working-class party. Philip, needless to say, does not agree with me.'

'Because you are not in the least working class yourself, my dear,' Dr Beaumaurice said silkily. 'You have simply no idea what the words mean. I have never noticed any desire on your part to demonstrate on the streets in favour of the poor and underprivileged.'

Verity grew more and more uncomfortable as husband and wife glared at each other, and said quickly: 'Peg is of the same persuasion. She is friendly with a young man who takes her to socialist meetings.'

'Oh – and don't you mind?' Mrs Beaumaurice seemed sur-prised.

'Not at all. I think variety in politics makes this country richer. Anyway my sister is nearly twenty-one and has a mind of her own, I can assure you.'

22

'But surely you think socialism is dangerous?' Dr Beaumaurice said. 'Look what has happened in Russia.'

'I wouldn't like to get into an argument about politics, Dr Beaumaurice,' Verity responded tactfully. 'I am not interested in the subject, or knowledgeable. I stick to what I do know something about, which is medicine. I am also most interested in painting and the arts.'

At this announcement Dr Beaumaurice suddenly leapt to his feet as if he had been stung by a bee, or had had an audacious idea, like Archimedes in his bath. He thrust out his chin and, standing in front of the fire, put his hands firmly behind his back.

'Miss Carter-Barnes, my wife is looking for a companion to accompany her on a sketching holiday in Italy. I shall be occupied at a medical congress in Verona, but there is no need to stay in that area. I wondered if by any chance you' – he looked across at his wife – 'would you think that a good idea, my dear?'

Mrs Beaumaurice appeared transformed. 'A splendid idea, Philip!' she exclaimed. 'Is it possible you would be able to come, Miss Carter-Barnes? I should be at a loss without Philip.'

'Well –' Verity tried to suppress a sudden surge of excitement. 'If I can get leave I should like nothing better. When would that be?'

'August.'

'Oh!' Verity looked downcast. 'My sister is getting married in August.'

'Oh, she's getting married!' Mrs Beaumaurice perked up again.

'That is another sister. I have three altogether: Peg, Addie and Stella. And one brother, Edgar,' Verity added. 'Addie is the one who is getting married, to a schoolmaster. She teaches too.'

'What date in August?'

'I am not quite sure.'

'My congress is late in August. In fact, I think it finishes in early September.'

'We would so love you to join us,' Mrs Beaumaurice's tone was almost pleading. 'Please do try and fit it in. Oh, and by the way, if your sister is *seriously* interested in journalism I could try and have a word with my brother.'

Mr Oliver Moodie was a tall, handsome man of about thirty-five, prematurely white-haired like his sister, whom Peg had met once when Verity brought her to tea one Sunday after the two elder women had gone walking in the park.

It was the greatest good fortune that Verity's new friend had a brother who was an influential newspaper owner. The *South London Gazette* was read quite far afield, and its premises, though not quite in Fleet Street, bordered on it, so it was only a short distance for her to go round in her lunch hour to Fetter Lane.

First Peg had been interviewed by a formidable woman of indeterminate age who was in charge of the typing pool, and gave her a test which she passed with flying colours. She had then been taken up to another floor and asked to wait in a small room with walls the colour of tobacco, which had a table covered with a brown baize cloth and several chairs stuffed with horsehair. It looked like a rather bleak parlour in a suburban house.

Peg had begun to feel anxious about the time, should Reg return early for some reason or another from his lunch. It was unlikely, but it was always a possibility, and she no longer had accommodating, loyal Alan to cover up for her. He had now joined a national paper as a fully fledged reporter. However, she had not been there long before a woman of about her own age appeared and introduced herself as Mr Moodie's secretary. She had then taken Peg to a door right next to the small room which she opened, announcing: 'Miss Hallam, Mr Moodie,' and gently ushering Peg in.

Mr Moodie had come towards her and, after shaking her hand, led her to a chair in front of his imposing desk. She liked the look of him. He had an open, frank expression and a ready smile. He wore a black pin-striped suit and a pearl-grey tie, and a golden watch chain was strung across his waistcoat. On his little finger was a heavy gold ring.

The room at the top of the building overlooked the Public Record Office and was furnished like a comfortable gentleman's study with polished mahogany desk and bookcases and leather armchairs. The prints on the walls mainly depicted racing scenes, though there was a large portrait of a distinguished-looking elderly man who might possibly have been Mr Moodie's father. Smoke from a cigar rose from the ashtray on Mr Moodie's desk, which was covered with papers and long galley proofs.

'I'm very happy to meet you, Miss Hallam,' he said, occupying the upright chair on the other side of his desk. Then, holding up a sheet of paper, he said: 'Your shorthand and typing speeds are excellent, but I understand you are after a more senior position?'

'I would like to be a journalist,' Peg said firmly, joining her hands tightly in her lap. They felt clammy and she hoped Mr Moodie hadn't noticed. She rubbed them surreptitiously on the sides of her dress. 'It is the only thing I am interested in.'

'But you have had no experience, have you?'

'No,' Peg said. 'None at all.'

'In that case, how do you propose to learn?'

'Through experience. I have a friend, a man who used to work with me, who learned by being sent out on assignments and writing them up. He started with small things and progressed to bigger stories.'

Mr Moodie smiled.

'I like your attitude, Miss Hallam. I like your spirit. By the way –' he paused, glancing again at the sheet of paper on the desk before him – 'how is it that you have a different name from your sister?'

'Verity was adopted and took the name of her adoptive parents, which was Carter. Barnes was our father's name. Mother married twice and we children of the first marriage took the name of my mother's second husband.'

'I see.' Mr Moodie tapped his desk thoughtfully. 'You realise, don't you, that the job of a reporter can be a dangerous one? That's why we are reluctant to send women on news assignments. There are very few women journalists, you know.'

'That's why I would like to be one.' Peg defiantly met his eyes. 'Just because there *are* so few.'

'Your sister sent me some stories you wrote –' Mr Moodie began and Peg, blushing violently, put her hands to her inflamed cheeks.

'Oh dear, I wrote those years ago. I was very young.'

'Nevertheless,' Mr Moodie said, 'they show promise, an interesting writing style. Have you written any more since?'

'A few.' Peg bowed her head, realising that a tough, bold woman journalist wouldn't behave in this schoolgirlish manner.

Mr Moodie got up and sat on the edge of his desk, papers still in his hand, looking kindly down on her.

'I am prepared to offer you a position, Miss Hallam, but in the first instance it must be in the typing pool where I am certain you can hold your own. We have no women reporters here, and I can only say that if and when an opportunity occurs and I think the assignment is a safe one I am prepared to let you go out with a more experienced reporter and see how you deal with it. Can't say fairer than that, can I?'

Peg looked away from those penetrating blue eyes, bit her lips and swallowed.

'Or would you prefer to think about it?' Mr Moodie got to his feet and looked towards the door.

'I'll take a chance,' Peg said, also rising. 'But it mustn't take too long. I'm getting old, you know.'

Mr Moodie smiled gravely and walked her to the door as though to indicate the end of the interview.

'Miss Clark, the head of the typing pool, who conducted your test, will be in touch with you by letter,' he said, pausing on the threshold to shake her hand. 'And I look forward to seeing you again, Miss Hallam. Goodbye.'

*   *   *

Exactly on the dot of five thirty later that day Peg put the cover on her typewriter, got her overcoat and hat and ran downstairs and out of the front door. She looked both ways, but there was no sign of Alan, and she had begun walking towards Fleet Street when she saw him turn the corner. He broke into a run when he saw her.

'How did you get on?' he gasped as he came to a halt.

'I think I got the job. They're going to write to me.' Peg's face fell. 'But only in the typing pool. Mr Moodie says I have to start somewhere.'

'You saw Mr *Moodie* himself?' Alan looked impressed.

Peg nodded.

'You know he's the owner?'

'My sister is friendly with his sister, Mrs Beaumaurice.'

'So you said, but I didn't think the great man would see you himself.'

'Is he such a great man?'

'Of course. He owns the paper.'

'He's quite young. But nice. He was very nice to me.'

'The Moodies are a very rich family,' Alan said gloomily. 'They own a lot of papers and magazines throughout the country. You're very lucky.'

'Don't be jealous, Alan.'

'I'm *not*,' he said, angrily averting his face. 'Of course I'm not.'

But she thought the mood had changed and he hurried along Fleet Street slightly ahead of her. Peg felt upset and quickened her step to catch up with him.

'What's the matter? Aren't you pleased?'

'Of course. It's what you want.'

'You don't show it. I thought you would be.'

'We must hurry or we'll be late,' Alan said, looking at his watch, and he took her arm and propelled her towards Red Lion Square.

The speaker that night was a woman who had been prominent in the suffragette movement. The occasion was the passage of the

Matrimonial Clauses Bill which allowed wives to divorce their husbands for adultery. Previously only the reverse had been possible.

In the opinion of the speaker it did not go far enough. Women were still unequal. In Cambridge women still did not qualify to receive degrees; women were paid less than men, their opportunities to advance in the workplace were negligible. They were slaves to the home, in bondage to their husbands.

Listening to her Peg thought that a lot of what she said was true. She could only achieve a place in the typing pool because as yet there were so few women journalists. It was considered a man's occupation, and female journalists were unflatteringly called 'mannish'. She also felt that Alan *was* jealous because, despite his socialist pretensions, he did not want her to be as successful as he was. She kept on trying to catch his eye, but he avoided looking at her.

After the lecture they walked up Southampton Row, as they usually did, only this time in a silence that was not companionable, as it usually was, but strained and somehow awkward.

It was a balmy June evening and the heat from the streets seemed to rise up and hit them. When they reached their usual cafe and paused outside Peg said, 'I think I'll go straight home and not bother with tea.'

'But why?' Alan sounded despairing.

'Because you're in a mood.'

'I am not in a mood.'

'There *is* something wrong,' Peg insisted. 'Is it something to do with me?'

'In a way,' he said grudgingly.

'Have I hurt or upset you? Is it something I said? I only ask that question because your attitude is so odd tonight. I'm sorry I suggested you were in a mood.'

'It's not that.' Alan angrily pushed a lock of his hair away from his forehead, his pale face unusually animated. 'It's us.' He paused and gazed at the pavement. 'It's about us.'

'*Us?*' Peg felt a sudden sense of shock. 'What about us?'

'Well, we've been going out for some time to these lectures . . . but we never seem to get any further.'

'Further in what way?' An unwelcome flush slowly stole up Peg's cheeks.

'You know. I would like . . . I wondered . . .'

'Oh, *Alan*.' Peg reached for his hand. 'Don't spoil it. We have such a *nice* relationship. We're good friends. I don't feel ready for anything else yet, honestly. I'm only twenty, you know.'

'I know. I understand but, do you think . . . ever?'

'Alan, I don't *know*.' Peg, feeling suddenly agitated, looked round for the bus. 'Look, I must go or Verity will be really worried.'

'But do you *like* me?' Alan asked with an air of desperation.

'Of course I like you, silly.' Peg's bantering tone suddenly changed and became solemn. 'But don't spoil it. Please don't spoil things, Alan. *Please.*'

Three

T hough five years separated Peg from her sister Addie, they had been thrust together after Verity left home and had become very close. That is until, at the age of eighteen, Addie mysteriously went to stay with Aunt Maude and Uncle Stanley. She never really came home to live again.

Some months later Mother had arrived back from a visit with a baby who, she said, was the daughter of a distant relative who had been left without means. It sounded like history repeating itself; Mother and Verity all over again.

As all the children were submissive towards their mother and would never have dreamt of interrogating her, the parentage of the baby, who was called Jenny, had never been questioned. It was a lot later that Peg, accidentally eavesdropping one night outside her mother's bedroom, had heard that Jenny was her sister's child and that the shame had been concealed from the family.

She had only been fifteen at the time and had kept such momentous news to herself, only confiding at last in Verity.

Peg had never felt able to talk to Addie about the baby. There were certain things that, even as sisters, they couldn't discuss. An impenetrable, invisible veil seemed to have fallen between her and Addie and from the time she went to stay with Aunt Maude and Uncle Stanley onwards they were never to be as close again.

But now Peg was to be a bridesmaid to Addie and she had

30

come home a few days early to help prepare for the great event.

On the day following her arrival Peg woke soon after dawn and lay in bed listening to the familiar country noises that came from outside: the rattle of cart wheels as farmers took their wares along the road to market, the bleating of sheep, the sound of birdsong.

Often as a little girl Peg had lain awake listening to the song of the blackbird, a lilting, triumphant song of courtship lifting the gloom from late winter until well into the spring. Now the mating season was over and for a time the blackbirds were silent.

She slipped out of bed and went to the window to look for her friends, a family of blackbirds who lived in the copse nearby but who came regularly to forage for food in the garden, and had done ever since she could remember. And there they were, hopping about on the lawn, digging for fresh worms in the soil that Frank had dug over the day before, until Mother should appear at the back door with their breakfast of a handful of crusts or a scatter of crumbs.

It was a peaceful, bucolic scene that filled Peg with nostalgia, for hers had been a happy childhood and sometimes she wished she was a child again.

In front of the cottage was the drive winding up to the castle. On the other side a road led to the town of Sherborne. Beyond that was a field full of plump, peacefully grazing sheep and higher up the copse where the blackbirds lived.

With a sigh Peg turned to look at Addie curled up in bed, face a little flushed, still fast asleep. It was difficult to think of Addie being married, with all the responsibilities that the state entailed, and especially difficult to think of having her fiancé Harold for a husband. He was over forty, pernickety, precise and set in his ways. He lacked the spontaneity of a younger man, and he was nothing to look at: tall, thin, angular, hollow-chested, pale, sallow-cheeked and with his spectacles always on the end of his nose, which gave him a myopic air. He did have a head of fair, slightly wavy hair, easily his best feature, was obviously proud of his appearance, maybe even thought himself handsome, and was always, unlike Alan – whom in some ways he resembled – well groomed.

But Addie must love him, Peg supposed, or she wouldn't want to marry him. They had been engaged long enough for her to change her mind.

Addie opened her eyes and stared into those of her sister.

'What time is it?' she murmured drowsily.

'After six. I was looking at the blackbirds. They're still there.'

Addie sat up and rubbed her eyes, blinking rapidly several times.

'I had such a funny dream,' she said, settling back on her pillow. 'I dreamt Harold and I weren't getting married. I don't know why . . .'

Peg sat gingerly on the side of her bed. 'Would you care?' she asked softly.

'Of course I'd care!' Addie looked at her indignantly.

'Sorry. I didn't mean –' Peg paused, not knowing really what she had meant, regretting her impulsiveness.

Addie went on, measuring her words with unusual care. 'Harold *is* a very nice person, kind and concerned. It may not be apparent to everyone, but he would never let you down or do anything mean or underhand. Not a bit like Jack or even, I suppose, our father.'

'Can you remember Father?'

Addie shook her head.

'No, not at all. But I do remember when Jack started courting Mother and took us to the garden of the Tempest Newtons, where he used to work. You were tiny – Mother had you in a pram. I quite liked Jack, at first.'

Her voice trailed off. None of them had liked her mother's second husband for long, or cared when he went off with someone else.

'There's a man in London,' Peg said suddenly, then stopped as abruptly.

'Oh?' Addie's eyes lit up.

'Oh nothing. I mean, not to *me*, but I like him. He just didn't . . . well, I wouldn't like to marry him, if you know what I mean.'

'What's his name?'

'Alan. Alan Walker.'

'I think you mentioned him before?'

'We worked together at the agency. Now he's a reporter with the *Telegraph* and I see him from time to time.'

'So what makes you bring him up?' Addie had a mischievous glint in her eyes.

'Well, because he reminded me a bit of Harold. I mean, he is very nice . . . but that's not enough, is it?' Peg realised that she was being clumsy, but blundered on. 'I mean, you have to be attracted to someone, don't you, and I can't see how you're attracted to Harold.'

Suddenly Addie looked agitated and began nervously turning the engagement ring round and round on her finger. Then, to Peg's consternation, she burst into tears.

Feeling inadequate, realising that she was desperately at fault, Peg tried to put a comforting arm on Addie's shoulder, but Addie shook her away. Then she grabbed a corner of the sheet and attempted to dry her eyes.

'You're quite right,' she said between sobs. 'I'm not attracted to Harold. I don't even *love* him, not in the way I loved—'

'I know all about Lydney Ryland.' Peg felt as if a great weight had at last been lifted from her mind.

'How do you know?' Addie demanded.

'Verity told me.'

'Verity shouldn't have told you. She had no right.'

'She thought I knew. She didn't know we never talked about the baby, or Lydd.'

'Then how *did* you know?'

'I've known for years. After Jack came home I overheard him tell Mum he didn't want Addie's bastard in the house. I knew

33

then that Jenny was your baby and that's why you went away. It was never explained to us.'

'But why did you never ask?'

'Because you never said anything.'

'I didn't want to talk about it.'

'That's what I thought. So I didn't say anything either.'

'I wanted to put it out of my mind, not Jenny but Lydd, to try and forget him. Only I never have.'

'He was very nice-looking,' Peg agreed, thinking of Lord Ryland's handsome heir, Lydney, passing the lodge on horseback or in his open motor car. He had been killed in the war, but by that time Addie had been with her aunt and uncle and Peg had never made an association between the two.

'I could never forget Lydd' – Addie started to sob again – 'but I don't want to be an old maid like Ver. She'll never marry, will she?'

'I don't expect so.' Peg paused. 'There *is* someone in London she likes, but he's married. She likes his wife too,' she added quickly. 'It was through her I got the job on the *Gazette*. The proprietor is her brother.'

'Well, I don't want to end up like Ver, and Harold has a lot of good points. There is more to life than looks, as Mum says.'

'Does Mum know you don't love Harold?'

'I think she guesses. Mum knows everything, doesn't she? But Harold is a clever, educated man with prospects and that means a lot to Mum. And to me,' she added after a while. 'I can see Harold and me settling down quite happily.'

'And he knows nothing about Lydd?'

'Oh no!' A shadow passed across Addie's face. 'Or Jenny, of course.'

As if on cue there was a thump on the door and Jenny's head appeared as it opened.

Five-year-old Jenny was the pet of the family. She had tight blonde curls, blue eyes and a stubborn little chin. She was very like her father, the handsome Lydney Ryland. Like him too she radiated energy and happiness because she had always been indulged by Cathy, whom she thought of as her mother. The others were rather vague, unspecified relatives and she called both Verity and Addie 'aunt' because they were so much older. Jenny had always been a little awkward with Addie, maybe because Addie was awkward with her, but she adored Peg and she now threw herself on the bed beside her and planted a kiss on her cheek.

'One for me too,' Addie said, still wiping her eyes.

'You've been crying.' Jenny looked at her gravely. 'Why has Aunt Addie been crying?' she asked Peg, as if Addie couldn't answer for herself.

'She's so happy,' Peg replied glibly. 'She's going to be married.'

For a few seconds Jenny regarded the woman in bed and then shook her head. 'She doesn't look happy,' she declared. 'Are we going out to play?'

'Not just yet. I have too much to do. Maybe later,' Peg said, getting off the bed. 'Now you go and get dressed and after breakfast we'll try and think of something nice to do.'

And she took her firmly to the door and gently pushed her outside.

Addie looked on the verge of tears again.

'She doesn't like me.'

'Of course she does,' Peg said robustly.

'I've never got on with her as well as you have. Every time she sees me she goes away and hides. Why do I make her nervous, Peg?'

'Maybe because *you* are nervous. Now look' – impulsively she sat down on the bed and tenderly stroked her sister's brow – 'stop brooding. Think of being *happy*. You will be. They say love comes and I am sure that it will with Harold. Anyway, the die is cast and it's much too late to change.'

For an awful moment as she walked up the aisle on the arm of her stepfather Frank, who was giving her away, the bride faltered, almost stopped, and the little procession of bridesmaids close together nearly fell over one another. Peg saw Addie glance at Frank, saw him press her arm tightly and murmur something to her, and they continued until Addie joined Harold at the altar. Frank took his place beside Cathy in the first row of pews and the ceremony began.

Peg kept a watchful eye on Jenny, who outshone them all, angelic in her lemon-coloured bridesmaid's dress, fresh flowers in her golden hair. The other bridesmaid was Stella, who was just fifteen and the offspring, together with her brother Ed, of Cathy and her second husband Jack. She was the youngest sister, five years Peg's junior and very different in temperament: sweet-natured, timid and always rather eclipsed by the ebullient Peg with her flamboyant good looks and extravagant style.

But all the sisters were fond of one another, and united in their love for their mother, who now sat in the front of the church dressed in the blue suit she had worn for her marriage to Frank, with a broad-brimmed straw hat hiding her luxuriant brown hair. At forty-nine, despite her five children and her hard life, Cathy managed to look years younger. Perhaps her recent marriage to Frank had helped erase the memories of all those years of hardship: the death of one husband, the flagrant infidelity of another and the abuse she had experienced at his hands. She was small, trim with soft, warm brown eyes and cheeks which dimpled becomingly when she smiled. She still exuded an air of sexual allure which had attracted Frank, a lifelong bachelor, and led to a very happy union for both.

However, Jenny was Cathy's weakness. She loved all her children, but adored this special grandchild whom she feared she would lose after Addie and Harold set up home. During the ceremony she kept glancing anxiously at Jenny, who grew increasingly restless as the service progressed but was kept well in control by the reliable Peg.

Oh if only all her daughters were as even-tempered, as capable, as her beautiful Peg, how much simpler life would be, Cathy thought, waving her order paper to fan herself on this very hot day.

Dear Verity was a stoic, but she conspicuously lacked either beauty or charm. She had taken the breakdown of her engagement well, but Cathy knew her heart had been broken and she would probably never have another chance. A chill had entered that heart and would surely help to freeze would-be suitors. So many eligible men had been killed in the war that there were few on the ground, and enough nubile and willing younger women anxious to ensnare them. Poor Addie was surely making a compromise in marrying Harold, second best to the glamorous Lydd. Stella, also dark and petite, shared her mother's good looks, yet she was still too young to think about men – though surely she would have no difficulty when the time was right.

Ed read the lesson. He was only seventeen but nearly six feet tall, dark and good-looking like his father, with the same unusually bright blue eyes that presented such a striking contrast to his dark skin. People had always thought there was something of the gypsy in Jack, maybe a throwback to ancestors of long ago who had crossed the continent from the east to find a home in England. Like his father Ed could charm the women, yet he wanted to be a priest and as his sonorous tones boomed out confidently in the church Cathy thought he would be a good one. He was a scholar, naturally not falsely pious, and perhaps a future adornment to the senior ranks of the Church of England clergy?

Cathy was proud of her children, all of whom, with no advantages of birth, had done or were doing well. Addie was the first one to be married, *and* to a professional man.

Cathy was roused from her reverie by a nudge in the ribs from Frank. She rose hurriedly to her feet as the vicar pronounced the blessing upon the newlyweds. She and Frank and Harold's mother Rose then joined the bridal couple to sign the register, after which, to the triumphant sound of the organ, Addie and

Harold emerged into the sacristy and walked down the aisle, man and wife.

By evening the festivities were well advanced. The reception had been held in the castle hall by kind permission of Lord and Lady Ryland, who had been unable to attend the wedding as they were away in Scotland. However, their daughter Violet had been kind enough to call in on her way to a dinner engagement, delaying a little the departure of the bride and groom, who were to travel to London before departing by boat-train to the continent.

Long before they got into the car Addie paused and, aiming high towards the throng gathered on the steps watching the departure of the newlyweds, threw her bride's bouquet in the direction of her sister Verity. She, however, skilfully managed to dodge it so that it was caught by Peg who, nonplussed at first, then burst out laughing and ran down the steps towards the car.

'You will be next,' Addie whispered to her. 'I hoped it would be Ver, but it seems it's not to be.'

'Please, take care,' Peg said, kissing her. 'Have a wonderful time.' She then stood back, waving frantically after them as Lord Ryland's Rolls Royce, driven by Frank, proceeded solemnly down the drive.

Since then Peg hadn't stopped dancing, much sought after by the young men present. She had a multiplicity of cousins, mostly on her mother's side, some of whom she had not seen since her grandfather's funeral three years before.

One, Arthur Swayle, debonair with sleeked-back black hair and a formidable handlebar moustache, tried to monopolise her. Indeed, there was a certain raffish air about him that she found attractive, so she returned to him for dance after dance.

However, when, during an interval, Arthur invited her outside for a cool glass of beer on the lawn, his demeanour changed and his attentions became obvious, and unwelcome. His arm tightly encircled her waist and his mouth came close to her cheek.

'I see you caught the bride's bouquet,' he whispered, slurring his words. 'You know what that means, don't you?'

'Don't touch me,' Peg said, angrily trying to push him away. 'You're drunk.'

'I am *not* drunk,' Arthur protested. 'Playing hard to get, are you, my beauty? I thought from the way you kept on dancing with me that you fancied me. Don't pretend you didn't.'

Imagining that she was being playfully provocative, Arthur grew more amorous and threw his other arm around her so that she was held in a vice-like grip. Peg wriggled furiously, attempting to free her pinioned arms, but to no avail. Arthur's beery mouth was about to bear down on hers when he was violently grabbed from one side and almost felled by a blow on the cheek which caused him to stagger away from Peg, practically losing his footing.

He looked round furiously for his attacker, who was a tall man in evening dress who appeared to have got out of a car parked in front of the house.

'What the—' Arthur began but the man ignored him and turned to Peg.

'Are you all right? I hope I did the right thing.' He looked across at Arthur, whose hand was pressed against his cheek.

'Thank you,' Peg said. 'I'm sorry you were troubled, Mr Ryland.'

In the dark she was blushing, red-faced and furious that Arthur had made such a fool of himself and her. For her rescuer was none other than Lord Ryland's heir, Hubert, who obviously had been returning from an evening function.

'That's no trouble. May I escort you back to the hall? I take it you are part of the festivities for the wedding of Addie Barnes. As for this man –' Hubert once more looked threateningly at the discomfited Arthur.

'It's quite all right. He won't do it again.' Peg gazed at him contemptuously as, still nursing his bruised cheek, he slunk off between the trees, perhaps to try and make his way home, though he had a long way to go. 'I am *very* sorry, Mr Ryland, that you should have been so troubled, but thank you.'

By this time Hubert was peering at her closely.

'Aren't you one of Jack Hallam's daughters? Peg, I think it is.'

'I am Peg, Mr Ryland, and that man was a distant cousin who lost control of himself owing, doubtless, to the amount of liquor he had consumed. I am grateful to you and sorry. *Very* sorry. I feel humiliated.'

'I could see you were struggling, but I wasn't *quite* sure . . . one never knows at parties. All sorts of things happen, some quite innocent. Now, if I may escort you inside, I might be in time to congratulate the happy couple?'

'They have already left for London, Mr Ryland. But I'm sure my mother and Frank would be glad to see you, though I would much rather you didn't mention what has happened.'

'Of course.' Hubert playfully put a finger to his lips. 'Not a word to Mama.' Placing a hand lightly on her arm, he escorted her back to the castle hall. This was used for all sorts of great occasions as well as the servants' annual Christmas party, which was the only occasion when the Rylands and staff met socially. Peg, aware of this, felt mortified that Hubert Ryland had caught her in such a compromising situation.

Cathy looked towards the door as Peg came in, wondering where she had got to. When she saw who was with her she turned to Frank and tugged at his sleeve.

'There's Mr Hubert. I thought he wasn't coming?'

'Changed his mind.' Frank hastily buttoned up his jacket, extinguished his cigarette and walked towards the visitor, who was looking about him, a little bemused.

'How *nice* to see you, sir,' Frank said politely. 'Your sister was here a short while ago.'

'I came home early from a regimental dinner in Sherborne.'

'I was taking a little air, Frank,' Peg said fanning herself. 'It is very hot in here.'

'I'm sorry you missed Addie and her husband,' Frank said. 'But please come and say how do you do to my wife.'

Cathy, already looking flustered, got up and dropped a bob at the heir, who spent little time at the castle. He worked for a bank in London and was rarely seen on the estate.

'May I offer you something to drink, Mr Hubert?' Frank hovered anxiously.

'A beer would be nice,' Hubert said, looking around, 'and as everybody here already seems to have taken off their jackets I wonder if I may too?'

'Of course, Mr Hubert.' Frank was anxious to assist him, whereupon their unexpected guest divested himself of his jacket, followed by his bow tie. As the band, who had been resting, struck up a waltz, he turned to Peg with both hands extended.

'I wonder if I may have the pleasure of this dance?'

Peg accepted him gaily and they swung on to the floor to be swallowed up in the throng.

Hubert Ryland was little known to most of the staff. He was tall and slim with fair hair sleeked straight back from his forehead and a blond moustache. After the war, in which he had served with distinction, gaining the Military Cross, he lived for most of the time in London.

'This is a nice party,' Hubert murmured in her ear. 'Much nicer than the stuffy old regimental dinner I was just at.'

'Is that why you came down, Mr Hubert?'

'Yes. And please drop the Mr. Hubert will do.'

'You won't say a word to anyone about Arthur, will you?' Peg said anxiously. 'He just had too much to drink. He didn't mean any harm, I'm sure.'

'There's nothing between you, is there?' Hubert held her away from him for a moment, looking into her eyes, and she thought how attractive he was, almost with the charm of his elder brother. 'I didn't disturb anything?'

'Nothing.' Peg shook her head vigorously. 'I hardly know him.' She looked around. 'Most of these people are relations on my mother's side, the Swayles. They all live in or near Bournemouth and we scarcely ever meet.'

'And where do you live, Peg?'

'In London,' Peg said, pointing to Verity, who was sitting in a corner with some elderly female cousins and hadn't been on the dance floor once. 'With my sister, who is a nurse at the Royal Free Hospital.'

'And you? Are you a nurse too?'

Peg shook her head. 'I work for a newspaper. I hope to be a journalist one day but just now I'm a stenographer.'

'Well, that is most interesting,' Hubert said. 'There aren't many women journalists. Who knows, one of these days we may bump into each other.'

It was very nearly midnight and although some people were as energetic as ever, others were palpably tiring. Most of the Bournemouth contingent were being accommodated locally by friends or relations; some had hired a bus to take them home. Others, mostly the young, were going to hang about and wait for the milk train, although already the bailiff was trying to clear the hall so that he could lock up the castle for the night.

Mr Hubert, after thanking Peg for the dance, seemed to dissolve in the mêlée and when the crowd had thinned out he was nowhere to be seen.

'Well, *that* was something, dancing with Mr Hubert,' Cathy said as she came up to Peg, the hand of a very tired Jenny clasped in hers.

'He seemed nice, I thought,' Peg said offhandedly. 'He says he lives in London.'

'And did he ask where *you* lived?' Her mother peered closely at her.

'I said I lived in London too, Mother.' Peg glanced impishly at her. 'But there's no need to worry. Someone like Hubert Ryland wouldn't take a second look at me.'

'Besides, he has a wife,' Cathy murmured. 'Although no one ever sees them together. They seem to lead quite separate lives.'

'Oh, *Mum.* Peg impulsively kissed her mother. 'You *are* silly. I'm not interested in Mr Hubert, or he in me. He's much older, anyway.'

Peg turned to say goodbye to an assemblage of cousins who were making for the door, but Cathy looked after her and then back at little Jenny as if she was thinking about the past, of the way Mr Hubert had looked at her beautiful daughter. She gazed down at Jenny as if wondering if such a thing could ever happen again.

Four

August–September 1923

Verity sat in the stern of the gondola, her hand trailing in the waters of the Rio di Palazzo as it passed under the Bridge of Sighs. In front of her Geraldine, a straw hat tied over her head with a chiffon scarf, sat busily sketching the side of the Ducal Palace, covering the paper with swift, skilful strokes. She was incredibly talented, with a far, far better gift than Verity, who had practically abandoned her sketch pad to soak in the sounds and sights of this miraculous city: Venice.

Geraldine turned and glanced at her.

'Penny for them, dear?'

'Just thinking how happy I am,' Verity said, smiling back. 'This is one of the happiest times of my life. I'm so glad you asked me.'

'And I'm so glad you came.' Geraldine leaned back and briefly pressed Verity's hand. 'It's made all the difference to me, too.'

Verity was also straw-hatted and wore a sensible blue cotton dress and white sandals. Geraldine, as usual, looked soignée in one of her flowing garments, a purple chiffon silk-lined ankle-length dress, gathered at the waist with a round neckline and long billowing sleeves. Her slim, tapered fingers, one heavily beringed, were fascinating to watch as her pencil skimmed across the surface of the paper.

The blissful holiday was nearly at an end. Philip's medical

44

conference would soon be over and they would join him in Milan to take the train back to Paris.

The friendship between the two women, begun in London, had deepened in this short time. Alone together they had discovered they had much in common: a love of art, an appreciation of beauty and the good things in life. They explored the churches and galleries: the glorious Byzantine interior of the Basilica of St Mark; the Carpaccios in the Scuola S' Giorgio degli Schiavoni; the Tintorettos in the Scuola S Rocco; the Accademia with its works by Bellini, Titian and Veronese. Each day was a sumptuous feast for the eyes and senses. Each day they were worn out with walking through the endless alleyways and piazzas that made up the unique city, free of traffic except for boats. Each night they returned to their beds weary but happy.

They both loved music and the opera, and the discussions they had often went on into the small hours of the morning, both of them sitting on the balcony of their small hotel overlooking the Grand Canal, where they occupied adjoining rooms.

The gondola emerged into the Canal and made its way slowly past St Mark's Square, past all the palazzi and hotels that bordered that splendid thoroughfare, until it deposited them outside their hotel on the corner of the Grand Canal and the Rio di Meloni, just before the Rialto Bridge.

Geraldine put aside her sketch pad and sat for a moment looking around as if savouring the scene, while Verity grasped the hand of the gondolier stretched out to help her and jumped on to the platform, groping in her handbag for her purse.

Geraldine gathered up her sketching equipment and then, with the assistance of the gondolier, joined her friend on the jetty.

'Do we have enough money, dear?'

'Plenty.' Verity laughed, handing the gondolier a handful of notes and shaking her head as he prepared to count the change.

'Grazie, signore,' he said. 'Grazie, tanti.' He was obviously grateful for the generous tip, and he jumped lithely into his craft and set off the way he had come.

'Our last ride,' Verity said, sadly watching his progress downstream.

'We shall return.' Geraldine tucked a hand through her friend's arm. 'We shall return time and time again.'

That night as a treat they ate at a little trattoria they had found on the first night near the Palazzo Tiepolo. They had ravioli followed by osso bucco and a glass of wine. For Verity the whole holiday had been an adventure into the unknown. She had never been abroad and Italy had enchanted her, together with the company of the elegant and sophisticated Beaumaurices. She got on well with both of them. They made a pleasant trio and the tension and discord she had noticed between husband and wife when she visited them in London, as she had done often since that first meeting, had largely evaporated.

They had spent a few days in Verona with Philip and then he had seen them to the station to put them on their way to Venice. Five blissful days, now nearly at an end. And Geraldine was such a wonderful companion: knowledgeable and sympathetic, cultured and charming.

It was a little like being in love, Verity thought, slightly guiltily, only of course it wasn't. There was nothing the least bit *carnal* about it – though there were endearments and brief moments of physical contact as they touched or brushed against each other which gave one a slight frisson of pleasure. It was much more a spiritual affair, a meeting of true minds, a warm friendship based on an appreciation of each other's qualities and shared interests. She had certainly never felt this way about Rex.

'This time tomorrow' – Geraldine raised her glass and sighed deeply – 'we shall be on our way to Milano.'

'But as you said, we will come back.' Verity raised her glass in return. 'I can't thank you enough for inviting me. It has given a whole new dimension to my life.'

Despite their intimacy, and especially their proximity to each other on this holiday, the two women had exchanged few

confidences of a personal nature. Now the situation appeared to
be about to change as Geraldine looked archly at her friend.

'I find it strange that you have never been abroad, Verity.
Surely all these years . . .' She raised an eyebrow interrogatively.
'No *man* in your life?'

'There *was* a man.' Verity momentarily bowed her head to
gather her thoughts, then raised it to look across at Geraldine
with troubled eyes. 'Even now it hurts me to talk about it. His
name was Rex Harvey. He was a doctor at Charing Cross
Hospital, a very good surgeon, and I was theatre sister during
the war. He enlisted and was sent to the Balkans, and just before
his departure we became engaged. When he returned we arranged the date for our wedding. He was to go into practice with
his father in the Yorkshire Dales and I was to work in the
dispensary. Such a happy, fulfilled life seemed to beckon. I liked
his parents; they seemed to like me.

'Then, just two weeks before the wedding, when I was on the
verge of leaving the hospital, Rex told me he couldn't go through
with it. The war had affected him too much and he felt he was
unable to settle. He wanted to go to Africa, where he promised to
make a home for me and send for me when it was ready.'

Verity bowed her head again, aware that even after so many
years, the emotion, the sense of rejection she had experienced at
the time, threatened to overwhelm her. From across the table,
Geraldine, her eyes brimming with sympathy, reached out and
gently placed a firm, consoling hand over hers.

'Don't go on if it's too painful, dear,' she said soothingly. 'I
quite understand.'

'No, I don't mind at all now, after all this time. Well, a *little*
bit, maybe.' Verity groped in her sleeve for her handkerchief and
quickly dabbed at her eyes. 'Anyway' – she sniffed, tucking the
handkerchief safely away – 'Rex met another woman and that
was that.' She swallowed hard. 'I had to make a new life for
myself and I did, quite successfully I think.'

'Oh there is no doubt of that!' Geraldine said robustly. 'Philip

47

thinks the world of your professional capabilities, and of you as a person. Sometimes I suspect he prefers you to me, and I feel a little jealous.'

'Oh, that is *nonsense*,' Verity protested. 'My relationship with Philip is not in the same category as yours. You are husband and wife. I hope you don't imagine –'

'Oh, my dear, not at all.' Geraldine gave a slightly superficial, silvery laugh. 'I don't think *anything* like that *at all*. It is just that' – she broke a bread stick neatly in two – 'we, Philip and I, have so little in common. I am bored by his medical talk, and he is not interested in the arts. Why, you have never mentioned your work *once* all the time we have been away – from Philip, that is. In Verona he was talking about it all the time.'

'That's because he was to present a paper to the congress. He has done some very advanced and important research in the field of obstetrics.'

'Well, obstetrics is of no interest to me at all,' Geraldine said, firmly hitting the table with the flat of her hand. 'And *you* can keep it to yourself, and not bore me, so why can't he?'

'That's because I do love art – and I'm not in the same league at all medically speaking as Philip. He is a very clever man and you should be proud of him.'

'Oh I am, I am,' Geraldine said offhandedly. 'Shall we be very wicked and have another glass of wine?'

'Let's' – Verity giggled like a schoolgirl – 'though I hope I don't get drunk.'

'Oh, if only Philip could see us now, eating by ourselves in a restaurant, drinking wine. Don't you think he would be a little shocked?' Geraldine smiled mischievously. 'I do. He is such a very conventional man. Such a stickler for the proprieties. So tedious really.' She gave an artificial yawn which she tried politely to disguise with her hand.

'But you do love him?' Verity looked at her anxiously.

'Love changes, you know,' Geraldine replied. 'We were passionately in love when we first married. The first two years were wonderful, but now –' she thoughtfully tapped the table with her fingers – 'I'm not so sure. But there is no question of, you know, *splitting up*, divorce, that sort of thing. No question at all. We have a nice home and we have the girls. As you say, he will do well in his profession.' She looked long and hard at Verity. 'You know, my dear, you would have found the same thing most probably after a few years of marriage with your Rex. I didn't know him, of course, but I suspect most marriages of people in our position in life follow a similar pattern. As it is, you have happy memories to look back on.'

'No so happy,' Verity replied. 'Not really so happy. We didn't know each other very well before we became engaged. I suspected he wanted to think that there was someone at home who would wait for him. He never wrote me passionate letters, or letters of any length at all. Mostly scribbled messages on postcards. I took it that this was owing to lack of opportunity. With so little communication between us, when he returned from the Balkans it was difficult somehow to rekindle the little spark we had. It was more from a sense of duty, if you know what I mean, especially on Rex's part. I did want to be married and have a family. I love children and come from a large family myself.

'However, I wasn't even sure I loved Rex, to tell you the truth; but he was very suitable and I imagined that that sort of thing would grow. Well, as it happened,' she finished flatly, 'it didn't, and *he* can't have loved *me* very much, either.'

'Anyone else?' Geraldine raised an eyebrow suggestively. 'I mean after Rex?'

'No one else.' Verity shook her head firmly. 'Never has been and probably never will. I am afraid I'm destined to be an old maid and live through the lives of my nephews and nieces, perhaps my younger sisters, who knows?'

The two women walked slowly back to the hotel through the quiet streets of a city, one of the most beautiful in the world, which had survived the war but suffered from the same poverty and unrest as the rest of Europe. Lurking in the wings was the blacksmith's son from poverty-stricken Romagna, Benito Mussolini, who had declared himself leader of the Fascist party and set out to counteract the wave of communist-led strikes which threatened the country. Mussolini had been sending his squads of black-shirted followers to beat up the Bolsheviks.

Geraldine linked her arm through Verity's and squeezed it tightly.

'We have become such friends,' she said, 'haven't we?'

'Oh, *yes*.'

'With lots in common.'

'Lots and lots. As long as I don't talk about obstetrics.' Verity gave another girlish giggle.

Geraldine paused and gazed at her.

'I admire you, Verity. Seriously I do. Philip says you're the best nurse in the hospital and I believe it. You may have had great sadness in life with your Rex, but look what you have instead. And what do *I* have?'

'A husband,' Verity said quietly, 'a home, two beautiful children. You don't know how I envy you.'

'Do you really?'

'Oh yes.'

'Well, *I* envy *you*. My life is very dull. I find it pointless at times. I share my home with a man with whom I have nothing in common. Temperamentally and emotionally we are miles apart. As an obstetrician he claims to know a lot about women, but he knows nothing about me. And, what's more, I know that this is how it will be. Nothing will change until the end of my life.'

The holiday, which had been so happy and successful, thus ended on a solemn, thoughtful note, during which new, raw emotions had surfaced, more questions raised than answered. After an affectionate goodnight, the two women went quietly to their separate beds, rather late.

The following morning they were up early to pack and after breakfast paid their bill and set off for the station and the train journey to Milan, where the reality of their respective lives would intrude again.

November 1923

Peg's desk was in a row in the typing pool, which employed seven stenographers busily typing copy that was sent to them from all parts of the newspaper. The desks were arranged in rows of two like those in a schoolroom, and facing them at the front like a strict teacher, at a table on which was her own typewriter, was Miss Clark, a middle-aged lady with a fierce reputation, who had given Peg her test at her first interview.

Miss Clark did very little typing of her own but checked the copy typed by the girls and took great pleasure in reprimanding anyone she didn't feel was up to scratch. There were quite a few of these incidents and, as a result, a high turnover in the typing pool, many of whose occupants frequently left in tears.

Peg refused to be cowed by Miss Clark, was meticulous in her work and hardly ever laid herself open to a reprimand. Nevertheless, Miss Clark did her very best to pick on her, to find fault, though she was seldom given the opportunity. It was as though she resented the fact that, somehow, Peg was there because she was a protégée of Mr Moodie. None of the other girls in the typing pool had ever met him, let alone been accorded the privilege of a personal interview.

Miss Clark would try and engineer some excuse, like Peg being late, or her typewriter not being clean enough, but these occasions were very few, and she was never able to find a valid reason to criticise her work. Knowing the woman harboured a dislike for her, Peg was determined to avoid causing offence, and when she was told off was careful not to answer back.

Peg was frustrated by the typing pool and its tedium. She wondered if Mr Moodie had forgotten the promise he had made to her when he saw her. Shortly after she joined the paper she had

had a brief interview with the news editor, Mr Edwards, who clearly resented her almost as much as Miss Clark because she had somehow managed to find favour with the proprietor. For this very reason she was bound to cause jealousy and hostility.

He had pointed to the lack of females in the newsroom and said that when something came up, if it ever did, he would try and remember her. He gave the impression that this was a very remote possibility. That had been months ago and she was beginning to feel that her attempts at a journalistic career were doomed to failure.

This particular morning in early November Peg was feeling very flat. Verity had not been well, suffering from the after-effects of a prolonged bout of flu, and had been uncharacteristically difficult and demanding. The weather was foul, London covered in an impenetrable fog, and the bus to work had been crowded.

Peg had begun to yearn for a place of her own, a life of her own not dominated by her elder sister, yet she knew that such a thing was impossible. She loved Verity and knew she only had her interests at heart, but she had taken on the role of mother and Peg felt more like a schoolgirl than an independent young woman. She had not enough money to support herself and she was still under age.

She had made one or two women friends from work and she occasionally saw a friend from her job at the bank, but she avoided taking people home because Verity tended to grill them to make sure they were suitable companions for her sister. To some people this attitude was intrusive and offensive. There were no men in Peg's life, though one or two had made timid advances and she had once joined a mixed group who went dancing, telling her sister she was spending the night with a friend. This was partly true, because she had gone home with one of the girls whose life was more emancipated than hers. But she didn't enjoy the evening much and the episode made her feel guilty, because she hated telling Verity even half-lies.

She had seen very little of Alan since their awkward conversation in the spring. He avoided her for weeks afterwards and when he invited her out again the atmosphere was different. The evening followed the usual pattern, however: a meeting in Red Lion Square and a cup of tea at the cafe near Euston.

Peg genuinely missed their old rapport because she had liked him, but she knew why he behaved as he did: he was frustrated and disappointed that their relationship had not progressed the way he had hoped.

Her work was similarly unfulfilling. She always got the dreariest copy, usually about finance or the parlous state of the economy, subjects in which it was impossible to whip up much interest.

The girls had had their tea break on that November afternoon and Peg was just resuming her seat when Miss Clark summoned her to her desk.

'Mr Edwards wishes to see you,' the older woman said sharply. 'You'd better give your work to me.' She held out her hand imperiously.

Peg stared at the supervisor but knew better than to ask questions. If she was to hand in her work it looked as though she might not be coming back. A surge of excitement suddenly banished the negative feelings of the day.

Peg went back to her desk, removed her latest copy from the typewriter and, with a glance at the girls, all of whom were gazing curiously at her, left the room and made her way quickly to the office on the third floor just outside the newsroom. She had not seen Mr Edwards since her interview in the spring.

'Miss Hallam,' he said, looking up as she came in. 'You know I am not in favour of women reporters. I think I made that clear. However, I am short-staffed because of the outbreak of influenza. Do you know anything about politics?'

'A little.' Peg gulped.

'Well, as you know, the prime minister, Mr Baldwin, has called a snap election, and I want you to go to the East End and cover a political meeting there. A member of the Communist Party is attempting to unseat the sitting member, who is a moderate. I want you to take notes and give me a report. It will probably be as dull as ditchwater, but it is at least a start for you. By tomorrow morning, first thing please,' he said, looking at the clock. 'The meeting is due to start at seven. Do you know the Whitechapel Road?'

'No, but I can find it,' Peg said breathlessly.

'Take care now,' Edwards said gruffly. 'It's not really a fit place for a woman on her own, specially at night, but that's what you said you wanted to do and if you do want to be a reporter you must take what you get.'

'Oh yes,' Peg said, her face glowing with excitement. 'I know that – and thank you, Mr Edwards, for giving me this chance.'

She rushed back to get her coat and hat, collected a notebook from her desk without saying a word to Miss Clark or her fellow workers, who were all gawping at her, and made her exit. She felt very guilty about not being able to let Verity know. She would get a ticking-off for it, but work was work and there was nothing she could do about it.

This was her big chance.

The hall was run by the Salvation Army and was just off the Whitechapel Road, which had a reputation for poverty, deprivation and now radicalism. The working classes, who had rallied with enthusiasm to the ranks in 1914, were suffering the most from the after-effects of the war – those, that was, who had returned. Many of the demobilised had not found employment, swelling the ranks of beggars who made their way hopelessly to the West End and back every day hoping for a few shillings at most.

All sorts of left-wing political groups regarded East London as a breeding ground for revolution and the freedom of the enslaved masses, and wanted to have their say. Beyond Aldgate, London was a seething mass of discontent, and when Peg found the hall she was not surprised to find that it was crowded. As she walked in and found a standing place at the back it appeared that the speaker had already started, fists raised in the air, as he urged the unemployed workers to take arms against the business classes and manufacturers of armaments who were bent on ruining the world.

Squeezed up against the wall, Peg took out her pad and frantically started making notes. Her shorthand was a little rusty, as she seldom had occasion to use it.

Her excitement at this unexpected opportunity was mixed with apprehension. It was as though Mr Edwards had deliberately thrown her in at the deep end, perhaps with the hope that she would do a bad job. Well, she wouldn't. It was so important to give of her best.

As the speaker progressed, his rhetoric became more inflammatory and there were murmurs of approval and an air of restlessness among the audience. Some appeared to think he had gone too far, others that he had not gone far enough. Before the speaker had finished, barracking had begun on one side of the hall followed by counter-barracking on the other.

Suddenly, as the speaker urged all those present to take up whatever implements they had and march on Whitehall, the centre of a corrupt government, a man leapt on to the platform and threw an object at him. He dodged, whatever it was missed him, and then another man jumped on to the platform, followed by another and yet another who launched themselves on the perpetrators of the first attack. A general mêlée followed which was immediately imitated by some elements in the hall, who began fighting one another.

Suddenly there was a surge of bodies converging on Peg, who stood in the centre. Her precious notebook flew out of her hand and she made a dive to recover it. As she bent her hat was knocked off and someone made a grab for her hair, maybe to try and help her to her feet. But she had completely lost her footing and as she slithered to the ground she only just managed to grasp her notebook, which had already been trampled on.

Limbs seemed to close around her, over her. Someone kicked her savagely in the arm, but she endeavoured to surge upwards for a last desperate gulp of air, hoping to fill her lungs. Just as she was about to sink beneath the mass of fighting bodies, she saw a familiar face trying desperately to make his way towards her through the crowd.

'Alan!' she cried, trying to raise her hands for help, but finding her left arm wouldn't respond. It was impossible and, not knowing whether he had seen her or not, she was submerged beneath a sea of heaving bodies. She began to suffocate.

'Oh, please God,' she murmured, 'don't let me die.' She remained on the floor in a sitting position with one hand clasped protectively over her head, conscious of nothing around her but a jumbled, tangled mass of legs, stinking bodies, a terrible lack of air and a dull pain in her arm, which she thought was broken.

She began to feel light-headed, nausea swept over her, and she knew she was losing consciousness. Suddenly she felt herself being dragged to the surface by two strong arms while elbows were flailing in all directions. She emerged a limp rag doll, collapsed in the arms of her saviour: Alan.

'You have a visitor,' Verity said. 'I told him not to stay long.'

Nursing a broken arm, Peg had been devotedly looked after by her sister, who had taken time off from the hospital to care for her.

She had spent twenty-four hours in the London Hospital on Whitechapel Road undergoing careful examination of her injuries and being tested for possible internal damage, but emerged at last with nothing more serious than a broken arm and a black eye. However, before she was taken to the theatre to have her arm reset she had insisted on dictating her copy to Alan, who had accompanied her to hospital. He had promised to type it up and deliver it personally.

'And don't touch a word,' Peg had commanded. 'It has to be all my own work.'

'I don't need to touch a word,' Alan replied admiringly. 'It's splendid.'

Peg looked up as Mr Edwards entered the room, a large bunch of flowers in his arms. He turned to thank Verity, who had asked him if he would like a cup of tea, and said that he would. Peg felt overwhelmed and shyly thanked him for the flowers, which he thrust into her hand.

'You shouldn't have bothered,' she said, sniffing them. 'I didn't think you could get flowers at this time of the year.'

'Hothouse,' Mr Edwards replied. 'Mr Moodie had them delivered by a florist in Mayfair. He sent his warmest regards, and if there is anything you need –'

'Very kind of him.' Peg looked nervously at the news editor. 'I'm very sorry. I muffed it, didn't I?'

'You nearly got yourself killed, young woman,' Mr Edwards said, sternly taking the chair which Verity had put out for him by the side of Peg's bed. 'But you submitted a splendid piece of copy which we ran on the first page.' And, like a conjuror taking a rabbit from a hat, he produced the newspaper, which had a banner headline together with a rather charming picture of Peg taken when she was still at school, which Verity had managed to produce.

'HEROIC YOUNG WOMAN REPORTS ATTACK ON A BOLSHEVIK IN THE EAST END' ran the caption.

At the risk of her own life, our new reporter, Peg Hallam, the only woman journalist in the newsroom of this paper, delivered a graphic account of the attack on a Communist speaker in East London, even though she was badly wounded. Rushed to hospital, badly bruised and with a broken arm, she insisted on dictating the copy to a colleague before being taken to the theatre to have her arm set. Peg Hallam thus follows in the best tradition of British journalism.

There followed Peg's account which, she was pleased to see, was largely as she remembered writing it.

'That's very gratifying,' she said. 'Thank you, Mr Edwards.'

'You were a very silly young woman.' Mr Edwards attempted to sound severe. 'But a very brave one. Most of your colleagues in the newsroom are speechless with admiration. I think some of them are actually rather jealous and wondered why I sent you instead of them. But we were not to know it would end in fisticuffs.'

'The whole hall was in uproar. Frankly I think if it had not been for Alan Walker I would never have survived to file this piece.'

'He was the man who came to your rescue?'

'We worked together at the news agency. He is now a reporter on the *Telegraph*. I didn't know he was at the meeting until, just as I was about to go under for the second time, I saw him come towards me. He had seen me and I'm sure he saved my life.'

'I'll run a piece on him in the next issue,' Edwards said generously. 'This is a good story. But if I had had any idea you were to be placed in such danger I assure you I would never have sent you. I thought it would be a run-of-the-mill, rather boring meeting. As it is, it has caused headlines round the country about the threat of the Bolshevik menace when the sort of scenes are happening here that are happening in Germany.'

Entering the room with a tray of tea Verity, hearing the last remark, said, 'We saw or rather *heard* of the same sort of carry-on in Italy when I was there with friends in the summer. Only the Fascists were worse than the Communists. Tea – weak or strong, Mr Edwards?'

'As it comes, thank you, Miss Carter-Barnes.' He looked up with a smile. 'You have a very brave young sister.'

'Foolish in my opinion,' Verity said with asperity. 'She could have been killed, suffocated to death and, frankly, I would rather have my sister with me than a martyr to the cause of newspaper reporting. I am supposed to be looking after her, and my family would never have forgiven me. You can imagine what a shock I had to learn my sister was in hospital, injured, when I was already worried to death because she was so late home.' She looked across at her visitor with an expression that had quelled many student nurses or young medical interns. Then, more pleasantly: 'Milk and sugar, Mr Edwards?'

Five

January 1924

'This is Alan,' Peg said, pushing him forward. 'I think he saved my life.'

Cathy's large, luminous eyes immediately filled with tears and she threw her arms around the startled man, hugging him like a long-lost son.

'Oh thank you, thank you,' she said and gave him a resounding kiss on the cheek. 'I have been so longing to meet you and thank you for what you did for Peg.'

'It was nothing,' Alan mumbled shyly. 'I did what anyone would do.'

'Well, I wanted to thank you,' Cathy said, glancing at Verity and Peg, who stood in the hall watching the proceedings. She then kissed each of them, looking anxiously at Peg's arm.

'Is it all right now?'

'It came out of plaster last week. Just in time for my birthday.' She wiggled her arm around. 'I have to be careful.'

The front door was still open, admitting a biting January wind as Frank brought in the cases from the car in which he had driven them from the station.

'Here, let me help you,' Alan said, embarrassed at the warmth of his reception and grateful for the chance to have something to do.

'No, Frank will do it,' Cathy said, firmly taking his arm. 'You are our special guest and must be introduced to the rest of the family. They're all dying to meet you.'

60

She drew him into the living room where a little group waited awkwardly to greet their guest.

'This is Addie, my middle daughter, and her husband, Harold.'

'How do you do?'

'How do you do?'

Addie and Harold gravely shook Alan's hand.

'Stella, my youngest daughter,' Cathy said, passing to the next in line. Stella, as shy as Alan, proffered a limp hand.

'And this,' Cathy said, looking at the small girl dancing excitedly around, the only one in the room to appear to be acting at all normally, 'is Jenny, my adopted daughter.'

'Hello, Jenny.' Alan relaxed a little and smiled.

'She's very excited,' Cathy said, grasping her hand in an effort to try and keep her still. 'I don't think she slept at all last night, did you, pet?'

Jenny vigorously shook her head.

'Ed isn't home yet. He's my only son, busy at the moment with his studies. You must be hungry, Mr Walker. Did you have a good trip?'

'Very good, thank you.'

'Terrible weather?'

'Terrible.'

Cathy sighed inwardly. Hero he might be, but he would also be hard work as a guest. But nothing – no awkwardness, no silence, would ever destroy the gratitude she felt towards this man.

'Where is Mr Walker sleeping, dear?' Frank popped his head round the door.

'In Ver's old room. I hope you don't mind?' She looked up at her eldest daughter who, having divested herself of her coat, stood warming her hands at the fire. 'Is that all right, dear? I've put you three in Stella's room. It will be a squeeze but you'll manage just for a few days. Frank has put in an extra bed borrowed from the castle.'

'I feel I'm putting you to a lot of trouble,' Alan said apologetically.

'It's *no* trouble at all, Mr Walker. We can't do enough for you, can we, Peg? You don't mind sharing, do you?'

Peg had come into the room after Verity and shook her head. She had been a bit reluctant to have a twenty-first birthday party, but knew that arranging it had given her mother, and apparently Frank, so much pleasure.

Lord and Lady Ryland had once again offered the ballroom at the castle and, once again, it would be a gathering of the clans from both sides of the family, as well as a lot of friends and school contemporaries of Peg's.

'Jenny is coming in with me,' Cathy went on, still preoccupied by domestic details. 'Frank is going to stay over at the Burtons'.'

'Where are Addie and Harold sleeping?'

'Mrs Capstick is putting them up.'

'That's very kind of her. Everyone has been so kind.'

'She said it was no trouble.'

Mrs Capstick, who was the cook at the castle, had a cottage on the estate, and Mr Burton was head gardener.

'Mrs Capstick *is* very kind,' Frank said, again entering the room. 'She's doing all the cooking for the party. In fact, a lot of the staff are making little extras. It's very good of them all.'

He went out of the room again, Verity started talking to Harold, and Peg and Addie, having warmly embraced, tried to catch up with the news. It was the first time they had seen each other since the wedding. Cathy went out to get the tea and Jenny to help her.

Momentarily on his own, Alan looked round the room with its cheerful fire, feeling quite unnerved by the number of people waiting to meet him, though he had known Peg had a large family.

Finally Addie and Peg finished their conversation, Peg and Verity went off to help their mother with the tea and Addie joined Harold, who had wandered over to talk to Alan.

'And what do you do, Mr Walker?'

'I'm a journalist,' Alan replied. 'I work for the *Telegraph*. I was at the same meeting as Peg.'

'Oh yes, of course.' Harold thoughtfully studied the ceiling, hands behind his back. 'Personally I am not in favour of young women engaging in professions like journalism. It was Peg's first assignment, which I understand came about by chance, and it nearly ended in disaster.'

'I think it was a very *rare* thing to have happened.'

'Still, it happened, and it could happen again.'

'Harold doesn't think women should be working at all,' Addie butted in. 'Do you, dear?'

'No, that's not true, Addie,' Harold corrected her. 'I do not think that at all. But yes, I am of the opinion that *married* women should stay at home to look after the family. However, I consider there are other forms of employment suitable for unmarried women, such as teaching, nursing or secretarial work. I have no objection to that kind of thing at all. Journalism is a man's profession and should remain so. As it is, I think the paper exploited the disaster that overtook Peg to help sell more copies. Peg was a victim, not a heroine, and I hope she has learned her lesson.'

Unobserved by the speaker, Peg had returned to the sitting room with a teapot in her free hand and was standing just behind Harold, listening to him. Alan saw her flush as she carefully put the pot down on a table and turned to her brother-in-law.

'That's a nasty thing to suggest, Harold, and your views about women journalists are terribly old-fashioned.'

'I *am* an old-fashioned man, Peg,' Harold said, smiling blandly, 'and I am not ashamed to say so. A woman's place is in the home, if she is married – I am convinced of that – and if she is not, there are plenty of suitable occupations for her to be engaged in.'

Addie, who had become increasingly nervous, placatingly put a hand on Harold's arm.

'Dear, don't you think we should go and see Mrs Capstick and take our things over to her cottage? It's getting rather late.'

After tea Peg and Verity went up to the room they were to share, which was one of the larger of the four bedrooms. Now, as well as a double bed, it contained a smaller put-you-up borrowed from the castle.

Peg, glad to have a rest, stretched out on the double bed and put a hand under her head.

'Addie doesn't look very happy to me. Does she to you?'

Verity sat on her small bed, unpacking her neat suitcase.

'What makes you think that?' she asked, looking up.

'Well, what do *you* think? She's looking all drab again, as she did before Harold started courting her.'

'Oh, I don't think she's *drab*. Maybe tired after the trip?'

'Do you think, maybe –' Peg looked at her sister. 'An addition to the family, perhaps?'

'Maybe.' Verity shrugged. 'Too early to tell.'

'Well, they've been married six months.'

'Now don't you jump to conclusions.' Verity began arranging her brush and comb on the dressing table.

'But if she was having a baby she would look happy, wouldn't she?'

'The thing to do is to ask her,' Verity said practically, 'if you're so curious. We're here for a whole weekend so there should be plenty of time.'

'Better start getting ready for supper.' Peg jumped off her bed and, going across to the dressing table, ran a comb through her hair, talking to Verity as she did.

'I told you it was a mistake to ask Alan.'

'Oh, I don't think so.'

'You can see he's not comfortable. He's ill at ease. No one really knows why he's here. I'm sure they think he's my boyfriend.'

'Well, they'll soon find out he's not by the way you ignore him. You mustn't be so offhand, Peg, especially after all he did for you.'

'I am *not* offhand' – Peg rounded on her sister – 'and if he did a lot for me, I have shown him I'm grateful to him in every way I can, except . . . well, I don't want to marry him.'

Verity looked startled.

'Do you think he wants to marry you?'

'Yes, I know he does.'

'You never told me.'

'There was no need – the question didn't arise – but I didn't want to ask him to my home in case he got the wrong impression, and gave everyone else the wrong impression too. You asked him without asking me, and you shouldn't have done that, Ver.'

'Has he already asked you to marry him?'

'No, but that's because I haven't encouraged him. I know what's on his mind because he came very near to it once when we used to go to all those political meetings together. That's why I don't see him so much. I didn't think it was fair.'

'You should have told me.' Verity bit her lip. 'I thought he was just a friend.'

'He is, and I want it to remain like that.'

'Well, if he doesn't think so, no wonder he feels awkward. Really, Peg, I don't know why you don't like him.'

'I do like him. I just don't want to marry him. Also I don't want to have this feeling of having to be *grateful* to him rammed down my throat for the rest of my life.'

And with that Peg flounced out of the room, leaving her sister looking bemused.

Alan stood at the back of the hall watching the couples dancing to the music of the small band. Tables had been pushed back and, as soon as the speeches were over and the music began, a crowd of men surrounded Peg and she was whisked on to the dance floor.

Alan was not a dancer, indeed didn't know how to dance, but he was still envious of the attention being paid to Peg. He was in love with her and had been since they worked next to each other at the agency. Only he knew so little about women, about love, and he knew he couldn't express himself very well. The declaration of emotions of this kind defeated even his journalistic skills. He had never known anyone like Peg, so beautiful, with so much vivacity. She was unique.

Alan was an only child, born to working-class parents in a suburb of Manchester. His father had been a bricklayer, his mother cleaned the houses of wealthy people in the more affluent suburbs of the city. Alan had been studious and had got a scholarship into grammar school, which had set him apart both from his family and the friends around him. He had experienced from that time a sense of alienation he had never succeeded in overcoming.

Alan did well at school and was expected to go on to university, but he knew the financial demands on his parents would be excessive, so he left after School Certificate and joined a local paper as a copy boy. Because of his background, the poverty he had grown up in, he had developed a passion for politics and until he met Peg this was all he had in life.

After supper Alan had been sitting between Verity and Cathy, whom he liked. Peg had sat between her stepfather and Harold, Addie's husband. She had hardly glanced at him across the table and he knew she hadn't really wanted him to come. But he couldn't resist the chance to be near her for such a long time and accepted the invitation.

'Would you like to dance?' As the music stopped he saw Addie, also looking a little shy and holding out her hand. 'It's all a bit bewildering, isn't it, with our relations?'

'It is a bit,' Alan confessed. 'There are so many, but I'm afraid I can't dance.'

'Neither can I. My husband can't either, but Verity has been dragging him round the dance floor, so I don't see why we shouldn't also.' Whereupon she propelled him out on to the floor.

'We're very *grateful* for what you did for Peg,' Addie murmured into his ear. 'I'm very glad you came.'

Alan began to feel more relaxed with Addie, whom he also liked. So far he liked all her family except, perhaps, Harold, whom he thought pompous and opinionated. He felt sorry for Addie, being married to someone with such old-fashioned, conventional views.

'I understand your husband's a teacher,' he projected, trying to be heard above the music. 'Do you teach too?'

'I did. That's how I met Harold.' Seeing the expression on his face, she added: 'He is really very nice, a bit severe, but very clever. He's just about to take up the headship of a school in Devon, so we're very busy settling into our new house. It's all most exciting. Of course I wouldn't have time for a job even if I wanted one. Besides, I haven't Peg's ambition.'

'Peg is very ambitious,' Alan agreed.

'Do you think she will do well?'

'Oh yes. She caused a sensation with her first job as a reporter. You can't do better than that, can you?'

'But you helped her.'

'I helped rescue her, that's all. I'm not sure I actually saved her life.'

'You're very modest. Peg seems to think you did. She said she was dying. She couldn't breathe.'

'I think somehow she could have made it. I'm getting a lot of praise I don't really deserve. Sorry,' Alan concluded apologetically, having stood heavily on Addie's foot and seen her wince. 'Look, maybe . . . I mean, this isn't really working, is it? I'm far too clumsy. Shall we sit it out?' His hands were sweaty and his throat was dry with the effort of trying to conduct a conversation in this noisy atmosphere.

'A lemonade would be nice,' Addie agreed, anxious to rest her bruised foot. They edged their way from the dance floor, around which were grouped tables occupied by all the guests, most of them red-faced and perspiring despite the cold outside. Many of the men had removed their jackets and were short-sleeved, and the women used improvised fans to wave in front of their flushed faces.

They were a large, rumbustious, good-natured crowd, mostly people who earned their living on or by the land. Cathy's forebears, the Swayles, had been farmers for generations. Her first husband had been a butcher, her second a gardener. Cathy's sister Maude had married into the middle classes, but neither she nor her husband were here, pleading illness plus the bad weather.

Peg, in a long taffeta dress of kingfisher blue, a colour whose contrast enhanced her golden hair, was the undoubted belle of the ball. Few of her female cousins or contemporaries at school could better her looks and, although she might have said she didn't want to have a party, she was clearly enjoying the attention she was getting.

Alan knew he would never get a look-in and wished he had not come. Sadly he looked away, resuming his conversation with his companion.

'These can't *all* be relations,' he said as they approached a long table on which were jugs of lemonade and beer and an assortment of empty glasses.

'No. A lot are, but some are also Peg's friends.' Addie pointed towards the dance floor, where Peg was waltzing with a rather dashing-looking young man with thick black hair and a large moustache. 'That's a cousin from Bournemouth. I can't remember his name. Most of our cousins live in Bournemouth, where my mother and father came from.'

'Peg was always very popular, then?'

'Oh, always. She's so pretty. Don't you think?'

Alan mumbled something inaudible and Addie, trying to get under the skin of this rather enigmatic young man, looked at him closely. '*Don't* you think she's pretty?'

'Why, yes. Yes, I do.'

Now Addie looked across at her merry, dancing sister, the belle of the ball, and wished once again that she was more like her. Where did Peg get her looks from, her style, her sparkle? It really wasn't fair and, not for the first time, Addie had to suppress that pang of jealousy which so often surfaced when Peg was around, and which made her ashamed of herself. Why, Peg had obviously bewitched the luckless Alan, who was clearly enthralled by her, even though she had ignored him for most of the evening. Just then Harold came up, said he was thirsty and, as Addie moved to pour him a beer, began to talk to Alan, whom he seemed to like. Perhaps he sensed in him a fellow spirit.

As the music finished, Peg stood for a few minutes talking to the friend with whom she had been dancing. They had been at elementary school together and he was now a local farmer. Out of the corner of her eye she had seen Alan and Addie leave the floor, and she was aware that they were now standing drinking lemonade, and had just been joined by Harold.

Peg had been acutely conscious of Alan all evening and felt uneasy about him. She was annoyed he had come, but really it wasn't his fault. Verity's invitation had been so pressing. She liked Alan, but she didn't want to give him any false hope just because he had intervened in the mêlée at the political meeting, and perhaps saved her life.

Had she been too generous in that respect? Too emotional? It was easy to be wise after the event, and at the time she had felt she was dying; but maybe someone else would have managed at the last moment to haul her up. Peg by nature was a kind, generous young woman, however, and she thought her feelings about Alan, perhaps her lack of gratitude, were unworthy of her.

She was relieved when Addie had asked him to dance because the rest of the family seemed to be preoccupied: her mother with all the Bournemouth Swayle relations whom she only saw once or twice a year; Verity, dutiful as ever, with some aged aunts, after her dance with Harold. Stella had, temporarily at least, thrown away her shyness and had been enjoying herself. She hadn't missed a dance. Ed, who was not yet into girls, had gone into the snooker room with some friends and a plentiful supply of beer.

At that moment there was a small commotion beside the main door into the hall and Lord and Lady Ryland appeared, followed by their daughter Violet, a tall, handsome woman. All three were in evening dress.

Frank hurried towards them, accompanied by Cathy, who beckoned to Peg. But Peg felt rooted to the spot, conscious of the pace of her heart quickening as the important guests came through the door. First she had seen Lord and Lady Ryland enter then, after a moment, Violet. Her eyes remained fixed on the doorway, but the door was shut and the distinguished visitors moved to the centre of the room where Frank and Cathy greeted them.

No Hubert. Just as well. Peg threw her head back and crossed the floor to join her mother and Frank.

'How very good of your lordship and ladyship to come,' Frank said and, turning to their daughter, 'and you, Miss Violet.'

'We couldn't miss the birthday,' Lord Ryland said, jovially looking towards the door, 'and I think in a few moments someone is coming in with a cake and some champagne.'

'Your lordship.' Peg bobbed gracefully. 'How very kind of you.'

Lord Ryland stooped to kiss her cheek. 'A very happy birthday, my dear, and many more to come.'

'How pretty you look, Peg.' Tall, white-haired Lady Ryland also kissed her. 'Many, *many* more.'

The Rylands were a distinguished-looking couple in their mid to late fifties who had had their share of grief, having lost their eldest son, Lydney, in the war. Violet's fiancé had also been killed, and ever since she was known to have suffered from mental trouble, even to the extent of spending some weeks in a clinic for patients with nervous disorders.

Violet shook Peg's hand and also pecked her on the cheek, and then the double doors were flung open and Mrs Capstick, dressed in her best, appeared, followed by a footman pushing a trolley on which was a large cake with twenty-one candles blazing away.

As if that wasn't enough two of the castle footmen entered with trays on which were glasses of champagne, which they distributed among the guests. The men instantly rolled down their sleeves and put on their jackets, and the hands of some of the women flew to their hair, which they patted anxiously, making sure every strand was in place.

Peg was pushed forward and, to a resounding chorus of 'Happy Birthday', managed with one large puff to blow out all the candles to cheers and applause.

After this ceremony Lord Ryland held up his hand. Instantly the chattering stopped.

'Good evening, everybody,' he said. 'I am Edward Ryland and this is my wife Penelope, and my daughter Violet. We are very happy that you were able to attend this splendid party tonight given for Peg Hallam, who I and my family have known since she was a very small girl.' He bent down and levelled the palm of his hand about three feet above the ground.

'Now she is of age, a grown woman and a very pretty one if I may say so.' He smiled at her and Peg lowered her gaze, almost overwhelmed by this turn of events. 'But, more importantly, she is a charming and delightful person and I hear also that she has already achieved some eminence in her chosen profession, which is journalism, and that she acquitted herself in an exemplary fashion when in a very dangerous situation.

'My family and I are close to Frank and Cathy Carpenter and their family, who suffered as we did, as many of you did, in the war. Now the family are grown up – well, almost.' He looked across at Jenny, holding tightly on to her mother's hand. 'Addie is happily married, Verity is carving a career for herself as a nursing sister after distinguishing herself in the war. We know what Peg does and Ed and Stella will no doubt carry on the family tradition of hard work and service to their country and the community.'

Lord Ryland raised the glass in his hand. 'So I give you a toast: to Peg and all her family. God bless her and God bless them.'

'Peg and her family,' chorused the enthusiastic, perspiring crowd, most of whom had never seen a lord, and were doubly impressed by the presence of the nobility, their largesse and the obvious favour in which their Hallam relations were held.

As the glasses were lowered Frank, facing the crowd, called for silence and then cleared his throat noisily several times, his finger travelling uneasily round the inside of his rather tight collar, while Cathy looked on anxiously.

'My lord,' he said, 'Lady Ryland and Miss Violet. My family and I are very honoured by your presence here this evening, and speechless at your generosity.' He pointed towards the cake, which Mrs Capstick was busily cutting. 'This splendid cake, the champagne. We can't thank you enough.'

Frank cleared his throat again and once more ran his finger round his collar while his face grew ever more puce.

'It *is* true, as his lordship has said, that we have all suffered in the war. His lordship and her ladyship lost a beloved son, and we have had personal tragedies in our family too. But now we have the peace that was so hard fought for – and which still seems so hard to achieve – and here on this night we are gathered together for one purpose: that is to wish my dear stepdaughter Peg Hallam the happiest of birthdays. She is now twenty-one, a woman we love and are all proud of, and what a lovely young woman she is, not only pretty but good and kind.' He looked fondly at her and held up a hand. 'Oh, I'll spare your blushes, Peg. I'll say no more but wish you the very best in your future life.'

By this time Frank had obviously got into the swing of things, relishing his role as a speaker capable of commanding the attention of an audience, perhaps for the first time in his life. He took a deep breath and seemed about to continue when Cathy surreptitiously tugged at his sleeve, and before he had time to open his mouth again Lord Ryland said: 'Thank you, Frank, for a very gracious speech. Now, please have your cake and champagne and enjoy it.'

'Thank you very much, Lord Ryland.' Peg sounded breathless, her eyes sparkled. 'And thank you, everyone' – she gestured towards the crowd – 'all my friends and relations who are here, some of whom have come a long way in very bad weather. Thanks to Mum, Frank, my brother and sisters, and thanks to Alan Walker, who made sure I was here to celebrate my birthday.' She turned towards the astonished Alan and gave him a brilliant smile. There was special applause, for everyone knew the story, and Alan stood there bemused and blushing. At the same time he felt proud of himself and glad that, at last, Peg seemed to wish publicly to acknowledge him.

Frank then took him by the arm and introduced him to Lord and Lady Ryland and their daughter, and explained Alan's role in Peg's rescue.

'You must bring your young man up to the castle before you go back to London, please, and show me all these newspaper reports I have been hearing about,' Lord Ryland told Peg.

'Yes, Lord Ryland.'

'How is little Jenny?' Violet looked at the shy child clinging to her mother's dress.

'Very tired,' Peg said, 'as you can see.'

'She should be in bed.' Cathy tried to urge the little girl forward, without much success, 'but everyone wanted to come to the party, so there is no one to look after her. Say good evening to his lordship and her ladyship, Jenny.' But Jenny shook her head and buried her face deeper in her mother's dress. Lord Ryland smiled and put a hand protectively on her head.

'What a sweet child,' he said, his hand resting there for a moment. Then, more briskly, 'I think we too should all go to bed. It is very late.'

'One final dance,' Frank declared. 'Would you and her ladyship not have a spin around the floor, my lord? And if I may –' He turned to Violet, who graciously took his arm, and they stepped out on to the floor, which gradually filled up with couples for the last waltz.

Alan looked at Peg ruefully. 'I can't dance,' he said.

'So I saw.' Peg tugged him on to the floor. 'Now follow me. One step at a time, you big oaf.'

Six

Despite the lateness of the hour at which they had gone to bed, Peg was awake early. It had been such a cold winter that it was still too early for the blackbirds' song, but the great tits and the song thrushes had started their dawn chorus and it always seemed to her then that spring wasn't very far away.

It had been a wonderful party and she did feel different. She was twenty-one, independent, on the verge of a new and exciting career. She had felt good, knew that she looked good, by the number of young men who thronged about her asking her to dance.

Momentarily her mind lingered on Hubert Ryland and her acute feeling of anticipation, and then the disappointment when he failed to follow his family through the door. But she refused to let her mind dwell for too long on the Ryland heir. It had just been a rather foolish, romantic notion that he would be there once more and they would dance again. Hubert meant nothing to her, or should mean nothing to her. Her sister Addie had been seduced by Lydney Ryland and Jenny would probably never know the identity of her true father or, perhaps, her true mother if this strange pretence continued. One romantic brush with the aristocratic Rylands was enough; another would be disastrous.

Stella and Verity were still fast asleep but Peg felt restless and, despite the bitter cold, she crept out of bed and fumbled for her clothes. She left the room and went downstairs to the kitchen, where she put on the light and started to light the fire.

She got it going, put the kettle on the hob and cut some slices of bread from the loaf in the bin. Then, fetching her overcoat from the hall, she opened the front door and stepped out on to the lawn.

There had been a frost and everything was eerily still. However, the dawn peeping over the hill slowly but inexorably bathed the garden in its soft light. A couple of her blackbird friends, flying over from the copse, landed close by and she threw them pieces of the thick bread which were soon eaten. Then a robin and a couple of tits joined in the feast until a large indignant magpie flew in and chased them all away, greedily gobbling up what was left.

Peg opened the garden gate which led on to the drive and began to walk up towards the castle when she saw a figure coming towards her, shoulders hunched against the cold. For a crazy moment she thought it might be Hubert, but as it got near the tall familiar outline was unmistakable.

'Alan,' she said, 'what are you doing out so early in the morning?'

'I could ask you the same thing.'

'I always get up early.'

'So do I. It's so lovely here.' He looked around. 'I envy you having grown up in such a place and always having it to come back to.'

'Yes, I'm lucky. But I love London too.'

'So do I, but when I see countryside like this I think how I would like to have been a country lad. I come from a smoky city just like London.'

'Well, you must come here whenever you like,' Peg said, impulsively tucking her arm through his. 'Let's go back to the house and have a cup of tea.'

'But weren't you going for a walk?'

'It *is* cold,' Peg said, shivering. 'I just lit the fire and put the kettle on. Maybe I'll go out later. Shall we go up to the castle and see Lord Ryland, as he invited us?'

'I have to get back to London,' Alan said.

'Oh. I thought you were staying over?' Peg looked surprised.

Alan shook his head. 'I'm on an early shift tomorrow. I think Verity is going back too, and I said we'd go together. Besides—' He stopped.

'Besides what?'

'Nothing.'

They reached the house and Peg pushed open the kitchen door. The fire was well alight with the kettle bubbling over it.

'Besides what?' she repeated, putting some tea leaves in a large brown pot and pouring water over them.

'I don't have any time for the aristocracy. Surely you realise that?'

'Oh!' Peg finished her task, got out two cups and saucers, put in the milk, added the tea. Then she handed Alan his cup. 'I don't think of the Rylands as aristocracy. They're very friendly employers. Frank has worked for them since he was a boy and regards them highly. They always gave us children money on our birthdays and a large party at Christmas and midsummer for all the staff.'

'But did they ever ask you for dinner at the castle?'

'I don't understand.'

'I think you do. They do not regard you as equals, as friends.'

'Well, we're not.'

'I found Lord Ryland's remarks last night horribly patronising. I have no time for that sort of thing.'

'Then perhaps it's just as well you didn't grow up in the country. Frankly, I'd rather be patronised here than have to live in a horrible smoky Manchester suburb, as you did.'

'Well, I wouldn't. We were free. The countryside is beautiful, but it is an illusion.'

'A moment ago you said you'd like to live here.'

'In theory, yes, I would – it *is* lovely – but not as the servant of Lord Ryland.'

'We are not servants,' Peg said hotly.

'You *are* servants. I bet the parties in summer and at Christmas are the servants' balls, aren't they?'

Peg bit her lip. 'We never think of them like that.'

'Because you were conditioned not to think. "The rich man at the castle, the poor man at the gate." '

'We were never "poor". My stepfather was head gardener; Frank was a groom and is now his lordship's chauffeur. This house comes with the job, it's true, but I don't think that if, for any reason, Frank couldn't work Lord Ryland would eject them. He'd find them somewhere else or let them stay on here. Mother thought we'd have to move when she married Frank, but she loved this house and Lord Ryland said they could stay and the new groom could have Frank's house up the hill. You see, they *do* care what people think and feel. They *are* concerned. After all, we all have employers, you and I as much as anyone else. The Rylands are kind, thoughtful people. Some aristocracy may not be so nice but the Rylands are different. My sister—' Peg stopped.

'Your sister?' Alan had been listening carefully.

'She was very friendly with Lord Ryland's son, the one who was killed.'

Alan looked astonished. 'And didn't Lord Ryland object to that?'

'He didn't know.'

'Ah!'

'Don't try and be so clever, Alan. You're so obsessed by theory. Sometimes I think you don't know what goes on in the real world.'

Later in the day Frank drove Verity and Alan to the station in Sherborne, but Peg didn't go and see them off. Alan had gone to his room after their rather acrimonious conversation in the kitchen, reappeared at breakfast then returned to his room until lunchtime, when Addie and Harold had also arrived. The younger girls spent the morning in the kitchen helping their mother, while Verity sat in the parlour sewing and trying to keep Jenny entertained. Although everyone was rather tired, the meal had been a proper Sunday lunch: a roast with plenty of vegetables and a plum pudding left over from Christmas.

Again the womenfolk did the washing-up, Verity and Alan went up to pack and then came the goodbyes. Alan had been vociferous in his thanks to Cathy and Frank for their hospitality, and Cathy had once more embraced him warmly, thanked him for what he had done for Peg and told him that he was always welcome.

Then there had been a long leave-taking of Verity.

'Don't you want to go and see Alan off?' Cathy had asked, but Peg had shaken her head. She didn't even stand on the doorstep to say goodbye.

After all the excitement it seemed rather flat in the house, and the two older sisters went into the parlour, where there was a fire, with their mother while Stella, Ed, Jenny and Harold went off for a brisk walk. The frost had not let up all day.

'Why didn't you want to see Alan off, dear?' Cathy asked Peg, stoking the fire. 'I think he was a bit hurt. He was very quiet.'

'Alan is a very quiet man,' Peg said, settling in a chair. 'He doesn't show much emotion.'

'I liked him,' Cathy said firmly. 'A nice, sensible kind of man. I should think he's very capable.'

'Mother, we are not a *couple*,' Peg insisted angrily. 'You keep on behaving as though we are.'

'I don't think that at all. I just think he is a very nice man and, as he was your friend and you brought him, you might have wanted to see him off.'

'Well, I didn't. And I didn't bring him. Verity asked him, actually, and he has gone back with *her*.'

'I see. That's it, then.' Cathy rose from her knees and yawned. 'I think if you two girls don't mind, I'll go and have a little sleep. It was a very late night. Maybe you'd like a nap too?'

'No thanks, Mother.' Addie slipped into the chair next to Peg. 'I may drop off here.'

'What time are you and Harold leaving tomorrow, dear?'

'Quite early. Harold has to prepare his timetable.'

'I shall miss you,' Cathy said, touching the top of Addie's head as she passed. 'Is everything all right with you, dear?'

'Of course, Mother. Why?'

'I just thought you seemed rather quiet.'

'I have been tired. There's so much to do in the new house.'

'But happy?'

'Of course.' Addie gave her a reassuring smile.

'Maybe we'll have a little chat before you go?'

'I'll bring you up a cup of tea, Mum, when the others come back. We can talk then.'

Cathy went out, closing the door, and the two younger women sat silently for a few moments, gazing into the fire.

'What does Mum want to talk to you about?' Peg asked after a while.

Addie shrugged her shoulders. 'Maybe about Jenny.'

'I understood you weren't having Jenny for the time being?'

To her consternation and surprise Addie suddenly burst into tears and Peg immediately rose and sat on the arm of her chair, putting an arm around her sister's shoulders.

'Not now. Not ever.' Addie frantically groped for her handkerchief and wiped her eyes. 'Harold doesn't want Jenny, *ever*. Didn't Mum tell you?'

'She said "for the time being"!'

'She was being tactful.' Addie leaned her head against her sister's breast. 'Harold was beastly on our honeymoon. At first things went well and then one day I told him Jenny was my daughter and he lost control of himself. He said he would never have married me if . . . he'd known.' She started to sob quietly again.

'What a horrible thing to say!' Peg burst out indignantly.

'I felt I'd been foolish.' Addie sniffed. 'I should have told him before the wedding. Mum said I should have told him. But I didn't. You see' – she looked furtively at her sister – 'I felt if he

knew I wasn't . . . you know, that I had slept with someone –
well, men are like that, aren't they? And I *did* want to get
married. I didn't want to be like Verity.'

'So you said.' Peg remembered their conversation before the
wedding. 'At the time I didn't think that you were really in love
with Harold. I still wonder; but if you had such a bad time it
explains everything.'

'Explains what?'

'Ver and I both thought you've been looking a bit off colour,
quieter than usual. Mum obviously thinks so too.' She looked
closely at her sister. 'We *had* wondered if perhaps you might be
expecting?'

Addie's laugh became a little hysterical. 'Nothing like that, I
assure you. Harold doesn't even want to touch me.'

'Oh!' Peg looked shocked.

'He said maybe in time he'll come round; but since our
honeymoon he feels he can't bear to share a bed with me. I'm
hoping that as things settle down he'll change his mind.'

'But how can you *stay* with someone like that?' Peg was
aghast.

'What choice do I have?' Addie smiled ruefully. 'Should I
admit my marriage is a failure and come crawling home? Imagine
the humiliation. Who would want me, what should I do with
myself? It isn't that I can't *bear* Harold. I think he has a lot of
good points. He is clever and capable, a most intelligent man, but
he is also cold towards me and that makes me very unhappy. I
can understand that I shocked him, deceived him even, and now
I'm having to pay for it.'

Addie gave herself up to a fresh torrent of weeping and for a
while Peg just hugged her, wishing that they were children again
and had never had to grow up.

'He'll be back soon.' Addie looked almost fearfully out of the
window, as if afraid that Harold somehow knew of her disloyalty
in talking about him. She frantically tried to dry her eyes. 'I
mustn't let him see me like this.'

'I worry about you,' Peg said gently, stroking her hair. 'I shall worry more than ever now.'

'I think Harold *will* eventually be all right. On one occasion when we made love on our honeymoon it was very good. It was blissful. It gave me a wonderful feeling of togetherness and tenderness that made me want to tell him about Jenny. I felt so close to him. It is a lovely experience, Peg.' She looked at her sister, eyes bright with emotion. 'You don't know, do you?' And, as Peg shook her head: 'It *is* wonderful when it goes well. It went well with Lydney and that one time with Harold. And because it was so good and special and I thought we really loved each other I made the mistake of spoiling it. You see, he hadn't had any experience with women, although he was over forty. I was the first. He really didn't understand passion.'

'Nor do I,' Peg murmured.

'Oh?'

'I've never really felt attracted to anyone in that way.'

'Maybe you're not ready. Maybe you haven't met the right man.'

Fleetingly the image of Hubert Ryland sprang to Peg's mind, but never in a thousand years would she confide such a thing to her sister. Instead she nodded in agreement. 'Maybe I haven't.'

'Not Alan?' Addie looked at her slyly. 'I do think he's very keen on you.'

'Did he say anything?'

'Not really, but it was the way he looked at you. His eyes followed you around when you were dancing. You once said he was like Harold, but I think he's very nice.'

'He is very nice, but he doesn't excite me.'

'I think there's more to love than excitement.' Addie paused. 'I mean, I think if Harold and I hang on and can straighten things out we have a chance of being very happy.'

'Even if you don't love him? Strange.' Peg gazed deeply into the fire.

'When we made love that hot day in Spain and it was so good I

82

felt I did love him and he loved me. Maybe it could happen again. He wants children. He said he did. I am prepared to give it time. To hope for the best.' Addie looked at the clock. 'Heavens, they'll soon be back from their walk! I'll go and get the things ready for tea.' She gazed wistfully across at Peg. 'You know, I do envy you.'

'Oh. Why?'

'You have everything ahead of you: love, work that you like, your independence. Sometimes I think that it's all over for me.'

And before Peg had a chance to reply Addie quickly left the room.

After her birthday Peg returned to London and immediately became absorbed in her new job. Soon everyone forgot that she was a heroine, and she was given the run-of-the-mill jobs usually given to a cub reporter, but she worked hard and learned quickly.

As the only woman in the newsroom Peg knew how important it was to gain the goodwill of her colleagues, many of whom were jealous and resented her position, believing she was under the protection of the proprietor. Even the news editor, whom she had once thought of as an ally, appeared to resent her and would have liked to see her fail. She had to tread carefully, and she knew all the time that she was learning: in every sense of the word she was on probation.

One day in late March, after two rather trying but interesting months, Peg was just leaving work. It was quite late and she was anxious to get home and put her feet up. She had been writing up a story about a fire in Clerkenwell, had put the finishing touches to it and filed it, and with a brief nod to those of her colleagues who remained, she put on her hat and coat and walked swiftly down the stairs to the lobby.

There a man stood with his back to her, reading the notices on the board. He turned as she reached the last step and to her surprise she saw it was Alan. Yet, somehow, he looked different.

'Alan,' she said in astonishment. 'What are you doing here?'

'I was hoping to see you,' Alan said diffidently, walking towards her. 'It seems to have been such a long time.'

'You've got new glasses,' Peg said studying him, 'and somehow you've changed.' His hair was neatly brushed back, no longer hanging in lank dull locks over his forehead, and he was freshly shaved. He wore an overcoat over a grey striped suit, a white shirt with a crisp clean collar and a blue tie. 'You've smartened yourself up, Alan,' she concluded.

'Never one to mince words, Peg.' He looked at her fondly.

'No, you have. I mean, well, you were a bit of a mess.'

'Would you like me better now?'

'I always liked you,' she said guardedly.

'It *is* good to see you again,' he said.

'And you.' Peg felt a sudden, unexpected surge of affection for him. 'What kept you away for so long?'

'I didn't really know if you wanted to see me. We didn't part too well.'

'We had an argument about the aristocracy,' Peg remembered, 'or rather *my* aristocracy: the Rylands. It seems a bit trivial now.'

'I wondered if you'd like to have supper or if . . . will Verity be waiting for you?'

'Verity's away. She's gone somewhere with her friend Mrs Beaumaurice. Penzance, I think. Tonight would be very good. In fact I'm hungry.'

Alan made no effort to conceal his pleasure. 'There's a new Italian restaurant in Farringdon Road. Would you like to try that?'

'Sounds fine,' Peg said and they stepped out on to the pavement and started walking towards Ludgate Hill. It was chilly, and Peg shivered.

'How long had you been waiting?'

'Oh . . . about an hour.'

'You should have told Reception. They would have phoned up to me.'

'I thought you might not want to see me.'

'Alan, why should I not want to see you?'

'Because . . .' He looked at her and shook his head. 'I don't know. It's just that when we do see each other we seem to argue.'

'Well, we haven't seen each other very often in the past months and, truthfully, I've missed you.'

'Have you?' He looked surprised.

'Of course I have. We're old friends.'

They reached Ludgate Circus and turned into Farringdon Road, walking under Holborn Viaduct on the left-hand side until Alan stopped outside a brightly lit restaurant, its window running with condensation, and pushed open the door.

It was small with about half a dozen tables covered with pretty red-and-white checked tablecloths. Half the tables were already occupied, but Peg and Alan were greeted by a friendly, softly spoken waiter who took their coats, showed them to a corner table and presented them with a menu which they studied, heads close together.

'Looks good, smells good,' Peg said, smiling cheerfully at Alan. 'What a nice surprise this is. I hardly ever get taken out. It's a treat.'

'I'm sure you've had all the men in your office after you.'

'On the contrary. They rather resent me being there and would like to get rid of me. They're just waiting for me to make one tiny mistake, and then' – she snapped her fingers – 'out.'

'But why?' Alan looked puzzled.

'Have you any women in your newsroom?'

'A couple.'

'And are they accepted?'

'I think so. They were there before I came. They do a first-rate job.'

The waiter came across and they ordered.

'Would you like some wine?' Alan asked Peg.

'Of course.'

'Spaghetti Bolognese twice, please, and could we have a bottle of Chianti?'

The waiter moved off and came back with a bottle which he uncorked. He poured the wine into their glasses.

'Cheers.' Peg raised hers. 'And let's hope we see each other more regularly.'

'Do you mean that, Peg?' Alan put aside his menu, leaned his elbows on the table and gazed at her.

'I mean it,' she said putting down her glass. 'But I mean it as friends. Just friends.'

'Have you got—'

'No, I haven't got anybody, if that's what you were going to ask. I haven't time. My work is very demanding. I have to be on my best behaviour all the time, careful not to make mistakes. It's very taxing.'

'And how is Verity, to change the subject?'

'Verity is very well. Very friendly with the Beaumaurices, especially Mrs Beaumaurice. They go on painting weekends together.'

'Does Verity paint?'

'She sketches just to keep Geraldine – Mrs Beaumaurice – company, I think.'

'And what do you do at weekends, Peg?'

'I try and catch up on my sleep. I must say I've found it hard work. All the time I have to remember I'm a journalist, not a woman. There are a lot of men in the newsroom who are determined not to like me. I have to tread warily.'

'Our women are both very good, older than you. They do seem to concentrate on features and not go out so much after stories. They've served their apprenticeships. Soon it will be quite common to have women reporters.'

'How about politics?' Peg looked at him. 'Still the same convictions?'

'Of course, and now that we have a Labour government, more so than ever.'

In January 1924 the first Labour government, though a minority one, had been returned under the leadership of Ramsay

86

Macdonald. Winston Churchill had called it a 'serious national misfortune', and the prediction was that it wouldn't last long.

'It *is* a tremendous triumph,' Alan went on, 'but for me it's not socialist enough. I'm beginning to ally myself with the forces of the left, with the object of one day bringing true socialism and an end to all injustice about. I'm coming more and more to respect what is happening in Russia. That's *real* socialism.'

Peg listened to him carefully. She found him impressive. He seemed invested with a new authority. His political views had crystallised. Despite her roots in the countryside and her devotion to the Ryland family, she did sympathise with a lot of what Alan said. There was much poverty and deprivation about but, more than that, Labour, she felt, were on the side of women, who were still held down in the workplace and oppressed on the domestic front. Her male colleagues were resentful, jealous and either tried to hinder her or ensure that she got the most menial jobs: minor fires, burglaries, unimportant incidents which often didn't even make the news pages after she had spent hours writing them up.

'I can't help agreeing with you,' Peg said. 'I wouldn't go as far as communism or extreme socialism, but Labour seems to me the best hope for the future of this country, and not only as far as institutions are concerned, but the place of women too. In many ways we have betrayed the sacrifices of the suffragettes.'

By the end of their meal, slightly tipsy on wine, Peg began to see Alan in a different way from the one in which she had seen him before. He had undoubtedly developed a stature and a maturity that made him almost attractive.

Alan got out his cigarette case and passed it to her.

'Do you?'

'Of course,' Peg said taking one. 'They smoke like chimneys in our newsroom.'

'Ours too.' Alan lit their cigarettes and poured the remainder of the wine into their glasses, looking ruefully at the empty bottle.

As they continued to discuss domestic politics and the international situation, Peg thought how nice it was sitting here with Alan, smoking and drinking the rest of their wine with the waiters moving quietly about between the tables. She thought it was a very sophisticated and grown-up thing to do. And they *were* grown up.

'I think it's time I moved away from Verity,' Peg said, stubbing out her cigarette.

'Oh?'

'She still makes me feel like a child.'

'Do you also have to ask her permission to do things and tell her everything?'

'In a way. I know she means well, and it's only because she loves me and worries about me. Only if I say I want to move out it will hurt her terribly. You must come up and see Ver again, Alan. She likes you.'

'And I like her.' Alan looked at his watch. 'And if you are to get the last bus we must put our skates on.' He called the waiter and asked for the bill. 'I'll have to see you home.'

Peg shook her head. 'No, that's not necessary.'

'Oh yes it is. I wouldn't dream of letting a young woman, or any woman, walk alone through the street at this time of night.'

'But how will you get back?'

'Don't worry about me.' Assured, confident Alan smiled reassuringly as he got up.

The bill paid, they hurried back on to Farringdon Road and got to the bus stop with seconds to spare before the bus came.

'I feel bad about this,' Peg said as they clambered aboard and took their seats. 'How will you get back?'

Alan reached in his pocket for the change to buy their tickets.

'I'll find a way. There are late-night buses.'

The bus stopped a little way from Peg's destination and she was glad that after all she had Alan to accompany her. At one stage she slipped an arm through his, and it seemed such a natural thing to do that when they stopped outside the gate of the house and he lightly kissed her cheek she didn't feel that it was an unwelcome gesture.

'Thank you for coming all this way,' she said.

'It was worth it to see you.' Alan kissed the other cheek and then stood back. 'Can I see you again?'

'Of course.'

'Let me watch you go in through the door.'

'You're getting like Verity,' she said in a light, bantering tone and then, with a confusion of emotions, a strange feeling of happiness, went up the path. Once she had opened the door, she turned to him and waved. He waved back and only then did he leave her, walking off through the dark.

For some time Peg watched him before she went in and locked the door, thinking that he had a long way to go, probably on foot, before he reached home.

How Verity would have approved of such gallantry.

Seven

The still placid waters of Derwent Water reflected the deep blue of the sky, the gently undulating fells and mountains surrounding them. Occasionally a breeze, or the wash caused by a rowing boat, would ruffle the surface of the lake, causing the reflections to tremble as though disturbed by some subterranean force.

The leaves were burgeoning on the trees above them, and the birds flew back and forth feeding their young. Occasionally a fierce cacophony of sound would break out high up in the branches, as nesting birds fought fiercely to protect their young from predators such as jackdaws or magpies, or the occasional sparrowhawk.

Geraldine sat in front of her easel painting the lake in vibrant, brilliant watercolours. Verity had gone for a walk through the woods surrounding the lake and now set about unpacking the picnic they had brought from the hotel, which was hidden in the trees, a short walk away.

A small skiff with bright red sails was making its way towards the island in the middle of the lake where the celebrated Victorian art critic John Ruskin had once had a home. Possibly someone still lived there. Not far away in Grasmere William and Dorothy Wordsworth had lived and there they had been visited by Coleridge, Southey and numerous other poets and intellectuals whose names were now part of England's rich cultural history. With its many artistic and literary associations, the Lake District was a perfect place for Verity and Geraldine to enjoy a short

Easter break while Philip attended one of his numerous medical conferences, this time in Germany.

Verity spread out a rug on the ground and, flopping on it, began to undo the various packages the hotel had provided for them: cucumber and ham sandwiches, rich fruit cake, tomatoes, oranges and a thermos of tea. They had also purchased a bottle of white wine in Keswick the day before and it lay at the edge of the water, secured to the bank by a piece of string.

Verity drew the bottle out of the water, undid the string and skilfully extracted the cork. Then she poured the wine into two glasses and, handing one to her friend, said, 'I really feel I would like to live here, don't you, Geraldine?'

Geraldine removed her spectacles and thoughtfully sipped the cool wine before replying. 'I don't know. Sometimes I think I would prefer Italy. Venice would be lovely.'

'Oh, Venice would be marvellous.' Verity put her glass to her lips, thinking of the wonderful holiday they had had there when their friendship had really started to blossom: two very different women but with a surprising amount in common.

'Or even Florence.' Geraldine warmed to her subject. 'You have never been to Florence, have you, dear?'

Verity shook her head.

'We *must* go to Florence, maybe in the summer.' Geraldine cocked her head on one side, a rapturous expression on her face. 'Oh, how I would *love* to show you the Fra Angelico frescoes in the Convent of San Marco, and the Michelangelo statues in the Medici Chapel, and . . . oh, the Ponte Vecchio, the Uffizi gallery. Florence is wonderful. You would find it thrilling!'

She rose from her stool and joined Verity, who was exploring the contents of the sandwich box, on the rug.

'Cucumber, I think,' Verity said, inspecting it critically. 'They do look after us supremely well. Florence in the summer. Sounds wonderful.' She looked across at her friend, who had stretched out on the rug, her face lifted to the sunshine. She really was beautiful; so poised, with a wonderful sense of calm that seemed such an integral part of her personality. She always wore long skirts, loose flowing robes, fluttering chiffon scarves. With beautifully coiffured white hair, her opalescent skin, her hooded eyes, she seemed deeply remote and mysterious, a being from another planet.

Verity realised that Geraldine bewitched her and felt all too humdrum and earthbound in her presence.

'Do you think Philip will mind? I mean, I assume he won't be coming?' she said.

'Well –' Geraldine pulled a face. 'I suppose we will have to *ask* him. But really I prefer it so much more without Philip, don't you?'

Oh yes she did, but Verity thought it tactless to answer the question directly. 'Philip of course doesn't share our interests. He would much rather be at a medical conference.'

'Or at his club,' Geraldine said, a derisive note in her voice. 'Sometimes I think we could easily do without men' – she poured herself a little more wine – 'except, of course, for the purposes of breeding. It is that which makes the whole business necessary. Otherwise I would be quite happy to be like you, dear Verity.'

'I don't think you would,' Verity said sombrely.

'But why not?'

'It isn't an enviable position in this society to be an unmarried woman without children.'

'Oh, but things are changing so much. Look at all the women who follow professions that not so long ago would have been unheard of? Your sister, for instance, a successful journalist.'

'My sister would one day like to be married and have a family. She would not like to be as I am, unattached, alone. I know that my sister Addie married a man she did not really love because she didn't want to be like me' – Verity gazed sadly at her friend – 'and that is the truth.'

'Oh, my dear.' Geraldine impulsively put a hand over Verity's. 'I do wish you didn't feel like that. I assure you I envy you your independence. You can go where you like, do what you want, see who you wish. I am totally governed by Philip's wishes, except during the few days I am able to snatch occasionally to go away with you.' She lowered her voice. 'All my friends are married and unable to take a moment away from their husbands. Women are really enslaved to men. You don't know what your friendship means to me.'

'Thank you for saying that.' Verity squeezed Geraldine's hand tightly. 'It means a lot to me too.'

'Let it always be like that,' Geraldine said, moving closer and gently pressing her lips to Verity's cheek. Then she rose, briskly brushed the crumbs off her skirt and returned to her stool, firmly fixing her eyes on the half-finished painting in front of her.

Unnerved, trembling slightly, Verity sat for a few moments, deeply affected by the immediacy of Geraldine's presence, by that chaste but sublime pressure of her lips, the sense of physical desire that had almost overwhelmed her. Then she rose, tied the string round the bottle of wine and lowered it again into the cold, clear water.

Of course it was possible to love a woman and not be 'in love', Verity thought when, after the blissful few days alone with Geraldine, she was back again in London following the familiar routine.

But her relationship with Geraldine had changed, entered a new phase. She knew about love between women, as there was love between men, and she herself felt a strong attraction to her own sex, though she had never considered it to be primarily physical. There had been much camaraderie in the nurses' homes, especially during the war. The bond between women was very different from that shared with a man.

Verity knew she had wanted a physical relationship with Rex and had resisted because she did not think, at the time, that it was right. She was not so sure about that now. As a thirty-year-old virgin she realised she had missed out on one of life's meaningful experiences. She knew a little, but nevertheless enough, of the theories of Sigmund Freud and his fellow psychoanalysts to realise that it was possible to sublimate these natural feelings and become absorbed in one's work as, indeed, she was. But what if, like Geraldine, you had nothing to do except wait on the wishes and commands of your husband?

Once again she was back in the maternity ward, shortly, she hoped, to take over as sister in charge, a position of responsibility for which she knew Philip Beaumaurice had recommended her.

A couple of weeks after her return from Derwent Water, Verity was sitting in her room in the hospital writing up her notes when one of the junior nurses hurried in without even knocking at the door.

'Would you come quickly, please, Sister? Mrs Farjeon is in terrible distress.'

'Oh dear.' Verity got up and followed the young nurse along the corridor to the labour ward where the poor woman was twisting and turning in agony on the delivery couch. A young doctor with bent head and sweat on his brow was working away between her legs while two other nurses looked anxiously on.

'Stuck fast in the breech position.' The doctor, who had only recently qualified, raised his head, looking with relief at Verity. 'Oh, Sister Barnes, thank goodness you've come. Can you . . .'

Verity hurried over to assess the situation and saw that it was serious. One of the baby's legs was protruding from the woman's body and the other nowhere to be seen. By this time Mrs Farjeon's screams of agony were horrific and one of the nurses gave her a rag and told her to bite hard on it.

'Have you called Dr Beaumaurice?'

The young doctor shook his head.

'Call him immediately.'

'But he is not on duty.'

'Telephone his home,' Verity commanded. 'At once. Say that I asked and that it is urgent.'

'But what about Mr Watson?'

Mr Watson was the consultant obstetrician and Dr Beaumaurice's chief.

Verity ignored him. 'Call Dr Beaumaurice. Tell him to come at once.' She then donned a white gown and mask and joined the young doctor to do what she could to try and contain the situation until the arrival of Dr Beaumaurice in order to ensure not only that the baby was born alive, but that the mother survived as well.

Dr Beaumaurice had been having dinner at home when the call came and left immediately. Within half an hour he too was scrubbed and gowned. Chloroform was administered to the suffering mother and with the skilful use of forceps and an amount of cautious but fairly brutal manual strength he managed to deliver a baby which, though distressed and in need of resuscitation, was alive and in all probability would remain so. Mrs Farjeon, recovering from her anaesthetic, was stitched and wheeled back to her ward.

The paediatrician who had taken over administered to the newborn infant and Dr Beaumaurice, perspiring heavily, removed his mask and gown and went to make his report in Sister's room, where Verity was already sitting writing up her report of the night's emergency.

'Thank you so much for coming, Philip.' She smiled at him gratefully as he closed the door. 'The baby would have died without you.'

'Did you call Watson?'

Verity's head remained bent over her notes. 'You know I didn't.' She raised her head. 'I wanted that child to live, the mother to survive.'

'You should have called Watson. I might get into trouble. Strictly speaking he was on call and I was not. If questions are asked what do I do? What shall I say?'

'That you are a competent obstetrician and he is not, that his methods are still lingering in the nineteenth century. The sooner that man retires the better for all prospective mothers-to-be.'

'You know I can't say that.' Philip looked at her angrily. 'When I apply for a consultant's post his recommendation will be vital for me. I already think he is a bit jealous of me.'

Verity's hand flew to her mouth. 'Oh, Philip, I didn't think. I couldn't think. I'm sure mother or child would not have survived if it hadn't been for you. That is the important thing to me.'

'Isn't my career important to you?'

'Of course it is. Terribly important.'

'I don't want to be forced to apply to some second-rate hospital in the provinces. I want to be a consultant in a major London hospital, and in order for that to happen I can't offend my boss.'

Verity looked truly stricken. 'Oh, Philip, I am so sorry. What can I do to make it right?'

'If asked say you tried to find Watson and couldn't.'

'But that would be a lie.' Verity vigorously shook her head. 'I'm afraid that is something I couldn't do. If there is a fuss I will naturally take the blame. I'll say I made a mistake. I assure you I will take full responsibility because the last thing I want is to do you any harm.'

And with that she picked up her notes and left the room. She made her way to the maternity ward, furious with herself for harming the career of a man she not only admired but now considered a personal friend.

She made sure that Mrs Farjeon had recovered and that the baby was being well looked after, and then visited the other mothers who had been delivered that day, checking also on their babies.

That done she returned to Sister's room, aware that she was more than weary. To her surprise she found Philip Beaumaurice still there writing at the desk.

'Philip, why haven't you gone home?' she asked in surprise as she closed the door. 'It's very late.'

'I could ask the same thing of you.'

'I had my rounds to do.'

'I wanted to apologise to you.' Philip put down his pen and
looked at her. 'I'm sorry I upset you. I didn't mean to. Believe me
I'm grateful to you.'

'Why should you be grateful to me?' Verity put her papers on
the desk and sat in the chair facing him.

'Because, as well as being an excellent and perceptive midwife
and nurse, you are a family friend and I am enormously grateful
for what you have done for Geraldine.'

Verity looked surprised.

'What have I done for Geraldine?'

'You have been a good friend to her. She is a very lonely
woman with little to do and she is not interested in my work.'

'Oh, I think she is.'

'No, she isn't, and sometimes I think she is even hostile.'

'She's very proud of you, Philip,' Verity insisted, 'and she is a
most gifted artist who gets a lot of pleasure and satisfaction from
her talent.'

'You're very loyal.' Philip's hand rested on her arm, his gaze
affectionate, even fond. 'Geraldine is very short of friends. She
frightens them away. Something about her intimidates people.'

'Well, she doesn't intimidate me.' Verity, a little unnerved by
Philip's gesture, moved away.

'That's why I'm grateful to you.' Philip picked up his papers
and put them in his case. He clicked it shut and looked across at
her.

'It is very late, Verity. May I give you a lift home?'

Verity went to get her coat, strangely perturbed by Philip's
attitude, which seemed to her to verge on intimacy. His touch
had been impulsive, warm. He had kept his hand on her arm for
some time before she moved away, the first real physical contact
she had ever had with him. Their relationship, though increasingly friendly, had always been impersonal. It reminded her a
little of Geraldine's chaste kiss on the shores of Derwent Water,
which had also taken her by surprise, and seemed to change the
nuances of their relationship. She felt she was becoming too

involved with this strange, rather bewitching couple, and felt that maybe it was time to back away.

But could she? That was the question. Was she not a little in thrall to them both?

As the music surged through the hall Peg was conscious of a feeling of exultation, of uplift in tune with the notes of the great Brahms symphony. She glanced at the man standing beside her and knew that he felt the same. Instinctively their hands met and remained joined, fingers loosely clasped, until the music came to the end and the audience roared its approval.

Sharing a love of music, she and Alan had been to many of the Promenade concerts in the course of the summer, standing in the auditorium where the seats had been removed, enjoying the music with hundreds of other young working people like themselves, or the not so young but impoverished.

On a sunny day they would picnic in the park beforehand. For a more popular concert, one of them would try and leave work early to save a place in the queue that wound round the Queen's Hall.

It had been a good summer for Peg. Her work had gone well. She was increasingly accepted in the newsroom, her copy no longer savagely scrutinised for possible errors. She was taken off fires and burglaries and sent on more interesting assignments.

As social and industrial unrest in the country continued she often reported from Parliament or the courts, where the government had recently won an important battle with Poplar Council over the payment of relief to striking dockers. In Alan's eyes this was a betrayal of the people and not what a Labour government should have been about.

Her relationship with Alan slowly blossomed. She enjoyed his company, his erudition – extensive for a working-class man who had never been to university – and appreciated his steadfastness and good sense.

They met regularly, once or twice a week. Verity liked him and he often came for Sunday lunch, after which the three of them might walk on the Heath. On one occasion they had even all been to visit the Beaumaurices in Highgate.

Alan had become a kind of fixture in Peg's life, and she knew that if for any reason their association were to cease she would miss him.

They had never been intimate, never fully kissed, but increasingly their relationship became more tactile, full of involuntary movements like clasping hands. Alan would occasionally briefly encircle her waist with his arm when showing her something. Never pressing, never offensive.

The music of Brahms still echoing, they made their way through the crowd of fellow promenaders out on to Portman Place and began to walk towards to Euston Road where Peg would get her bus. It was still daylight, the July evening warm, muggy.

'It's such a lovely evening I feel like walking home,' Peg announced suddenly.

'It's too far. Verity will be anxious.'

'Verity is away. She's gone to Florence with the Beaumaurices.'

'Oh!' Alan appeared to consider this. 'Well, let's walk, then.'

It was a Saturday and the next day they could sleep in. They strolled along Albany Street, through Camden Town and up Haverstock Hill. It was a long way, but it didn't seem like it because their companionable silences, occasionally broken by conversation or an observation, were never awkward.

'You must come in and have a cold drink,' Peg said when they at last reached her front door. 'I can't let you walk all the way back.'

'Well –' Alan appeared to hesitate – 'if you insist.'

'I insist,' Peg said firmly, unlocking the front door.

Alan followed her up the stairs to the flat, Peg putting on the lights as she went.

'It seems strange without Verity,' Alan said, looking round. 'She seems very friendly with the Beaumaurices.'

'She is,' Peg agreed as she went into the kitchen. 'Would you prefer a cup of tea to a cold drink?'

'Cold, I think.' Alan sat down at the kitchen table. 'I'm quite tired. That really was a long walk.'

'But enjoyable.'

'Oh, very.'

'Pity you have to go all the way back.'

Peg poured lemonade into glasses and handed one to him.

'I might pick up a late-night bus.'

'You could stay the night. There's plenty of room.'

'Oh!'

'You can sleep on my bed and I'll sleep in Verity's. There's nothing wrong with that, is there?'

'Nothing at all' – Alan thoughtfully stroked his chin – 'if you're sure it's all right. Will the neighbours mind?'

'It's none of their business. We must be adult about these things,' Peg said matter-of-factly. 'We aren't going to do anything immoral. I can't let you go all the way back. I'll give you a rug to throw on my bed and you can cover yourself with that.'

She left the room for a moment, came back with a rug and gave it to him. 'It's a warm night. You'll be all right.'

'Thanks.' Alan, suddenly feeling nervous, quickly finished his drink. He looked towards the bedroom door. 'If you're sure I think I'll turn in. I'm awfully tired.'

'I don't have a spare toothbrush or anything.'

'I'll manage.' He looked at her awkwardly, saying brusquely: 'I enjoyed this evening.'

'So did I.'

'Goodnight.'

'Night,' Peg said and went into Verity's room.

Although he was tired sleep didn't come. Alan was acutely conscious of the fact that this was Peg's bed. He lay on the outside but he would love to have got between her sheets and imagine her being there with him. He closed his eyes in a fever of torment.

If only she knew.

But perhaps she did and she didn't care, or in some perverse way she enjoyed his suffering. His months of wooing Peg had left him at times with hope, at others in deep, deep despair. He didn't dare declare himself for fear of being rebuffed, as he had been before. It was better to see her like this than not at all: he preferred chastity and self-control to banishment.

Peg woke up late in the morning, rose, threw on a dressing gown and without combing her hair went into the kitchen where she found Alan, looking remarkably fresh and spruce, reading a day-old newspaper.

'Did you sleep?' she asked him.

'Excellently.' He put down the paper and smiled at her. 'Did you?'

'Oh, fine. I always do.'

Peg filled the kettle and put a match to the gas.

'I wondered if you'd like to do something today?' Alan said.

'Like what?' Peg got out a loaf of bread and began slicing it.

'We could go for a walk. Take a trip down the river.' He looked out of the window. 'It's such a lovely day. Pity not to use it.'

'I think the river sounds lovely,' Peg said enthusiastically. She buttered slices of bread, put them on a plate, got out a pot of marmalade and pushed everything towards Alan. 'Help yourself. I'm starving.' She made the tea and passed him a cup.

Alan found he was hungry too. 'We can get a boat at Westminster Bridge and go to Greenwich or Richmond.'

'I've never been to Richmond. What a good idea, Alan.' Her smile was radiant with approval. 'You *are* clever. This is nice, isn't it.'

Alan swallowed. 'How do you mean?'

'Well, it feels very adult. Us being together. I'm glad Verity was away.'

'So am I.' Alan was about to put a slice of bread to his mouth when he stopped abruptly. 'Peg . . . ?'

'Yes?'

'Do you think you could ever marry me?'

'Good heavens,' Peg gasped abruptly, putting down her cup. 'What a thing to ask at breakfast time.' Then, after a moment's thought: 'Do you know, I really don't know.'

Alan's heart bounded with hope. Cautious for so much of his life, some instinct had told him it was time to be bold.

'I love you, Peg. I think you know that. It was purgatory for me when I didn't see you all those months; but lately things seem to have changed between us.'

Peg nodded, avoiding his eyes. She felt a strange upheaval taking place inside her, but didn't think she could call it love, not yet.

'I wondered,' Alan went on hesitantly, 'if your feelings for me had changed at all?'

Peg nodded.

'Oh yes. But I don't know that it's love. I don't know what it is, except that I like you a lot and would feel miserable if I thought I wasn't going to see you again. I suppose that's a *kind* of love.'

Alan, scarcely believing his ears, nodded enthusiastically several times.

'Let's get engaged!' he exclaimed, jumping up and going over to her side.

Looking at his eager, trusting, familiar face, Peg reached up to him and put her hand against his cheek. 'I think it's a bit too soon, Alan, a bit premature.' She removed her hand. 'But ask me again. One day, perhaps?'

Alan, overcome with emotion, put his arm round her waist and pressed her close.

'I will wait for you for ever,' he said. 'I will never grow tired of you, Peg.'

At that moment Peg felt an intensity of emotion that she was sure was a surge of love for Alan.

But it was too soon to tell him.

She thought of it rather as a delicate flower that had to be allowed to grow until it was strong and free in case it withered and died.

Eight

Geraldine stood in rapt contemplation of one of the most famous pictures in the world. *The Birth of Venus* by Sandro Botticelli. Having read the details of its provenance to Verity in a loud whisper from the guide ('Sandro Botticelli, born Alessandro de Mariano Filipepi, the son of a tanner in Florence in 1445, one of the greatest painters of the Florentine Renaissance. The painting, tempera on canvas, was executed for Lorenzo di Pierfrancesco de' Medici'), she had been standing there for several minutes, apparently lost to the world, absorbed by the painting's undeniable beauty.

The enigmatic aquiline face of Venus seemed to Verity in many ways to mirror the inscrutability of Geraldine's expression, as if her friend was identifying herself with that mysterious goddess rising from the waves.

Verity, on the other hand, having tramped the length and breadth of the huge Uffizi Gallery, was desperate to rest her aching feet.

Florence was very hot. It had, perhaps, not been a good time in which to visit that beautiful city, but while others flagged Geraldine was indefatigable. They were out early every morning, even before most of the churches and galleries were open, and after lunch and a short siesta they were out again until well into the evening.

Within a week of their arrival Verity had seen almost

104

everything there was to see, though Geraldine assured her with gusto that there was plenty more. She had marched her round the Palazzo Pitti, the Convent of San Marco, the frescoes of Massacio in the Brancacci Chapel, the Medici Chapel with its sculptures by Michelangelo, and Michelangelo's house, the Casa Buonarroti. They had toured the Palazzo Vecchio, admired the Bronzino frescoes in the chapel of Eleanor of Toledo, visited most of the churches, inside as well as out, absorbed the beauty of the details of the Ghiberti doors of the Baptistry outside the Duomo and, of course, stood in awe inside the building gazing at the dome of that great cathedral which had taken six centuries to complete. And no wonder. The dome itself had marked a revolution in architectural construction.

They had been back and forth across the Ponte Vecchio with its dozens of small shops and gazed in admiration at the view along the Arno.

But, oh dear, it was hot.

Philip, who, after all, had decided to join the trip, had most sensibly accompanied them on only a few of their jaunts, arranging to meet them at some suitable rendezvous once their explorations were over. He had seen it all, he said, many times and did not share the cultural and artistic enthusiasms of his wife. But he was very content to enjoy the Florentine sunshine, read the English papers, late as they were, and drink coffee or a glass of wine.

'Geraldine,' Verity said timidly, 'Philip will be waiting for us.'

'Oh!' Her Venus-like serenity suddenly dissipated and Geraldine swung round on her heels. 'I do wish he'd stayed at home!' she hissed. 'You've completely destroyed my mood.'

'Sorry,' Verity said humbly, looking at her watch, 'but I think he might be worried. We agreed to meet him at noon and it's now 12.30. Besides, I think the gallery will soon be closing.'

'Closing?' Geraldine looked round. 'Does it close? I didn't think so. I could stay here all day.'

'They all close, dear, in the afternoon, you know that.' Verity tried to sound patient. 'I do think we should go and we can come back later or tomorrow.'

She took her friend's arm and steered her firmly out of the gallery and down the road, where Geraldine swept ahead, her long skirt swirling about her, a large straw hat protecting her from the sun. Verity was more demurely and practically dressed in a short cotton frock and sensible shoes.

Sitting at a table outside a café in the Piazza Signoria in a white straw hat, Philip looked remarkably unfazed and controlled, reading his paper and smoking his pipe. As he saw his womenfolk approaching, he put aside the paper and rose to greet them.

'There you are!' he cried good-naturedly, standing and pulling out a chair for his wife. 'Did you have a good time?'

'Oh, did *we* have a good time.' Geraldine raised her eyes heavenwards. 'Philip, you don't know what you're missing.'

'But, dear, we have seen it all before. We came here on our honeymoon,' he explained to Verity, turning towards her, 'and we have been back several times since, and to Venice and to Rome.'

'Well, you know I can never see enough of it, Philip.' Geraldine looked up at the waiter who hovered over them. 'I will have cold lemonade,' she requested in passable Italian. 'Verity?'

'The same for me, please.'

'Wouldn't you like something to eat, dear?'

'I couldn't eat a thing.' Geraldine shook her head and put a hand on her stomach. 'In fact, I have begun to feel a bit queasy. It came over me in the gallery and has slowly been getting worse.'

'Oh, my dear!' Philip immediately looked concerned.

'It's nothing.' She waved her hand airily. 'It will pass after I have had my rest this afternoon.'

Nevertheless, by the time they got back to the hotel Geraldine looked far from well and when she got up to her room Philip deduced she had a fever and asked the hotel to call a doctor.

'You can't be too careful in this heat,' he said to Verity, who hovered anxiously around the patient.

'I agree completely,' she said. 'Maybe it was something Geraldine ate?'

'But we all had the same thing last night. Besides, the symptoms would have presented a long time ago.'

'She *did* have an ice cream this morning,' Verity added thoughtfully, 'just before we went into the gallery.'

'That's it,' Philip said. 'Food poisoning.'

His diagnosis proved to be correct. Geraldine started vomiting as soon as she got to her room, and when he arrived and examined her the doctor prescribed medication and a day or two in bed with plenty to drink.

That night Verity dined alone while Philip dutifully stayed with his wife, keeping her under observation.

Before going to bed, Verity called to see how Geraldine was, but her condition was no better, and she passed a restless night. Sickness and diarrhoea in a foreign country were worrying symptoms.

Verity woke at seven and flung open the windows of her hot little room. The hotel behind the Piazza del Duomo was the one in which Philip and Geraldine had honeymooned. It was very much liked by English people, being considered suitably foreign yet with all the conveniences that the British appreciated.

Though situated in a hot narrow street, the hotel had a cool courtyard with a fountain. Geraldine and Philip had a suite overlooking the courtyard and double windows which opened wide to allow in plenty of air. Verity, on the other hand, had a small room which overlooked the street and was noisy as well as being airless. Consequently she was very glad to get out as often as she could.

Though she too had passed a disturbed night, Geraldine professed herself much better in the morning: weak, but the sickness had passed.

'Though not up to sightseeing today, Verity.' She smiled

apologetically at her friend. 'I am sure Philip will be pleased to accompany you.'

'Oh no, my dear,' Philip protested, 'I must stay with you.'

'Yes, Philip must stay,' Verity insisted. 'I'll be perfectly all right by myself.'

'I wouldn't *hear* of it,' Geraldine said firmly. 'Besides, I shall enjoy the rest and quiet and shall probably sleep a lot.' She smiled wanly at her husband. 'Frankly, I would prefer it, Philip, if I had a few hours on my own. As it is so hot, why don't you take Verity to somewhere out of the city, like Fiesole, and give her a spot of lunch after showing her the sights? When you return I will probably be well enough to join you for dinner, though I can't contemplate the prospect now.'

'Oh no, you must spend the day in bed or at least in this room,' Philip insisted. 'These stomach bugs are nasty and so often recur.'

'If you say so, dear.' Geraldine lay back on the pillows. 'How sweet you both are to me.'

'Well, that's it, then,' Philip said, looking at Verity. 'Would you like to go to Fiesole after breakfast? We can take a cab.'

'From there you have the most wonderful view of Florence.' Geraldine gave a deeply nostalgic sigh. 'Philip must take you to the Cathedral and the Bishop's Palace; and the museum, which is full of treasures from the Etruscan period, is a *must*. Fiesole is a very old Etruscan city which was wiped out by the Florentines in, I think, the twelfth century.'

At first Verity was a little nervous at being thrust into the company of a man she liked and admired but of whom she was still a little in awe. Of course she was very friendly with his wife, and she saw more of him socially than she had at one time, when they were simply colleagues. But after all, he was a senior member of the hospital staff and there still existed that gulf between medical and nursing personnel in which the latter were deemed to have an inferior status.

However, Philip proved to be an admirable and solicitous

companion. Soon after breakfast he strode out into the street, Verity following behind, and once in the piazza he commandeered a horse-drawn cab and ordered it to take them to the hills. It was, after all, delightful to be sitting next to Philip, admiring the magnificent countryside through which they passed, while from time to time he pointed out many things of interest.

Verity had always admired Philip, but she had thought it was because he was such a wonderful doctor, a skilled and thoughtful obstetrician, always considerate for the welfare of mother and baby. On the other hand, he was an undeniably attractive man: tall, dark-haired, greying a little at the temples, with a full moustache and deep-set piercing dark eyes. He had an air of confidence and strength which she thought contributed, with some justification, to the regard his women patients had for him.

She also saw how solicitous he was towards his wife. At close hand she was able to observe, in a way that had not been possible in London, the nature of the relationship between the two.

There was no doubt that Geraldine, as well as being beautiful and alluring, was also capricious and selfish. She enjoyed getting her own way, having people at her beck and call, particularly her husband. Her boundless drive and energy had an enervating effect on everyone else and Verity wondered if this was why she always felt so tired in Geraldine's company, much as she had loved and valued the experience of being introduced to the treasures of that great city.

The carriage reached the top of the hill and trotted into the main square where the driver, who spoke fluent but very broken English, pointed with some enthusiasm to a structure slightly elevated from the main square which he informed them was the Palazzo Pretorio. This square itself was, he explained, the Mino da Fiesole, the centre of the town, and they would find here many delightful sights, as well as fine places to eat.

He jumped out, helping Verity down from the carriage, then extended the palm of his hand for the notes Philip put into it as

he murmured his thanks. He obviously included a generous tip
because the driver seemed well satisfied, thanking him profusely
before he remounted and with a crack of his whip drove away.

It seemed just as hot up here as in the city and Philip drew out
his handkerchief to wipe his brow and looked round. Then he
dutifully took from his pocket the guide his wife had pressed
upon him, the places of interest marked by small pieces of paper
sticking out of the pages.

'I think we should sit down while we study this,' he said,
pointing to a cafe with tables outside shaded by trees, 'and have a
cool drink.'

'Good idea,' Verity agreed, thinking that Philip, the correctly
attired Englishman in white suit, university tie and panama hat,
looked very uncomfortable. 'Why don't you take your tie off?'
she suggested as they sat down. 'It's so close.'

'Would you mind?' Philip looked at her gratefully and tugged
at his tie, finally removing it and tucking it into his pocket.

'Oh, how *pleasant* this is,' he declared, sitting back after they
had ordered, and stretching his long legs in front of him. 'What a
splendid idea it was of Geraldine's to suggest we should come
here.'

'Couldn't be nicer,' Verity agreed. 'I do wish she had been able
to come with us.'

As if reminded of his duty, the unseen but almost palpable
presence of his formidable wife appearing to hover over him,
Philip opened the guidebook and turned to the marked pages.

'Now let me see. The palazzo which you see over there' – he
pointed to the tower-like construction above them on the hill – 'is
fifteenth century. The Bishop's Palace' – he squinted ahead of
him – 'over *there*, I imagine, is seventeenth century and next to it
is the seminary . . . Oh dear.' He tossed the book on the table as
the waiter appeared with their drinks. 'I can't really be *bothered*
with all this, can you? I mean, do you *really* want to trudge round
in this heat and see it all?'

Verity looked at him doubtfully. 'But what will Geraldine say?

At least we should take a look at the Etruscan remains to say we've seen something.'

'Well –' Grudgingly Philip picked up the book and turned again to the marked pages. 'Ah, Etruscan remains. Here we are.' He cleared his throat and started to read. ' "The Etruscan settlement of Fiesole was probably the centre of a zone extending right across the Florentine basin. Remains of the city wall and the temple can still be seen and the museum contains some of the most interesting and important discoveries from the Etruscan period: urns, clay and bronze statues . . ." Interested?' He paused to look at Verity, who had felt herself dozing off in the heat and quickly opened her eyes.

'Oh, yes. Very.'

'I don't believe you,' Philip said with a conspiratorial smile. He firmly shut the book, placing it once again on the table. 'Shall we be very naughty and play truant?'

A spasm of alarm shot through Verity and she looked at him in surprise.

'Whatever do you mean?'

'Oh, don't be alarmed.' His hand rested lightly on hers for a moment. 'I know of a lovely place in the hills with a very good restaurant: Hotel Primavera. Now why don't we treat ourselves to a leisurely lunch there and have a little walk in the hills before making our way back?'

'Well –' Verity looked at him guiltily. 'I must say it *sounds* very appealing, but what will Geraldine say? I think we should at *least* have a peep at the museum.'

'Very well.' Philip tossed back his drink, took up the guide-book and stood up. 'Let's get it over with.'

'I must say you're very *naughty*, Philip,' Verity said with a giggle of delight as she got up and they started to walk across the square in the direction of the museum pinpointed by the map in the guidebook.

The Etruscan remains were largely urns made of terracotta or alabaster, bronzes, coins, amphora and vases. There were busts

111

of Roman emperors and pieces of broken statutory. It was all exceedingly dull.

However, it was cold in the museum, which was a relief. Nevertheless, Philip's boredom was so obvious that when they were halfway round Verity tugged at his arm.

'I think we've seen it all, don't you?'

'We've seen enough.' Philip drew a deep breath. 'But I thought you were enjoying it?'

'I prefer the Uffizi,' Verity said as Philip took hold of her arm and steered her out of the museum and on to the baking street in search of a cab.

Under Philip's careful instructions they were driven further up the hill and out of the town to the gates of an imposing hotel set in the trees. Even from the gate they could see the terrace with people sitting on it in deckchairs.

'Cooler already, isn't it?' Philip cried as they alighted and he paid off the driver.

'Oh, it's *beautiful!*' Verity stared about her with wonder.

'I thought you'd like it.' Again he took her arm as they walked up the drive towards the main door and reception area, which was a large cool atrium with a fountain and palm trees. From the double doors at the far end they were able to see right on to the terrace and the breathtaking view of the city of Florence beyond.

Part of the restaurant opened on to the terrace. The maître d' hurried forward and showed them to a table partly set in the shade but with a commanding view of Florence. Once they were seated waiters were immediately summoned who hovered over them, one producing two menus while the other solicitously covered their laps with pink table-napkins.

'This *is* delightful.' Verity sat back with a deep sigh of satisfaction.

'Wait until you taste the food.' Philip appeared genuinely pleased with her enthusiasm. 'Do you like Parma ham?'

'Very much.'

'If I remember they have the finest Parma ham here I have had anywhere.'

'I'll have Parma ham, then.' Verity was anxious to please and show her gratitude.

'And then maybe veal? With a fine lemon sauce and zucchini. A bottle of Orvieto I think, as it's the middle of the day.'

The waiter returned and Philip gave the order, then he settled back and joined his hands.

He smiled at her. 'Yes, this *is* nice, isn't it?'

'It's a very special treat,' Verity agreed, then, sotto voce, 'but Philip, it seems *terribly* expensive. You must let me—'

'Oh, my dear, I wouldn't *dream* of it.' Once more his hand lightly fluttered over hers. 'Don't even *think* of such a thing. I meant you to be happy and have a happy day. You've been so good to Geraldine, and it's our special treat.'

'But will we tell Geraldine?'

Her question made Philip look thoughtful.

'I think we *may* keep it to ourselves. You see, my wife and I came here on our honeymoon too.'

'Oh!'

'We actually stayed the night and she said it was her favourite place in all the world.'

'I still think we should tell her. It would be deceitful not to.'

'As you wish.' Philip sat back and nonchalantly lit a cigarette. 'I see no real harm. I certainly don't want to be deceitful, but I don't want to hurt her either. She might get the wrong idea.'

A flush swept over Verity's cheeks. '"Wrong *idea*"!' she exclaimed. 'What sort of "wrong idea"?'

'Wives are such funny creatures.' Philip tried to make light of his remark. 'They can imagine the strangest things.'

Verity tried to make sense of this discussion, but at that moment they were surrounded by waiters again. One poured wine from a bottle which was then put in an ice bucket by the side of the table, and the other set before them plates of very thin Parma ham which he proceeded to cover with black pepper.

Just before they started to eat Philip raised his glass.

'Thank you again,' he said, 'for being such a good companion, such a true friend to Geraldine . . . and me,' he added as an afterthought. Then, more prosaically, he continued, 'Strange to think, isn't it, that this time next week we shall be colleagues again, back in the hospital?'

'I hope I shall have some news.' Verity broke into a bread roll.

'About your promotion?'

'Matron said we would know some time in August.'

'Oh, I have no doubt you'll get the job. You were easily the best qualified candidate. Of course I'm prejudiced, but I think the board were in general agreement.'

Philip had been on the selection panel that had interviewed Verity and other applicants for the post of sister in charge of the maternity unit a few weeks before. In the course of a long question and answer session, however, Verity couldn't help noticing that Mr Watson asked few questions and seemed anxious to avoid her eyes. Otherwise all the others – Matron, Philip and two of the governors – had been very nice and encouraging.

'I'm not sure about Mr Watson,' Verity said doubtfully. 'I think he knows I don't regard him too highly. Perhaps he feels the same about me?'

'Oh, I don't think that for a moment. You are imagining it. Drink up,' Philip said encouragingly, 'we have this bottle to get through.' And he refilled first her glass and then his.

The meal was delicious, the veal tender and beautifully cooked with a mild lemon sauce, courgettes and sautéed potatoes to accompany it. Afterwards they had ice cream and, somewhat to her surprise, Verity realised that they had also finished the wine, though she was sure Philip must have drunk most of it. Between courses he smoked and she began to feel more and more relaxed. It was indeed an occasion to remember: lunching at this grand restaurant set in the hills above one of the world's most beautiful and historical cities with an attractive and clever man, who was-

also an amusing and interesting companion. Somehow he made
her feel important, his gaze flattered her and she felt womanly in
a way that she had not for many years.

She knew she would remember this day all her life.

Verity was also surprised at how different Philip was away from
the rather daunting presence of his wife. Of course at the hospital he
was a different man completely, but she had never before seen the
one who sat opposite her now: relaxed, composed, almost intimate.

The lunch finished, they moved away from the table. Comfortable chairs were placed for them on the terrace. Philip
ordered coffee and asked for a cigar. Then, turning to her, he
enquired: 'Would you like a liqueur?'

'Goodness no!' Verity exclaimed laughing. 'I feel a little tipsy
already.'

'Oh, the coffee will soon take care of that.' Philip again
reached for her hand and patted it in an avuncular fashion,
then ordered a Strega for himself. 'I'm enjoying this enormously,'
he said. 'It makes a change from all those museums.'

'But they *are* very interesting,' Verity said guardedly, not
wishing to appear disloyal to Geraldine.

'I must say you share that with Geraldine, but not much else.'

'Oh?' Verity looked surprised. 'How do you mean?'

'Well, you're very different people. I'm very glad you have
befriended her because she doesn't make friends easily and I
worry about her. But she certainly took to you. Now –' as the
coffee and liqueur arrived he asked for the bill – 'I suggest a short
stroll in the grounds. They're really lovely and I can show you an
even more spectacular view of the city.'

'Shouldn't we be getting back?' Verity looked nervously at her
watch. 'It's nearly three. We said we'd be in time for tea.'

'I'm sure the rest will do Geraldine good,' Philip said reassuringly. 'She won't be missing us at all.'

'A stroll *would* be nice,' Verity agreed. She was feeling a little
light-headed. The exercise would undoubtedly be beneficial.
Maybe she had had more wine than she thought.

They finished their coffee, Philip paid the bill and they strolled off the terrace and round the side of the hotel, which was surrounded by trees.

'I expect this must once have been some grand house,' Verity said, 'lived in by a noble family. A lot of them were bankrupted by the war.'

'Oh, this was a hotel before the war. I told you we came here on our honeymoon.'

'I suppose it must have been very near the outbreak of war when you were married?'

Philip nodded. 'We were very lucky – 1913. I had only just qualified. The following year we were at war.'

'And you served all the time at the front?'

'In the field hospitals. It's amazing how one can get over such dreadful and troubled times.'

Verity nodded. She had a strange feeling of rapport with him that had been growing all through lunch, and now she was aware that Philip had casually put his arm round her waist. However, she thought it best to pretend that she hadn't noticed anything.

'I believe you lost your fiancé during the war?'

'But not *in* the war,' Verity corrected him. 'It was after. He didn't die. He merely . . . left.' She trailed off, not wishing to revive those painful memories all over again.

'Oh, Geraldine just told me you had lost your fiancé and I assumed . . . really, Verity, I know nothing about you.' He stopped and, his arm still round her waist, turned her towards him. With his free hand he casually brushed the hair back from her forehead, the expression in his eyes strangely unfathomable.

'Philip –' she began.

'It's nothing to be afraid of,' he said gently as, tightening his grip round her waist, he pulled her closer to him, inserted his knee between her legs and kissed her quite hard.

Verity submitted without a struggle, reeling with a rush of sensuousness, her mouth opening wide to receive him. It was the most passionate kiss she had ever experienced – certainly nothing remotely like those with Rex – and she felt as though her whole body and not just her mouth was being explored in the most intimate way by this man.

After it was over they clung together and she rested her head on his chest, aware that his heart was beating as rapidly as, if not more rapidly than, hers.

'I don't believe this,' she murmured. 'It is *very* wrong.'

'Nonsense.' His chin touched the top of her head, 'You know we attract each other, have done for ages.'

'No!' she protested.

'Oh yes. Why are you always sending for me instead of Watson?'

'Because you're the better doctor.'

'I think it is also because you like to see me. Any competent doctor can deal with even a complicated maternity case. You wanted *me*.'

'That is *not* true,' Verity protested weakly. 'I mean, I like you and I like Geraldine . . . Oh, this is *awful*.' As if suddenly aware of the situation, she tried to push him away.

'It's perfectly natural, darling,' he murmured. 'If you like I can get a room here for the rest of the afternoon. They're quite used to that sort of thing.'

'Philip, *no!*' Terrified, Verity backed away from him. 'How *can* you entertain such an idea?'

'Very easily.'

'But Geraldine . . .'

'Forget about Geraldine.' His voice betrayed a note of impatience. 'Just for once.'

'I can't, Philip.' She made a frantic effort to smooth her hair and pull down her skirt, which he had managed to raise without her noticing it. 'This is *very* wrong. I don't know how I can ever face Geraldine again. I feel I'm betraying the trust she has in me.'

'My dear' – Philip pulled open his cigarette case, lit a cigarette and leaned against a tree – 'Geraldine and I lead separate lives in the sense that we don't sleep together, and haven't done for

117

years. You can understand how difficult it is for a man like me to be faithful to a wife who no longer loves him or satisfies his needs.'

'But Geraldine—'

'You *know* Geraldine doesn't love me. You must have noticed. We irritate each other. Oh, all right, perhaps we're making a special effort for you, but the strain shows, doesn't it?'

'Sometimes,' Verity admitted, biting her lip. 'But I didn't realise things were . . . so bad.'

'Verity' – he drew her towards him again – 'I am not a man easily given to having affairs, I assure you. But I'm immensely attracted to you and thought you felt the same way about me. Don't you?'

Verity bowed her head and once again leaned it against his chest. She didn't know whether it was the effect of the wine or the excess of emotion, or something of each, but she felt very close to fainting.

All the talk had been about Etruscan artefacts, but Verity found it increasingly difficult to keep up the pretence. Philip behaved as though nothing had happened, but she avoided his eyes.

Finally Geraldine leaned towards her: 'Aren't you hungry, dear?'

Verity shook her head.

'I hope you're not getting my tummy bug,' Geraldine enquired anxiously.

'I think I'll go early to bed, if you'll excuse me,' Verity said, getting up from the table. 'I do feel a bit funny.'

'I think you tired yourself out today.' Geraldine looked sternly at Philip. 'Overdid the sightseeing, perhaps, did you?'

They had returned to the hotel at about seven and were now having a light supper in the hotel dining room. Geraldine was still pale and had picked at her food, but otherwise seemed much recovered. Philip's mood had been one of ebullience, so much so that Geraldine seemed to have concluded that they must have had a very good day, which sent Verity into a silent mood of remorse and shame, and she slunk quietly off to bed; but not to sleep.

For the rest of the holiday Verity felt she was in purgatory, and from the meaningful glances she kept getting from Geraldine, or imagined she got, she was convinced that she knew something had happened between her friend and her husband on those hills above Florence one hot summer's afternoon.

But a kiss was all it had been. Nothing else. The idea of adultery in a hotel bedroom, as Philip had suggested, was wholly abhorrent to a woman of Verity's upbringing and temperament. They had eventually driven back to the hotel in complete silence, wrapped in their respective thoughts.

But the mood of the holiday changed. Perhaps they were tired, or Geraldine hadn't quite recovered, or Verity felt too ashamed. In any case, the sparkle, the sense of adventure, had gone and they were all quite happy at the prospect of returning home.

Nine

Verity returned to London in a state of wild confusion, her relief at saying goodbye to the Beaumaurices knowing no bounds. The prospect of facing Philip again at the hospital was something she dreaded.

She was ashamed of herself and mortified that she had given in to him, undoubtedly under the influence of strong wine, on a hot afternoon. It was so unlike her as not to bear thinking about.

What must Philip think of her now as a woman, someone he respected, a nursing sister with a formidable reputation as a disciplinarian, a person whose emotions were always kept carefully under control?

It was a very good thing that she had had her interview for the post of sister in charge before the holiday and not after it.

As the senior nurse she would now probably see less of Beaumaurice, and she would certainly not be summoning him to assist in difficult deliveries. Now it would be Mr Watson or one of the housemen every time. Rules would be strictly observed.

Peg was glad to see her sister back, delighted she had had such a wonderful time, yet perturbed that she didn't look as well as she thought she would.

'It was so terribly *hot*,' Verity exclaimed, fanning herself at the memory of it as they sat at the supper table the day she returned home. 'One had to spend a good deal of time in the shade, and towards the end I think I did have a bit of an upset stomach, something I may have caught from Geraldine, who took to her bed.'

120

It was odd, Verity thought to herself even as she said the words, how easy it was to believe in one's lies. 'And what have you been up to, my dear?' she asked, glad to change the subject.

'Nothing very much,' Peg shrugged, 'same as usual.'

'Anything interesting at work?'

'I covered the jamboree of the Boy Scouts at Wembley, which was attended by the Prince of Wales. That was quite interesting.'

'And did you meet him?'

'Oh no. We were kept very far back. He is actually very handsome, though, better than he looks in photographs.'

'And how is Alan? Have you seen him?'

'Oh yes,' Peg said casually, 'we went to the Proms at the Queen's Hall.'

'I see.' Verity pursed her lips.

'There's nothing to be *disapproving* of, Ver,' Peg said indignantly.

'I was not aware that I was being disapproving.'

'It's just the look on your face. We like each other. We have a lot in common. That's all – and Ver' – Peg got up, looking very nervous, and started clearing the dishes – 'there *is* something I want to say.'

'And what's that?'

'I would like to have my own place. It's nothing to do with you, except that I feel sometimes you treat me as though I was a small child.'

'Oh I don't know how you can say that.' Verity, feeling very agitated, got up and lit a cigarette. 'That seems to me to be *very* unfair.'

Peg replaced the dishes on the table and came over to her sister, impulsively throwing her arm round her.

'I don't want to hurt you, Ver. I do love you, but . . . I want my own place and now that my wages are a little better I think I can afford it. Alan knows of a room with a kitchen near him and it will also be better for me for work. I needn't get up so early. Also, if Alan sees me home to here it is a very long way.'

121

'Oh, I see what's behind this.' Verity sat down again and crossed her legs, angrily puffing away. 'I suppose this has all to do with Alan, hasn't it?'

Peg flushed. 'Not at all.'

'I thought he was just a friend.'

'Well, he is.'

'You're seeing an awful lot of him.'

'But Ver, that has got *nothing* to do with you.'

'I just hope you're not doing anything silly – are you, Peg?' She looked anxiously at her sister. 'Remember what happened to Addie.'

'Ver' – Peg's face was stormy – 'I am twenty-one. Addie was seventeen. I am quite capable of taking care of myself, thank you. Anyway, there *is* nothing like that.'

As if suddenly aware of Verity's misery, Peg knelt beside her. 'I do love you really, Ver, but I've felt like this for some time.'

Sadly Verity stroked her sister's face while her eyes filled with tears. 'It's just that I'll miss you, Peg. I shall feel lonely.'

'I'll see you an awful lot, Ver. And Alan and I will come and have lunch with you every Sunday. Promise. Besides, you have the Beaumaurices.'

'Somehow I don't think I shall be seeing as much of them in future.' Verity realised she was very close to breaking down.

'Oh? I thought you enjoyed the holiday?'

'I did.' Verity stubbed out her cigarette with more force than was necessary. 'Very much. The trouble was that it just went on for too long. A week would have been perfect.'

Verity finished her ward round with the staff nurse. Everything had gone smoothly in her absence. No one had died. There had been no dreadful emergencies. It was nice to be back. The sister in charge of the maternity unit had left and Verity was deputising in a place it was assumed she would soon fill. In her blue uniform with its starched white collar and white cap she felt normal, at home. The folly of Florence was forgotten. When she saw Philip again she would pretend that nothing had happened and, she presumed, so would he. It had been a rush of blood to the head, the result of the hot sunshine, beautiful scenery and too much wine.

She would also pick up with Geraldine and, doubtless, in time they would resume their short breaks together while Philip went off to his medical conferences.

Nothing would change. Everything would soon return to normality.

She bent over the cot of the latest addition: a baby just two hours old. She never really got over the miracle of birth; the arrival of each new human being, however great or humble, filled her with silent awe. It was one of the great bonuses of her work, a cause for deep satisfaction.

The only sadness was that she felt she would never experience the happiness of motherhood herself. That had been sacrificed on the altar of treachery by Rex Harvey when he had terminated their engagement.

But there was no place in her heart for bitterness. She was a person of strong religious faith and she knew that God had a purpose for everyone, no matter how difficult it might be for the individual human being to understand it.

She tapped the baby's head, smiled at the nurse who was looking after it and made her way back to her room to write up her report.

It was good to be back in the old routine. Routine suited her. Holidays in a hot country with people who were really not of her sort were an aberration and must not be repeated, however tempting the invitation. It had been fun for a time to pretend she and the Beaumaurices were alike, but they weren't. They were very different. They were professional, upper middle class and wealthy, and she was none of these things. Her father had been a butcher, her stepfather a gardener. Geraldine's wealthy family owned a newspaper empire. Philip's forebears had adorned the higher echelons of the medical profession for generations. She was merely a nurse and had no money, other than some small savings.

Verity thought, in retrospect, that in many ways Geraldine had patronised her, pretending to find in her a soulmate when all she wanted was a companion to ease the boredom of a spoiled, pampered and basically dissatisfied woman.

As for Peg . . . well that was a sorrow, but if it was what her sister wanted there was nothing she could do about it. It was important to let the young have their wings, though she never felt that she was repressive towards her younger sister, and the implication that she had been had rather upset her.

At Peg's age she had been a theatre sister dealing with the most terrible casualties brought in by the war. On the other hand she had lived in a closely supervised nursing home; but she had also become engaged. By twenty-one she had led a much fuller, more independent life than Peg. Maybe it was time to let a young woman, as spirited as Peg, spread her wings. But she did so hope she wasn't doing anything foolish with Alan.

Verity was in the middle of writing her report when there was a knock and one of the hospital porters put his head round the door.

'I'm sorry for disturbing you, sister, but Matron wonders if you could spare a few minutes? She would like to see you in her room.'

Verity's heart skipped a beat. She put the cap on her fountain pen, rose and glanced at herself in the mirror to be sure not a hair was out of place, that she looked neat and composed.

'Thank you very much,' she said. 'I'll come directly.'

The porter held the door open for her and stood back to allow her to pass. With a feeling of excitement Verity hurried along the corridor and knocked at Matron's door.

'Do come in, Sister Carter-Barnes,' Matron said pleasantly, pointing to a chair, 'and sit down.' She glanced at a paper on her desk. 'I haven't seen you since you returned from holiday. Did you have a good time?'

'Very good.' Verity nodded. 'Excellent.'

'I believe you visited Italy with Dr Beaumaurice and his wife?'

'Yes, Mrs Beaumaurice is a particular friend of mine.' Verity swallowed, suddenly feeling acutely uncomfortable at the memory of that illicit, passionate kiss.

'Such a charming woman.' Matron nodded. 'I have had the pleasure of meeting her several times. She is most generous at the hospital fêtes. Now to the point.' Matron looked down at her desk again and then at Verity. 'Miss Carter-Barnes, I am very sorry to have to give you news which I know will disappoint you, but the appointment of sister in charge has been offered to another candidate.' She paused as if to give Verity time to absorb the shock.

Verity sat there as if suddenly mesmerised. When she spoke, her voice, though controlled, seemed to come from very far away.

'But I thought . . . I understood . . . that I was very well qualified? That I was in with a good chance?'

'Indeed you were.' Matron coughed apologetically. 'I am very sorry, but there it is. The woman who has been selected is also very well qualified. Miss Frobisher comes from a hospital out of London, and I am sure you and she will get on very well. I know you will do all you can to assist her and help her settle in.' Matron rose as if signifying that the interview was at an end. 'She will commence her duties at the beginning of September. In the meantime you may carry on as acting sister in charge until Miss Frobisher takes up her position.'

She looked down at Verity, who had not attempted to get up. 'I *am* sorry, Miss Carter-Barnes.'

Verity at last found her voice and this time it was stronger.

'But may I know *why?*'

'Well, strictly speaking, no reason is given, but I do believe you have not managed to hit it off with Mr Watson. It was he who was very much against your appointment, and as he is the consultant we could hardly oppose him.'

'But Dr Beaumaurice –' Verity paused. 'Dr Beaumaurice seemed to think I was an excellent candidate.'

'I'm surprised that Dr Beaumaurice mentioned the matter,' Matron said coldly. 'The selection was supposed to be confidential.' She put her head to one side and looked gimlet-eyed at Verity. 'Maybe not a very *wise* friendship, Miss Carter-Barnes, in the circumstances.'

'What do you mean?' Face aflame, Verity rose to her feet.

'I have always been of the opinion that the medical and nursing staff should not mix socially, and have avoided such temptation myself. I understand that it is Mrs Beaumaurice with whom you are friendly, but it has come to the attention of the staff and particularly, unfortunately, Mr Watson that you and Dr Beaumaurice do seem, well, rather close.'

'That is absolutely untrue,' Verity said vehemently. 'Whatever are you suggesting, Matron?'

'I am suggesting nothing. Of course I know you well enough to know you are a woman of the utmost integrity and would always observe the proprieties. However, I do understand you are on Christian name terms, and the fact is that people have noticed you always insist on sending for Dr Beaumaurice in an emergency.'

'But he is an excellent doctor. He has saved several lives.'

Matron nodded. 'I agree. He *is* excellent, and I am sure he will soon be promoted to consultant status, at which time he will move from this hospital. In the meantime, sister, I do urge you to be circumspect and not be seen to favour him over all the others, especially if he is not on call.'

She then walked calmly to the door and opened it. 'Believe me, Miss Carter-Barnes, I am very sorry, and I would be the last to blame you if you sought a senior post elsewhere, much as we would miss you.'

And with a sad, regretful little half-smile she held open the door, patting Verity gently on the shoulder as she passed her.

Verity hardly remembered returning to her room. She

seemed to come to sitting at her desk, and remained in the same position for a very long time, her head propped on her hands, staring at the unfinished report still on the desk in front of her. She had been passed over. She was the victim of gossip, spite, jealousy. Philip's misgivings had come true, only he was not the one to suffer, she was. Her career had been sacrificed, not his.

But was the woman not always the one to suffer, to take the blame? Was it not always the woman who lost out?

She tried to pull herself together and continue with her report. After all, she was strong; she had been trained to cope with disasters. Only the words wouldn't come. Finally she lay down her pen, put her head in her hands once more and allowed those tears to flow that had been pent up for so long.

Then, after a while, they stopped. She wiped her eyes, inspected her face in the mirror on the wall in case anyone should come in, and finished her report in her neat handwriting.

When she did her next round with the staff nurse she was again in command of herself. At least, she thought she was, but the memory of her interview with Matron kept on intruding. Try as she might, she could not prevent tears welling up in her eyes as she thought of her loss and the injustice of it all.

'Are you all right, Sister Barnes?' The staff nurse looked at her anxiously.

'Perfectly all right.' Verity got out her handkerchief and blew her nose. 'Unfortunately I think I have a cold coming.' She put her hand to her brow. 'Maybe a touch of fever. I think perhaps I should go home so that I don't infect everyone. Take over, please, will you, Staff Nurse? I shall ask Matron if I might be relieved for the rest of the day.'

And with an attempt at a smile she hurried out of the ward back to her room where another fit of uncontrolled sobbing overtook her.

The ward round, the routine of it all – a routine that she loved and within which she worked so well – once again reminded her of the extent of her loss. She would never be in charge as she had hoped to be in charge, not in this hospital at least.

And would the fact that she had been passed over affect any other applications she might make? Why was a woman so well qualified and experienced not given the most senior post in her own hospital? Might a potential new employer not delve into her personal life, and the connection with the senior registrar be revealed?

But what was so damaging about *that*?

Nothing generally, except that people had nasty minds and tongues would wag. A relationship, however innocent, between a nurse and a doctor was not encouraged in well-conducted hospitals. It was considered bad for morale.

The tears ceased once more and Verity quickly put on her coat and hat and, taking her bag, went to see Matron. She felt ashamed of her weakness, her failure to be able to go on, and rather dreaded Matron's reaction. Like her, Matron was of the old school. However, to her relief the deputy matron was sitting at her desk and smiled as Verity entered.

'Sister, are you not very well?' she asked, immediately noticing Verity's pallor, her agitation. She was older than Matron and a kinder, more motherly person, soon due for retirement. 'You look very pale.'

Verity blew her nose with conviction. Once more her hand flew to her brow. 'I wonder if I might go home, Matron? I feel I have a cold, a touch of fever, and –'

'Of course.' The deputy nodded her head. 'You mustn't pass any infection on to your charges.'

'I've told Staff Nurse.' Verity became agitated again. 'I am *very* sorry. It's not like me, as you know.' To lend even more conviction to her statement she blew her nose vigorously until her eyes watered.

'You run along home,' the deputy said soothingly. 'I'll give the message to Matron. I'm quite sure she'll understand. Go home and lie down and take care of yourself.'

Verity nodded, felt the tears about to recommence and hurried out.

She knew; the deputy knew; the whole hospital must know she had been passed over. And now they would also know that she couldn't take it. She simply could not accept it. She was out of control, something that had never happened to her before, except on that hot afternoon in Florence, and somehow she couldn't help thinking the two events were connected by one name: Philip.

Verity walked down the length of the corridor, seeing no one. It was early afternoon, a quiet time. The morning's rounds were finished. Patients sometimes rested, and nurses caught up with their work. Only the theatres remained busy and, of course, the work in the labour ward never stopped.

Running down the steps on to the Gray's Inn Road, not looking where she was going, Verity went headlong into someone coming the other way and stood back immediately to apologise.

'Verity!'

She looked up, her face still tearstained. She tried to brush past Philip, but he reached out and stopped her.

'Verity, what is the matter?'

'*Please* let me go,' she said. 'I don't feel well.'

'Let me take you home.'

'No.'

'Please. I have my car.'

'No!' she said again, this time more stridently, but he hung on to her arm.

'Oh, Philip, let me *go*,' she hissed. 'People will talk, they are talking already. Don't you see what harm you're doing?' She looked fearfully up at the hospital windows, afraid that someone might observe the fracas going on down below.

'I won't let you go until you explain.'

'Very well, then.'

Anxious to be gone from the hospital grounds, she allowed Philip to lead her to his car. She sat in silence as he started the car and drove into Gray's Inn Road, turning right towards Hampstead.

'Shouldn't you be on duty?' she enquired after a few moments, during which she felt she had recovered sufficiently to speak normally.

'No. I came in to look at a patient: Mrs Hudson.'

'She's all right.' Mrs Hudson had had a difficult delivery during the night and Philip had been called, but Verity had not been present.

'Oh good.' He looked relieved. 'And the baby?'

'The baby had a bad time but will be all right too.'

'You look terrible, Verity,' he said glancing at her. 'Whatever has happened?'

'I'm not being promoted.'

There was silence. 'You knew, Philip, didn't you?' she said accusingly.

Still silence.

'You *knew*, didn't you, Philip.' She raised the tone of her voice. 'You were on the board, and yet you allowed me to think –'

'I could see the way the wind was blowing, but I didn't want to spoil the holiday,' Philip said lamely.

'Oh, didn't you?'

Tears began to stream down Verity's face and she put her head in her hands. 'I don't know what is the matter with me,' she sobbed. 'I think I'm breaking down.' Philip put his foot on the car's accelerator and raced up the hill, but by the time they reached the house her tears had subsided. Philip put an arm round her shoulder, but she shook him off.

'I'm quite all right now, thank you, Philip,' she said, attempting a dignified smile. 'I feel much calmer. This was something I didn't expect and I took it badly. I'll be quite all right now.' She began to get out.

Philip jumped out too and went round to assist her, and for a second or two they stood awkwardly on the pavement looking at each other.

'Let me see you inside,' he said solicitously.

'Really, it's not necessary.'

'I think it is.'

'Well —' She looked at him uncertainly. 'Perhaps I can offer you a cup of tea?'

'That would be very nice.' Philip followed her up the path to the door where she fumbled awkwardly with the key, let them both in and hurried up the stairs.

'It's not the end of the world, Verity,' he said, taking off his hat as they entered the sitting room of the flat.

'It is, as far as I'm concerned,' she said bitterly. 'But I have been trained in a hard school and I will survive.' She removed her hat and coat and ran a hand through her hair.

Philip thought how seductive she looked in her uniform, with her firm bust adorned with the badges of her profession. Her tall upright figure was at once desirable and forbidding.

The atmosphere seemed charged and when she went into the kitchen to put the kettle on, Philip followed her.

'You don't know what Matron said, Philip.' Verity struck a match over the gas and put on the kettle. 'She inferred there was something between us, and it was that, and not my ability, that influenced the board's decision.'

'It was Watson,' Philip said angrily. 'He was very opposed to you. We all did our best to persuade him.' His arm encircled her shoulder. 'I am very, very sorry, Verity, but life must go on.' As his tone of voice changed, grew gentler, his arm tightened round her. 'Do you know how very attractive you look?' His mouth brushed her hair. 'Come on, Verity. Let's finish what we started in Florence. You know we both want it.' He turned his head towards the kitchen door. 'Which one is your bedroom?'

It all seemed so unimportant now, Verity thought, gazing towards the window. The tears, the emotion, the rage, the indignation had all been swept away in a few moments of passion. Utter release.

131

'You all right?' Philip opened his eyes and touched her arm.

Verity nodded, turned her eyes away from the window and smiled at him.

'Was it worth it?' he said.

She nodded again.

'I thought it would be.' He put his finger against her mouth. 'And not a *word* about Geraldine, or it being wrong. Do you hear? What time does your sister get home?'

'Not for ages.'

'Good.'

Then he snuggled down beside her and went to sleep.

Verity still couldn't believe this was happening but, after a while, she began to feel drowsy, gingerly put her arm round him, rested her head on his chest and went to sleep too.

Ten

October 1924

The doctor put his stethoscope down and then carefully palpated Cathy's chest, starting at the top and working his way down to her waist. He asked her to turn and did the same thing on her back. He then invited her to get dressed and, with a thoughtful expression, returned to his desk. When Cathy emerged from behind the screen he was busy writing.

'Please take a seat, Mrs Carpenter,' he said without looking up. He finished writing, folded a sheet of paper, tucked it into an envelope, sealed it and scrawled a name on the outside.

'How long have you been feeling like this, Mrs Carpenter?' he asked, sitting back and studying her.

'Several weeks,' Cathy said in a low, anxious voice. 'I've been feeling dreadfully tired, Doctor, no energy, and I'm usually such a busy person.'

'And the cough; you've had that for several weeks too?'

'It only became bad more recently, which is why Frank told me to come and see you.'

'Frank was quite right,' the doctor said and, leaning over his desk, handed her the letter. 'I want you to go and have an X-ray as soon as possible. I'll make an appointment for you and you must take this letter with you.'

The expression of anxiety on Cathy's face increased. 'Is there anything seriously wrong, Doctor?'

'Well, I don't like the sound of your lungs, particularly your right lung, and, yes, the symptoms are a little worrying. Have you any history of TB in the family, Mrs Carpenter?'

Although much of Cathy's life had been troubled, the last few years had been happy, particularly since her marriage to Frank, which had followed her divorce from her second husband, Jack, who had abused her and been unfaithful during the war. Frank, her two younger children, Stella and Ed, and her adored grand-daughter Jenny had formed the basis of her well-being.

There was always a little worry about Addie and her marriage to Harold which, though she said very little about it, did not seem happy. Verity had recovered from the collapse of her engagement and Peg was considered the high-flying member of the family with, possibly, a brilliant career in front of her.

Cathy was a woman who had been born on a farm and enjoyed country life. She loved her garden, she participated in local activities in the small village, and they lived a contented and relatively carefree life, Frank continuing to act as chauffeur to Lord Ryland.

Frank was very far off retirement – he was a few years younger than Cathy – and they knew they would never want, safe in the benevolent protection of the Ryland family. But Cathy had begun to feel unusually tired during the summer and a cough which had begun about that time had got worse. Always a good eater, she nevertheless began to lose weight and her husband had sent her to the doctor.

When she got home he was working in the garden and looked up anxiously as she opened the gate.

'All well, Cath?' he asked, going towards her, but she didn't stop and continued into the house. There she took off her hat, shook out her hair and sat at the kitchen table upright, though the shock on her face was clearly visible.

'Like a cup of tea, Cath?' Frank asked helpfully.

Cathy ignored his question. 'He's sending me to the hospital for an X-ray, Frank. Asked if there's any TB in the family.'

'Oh, my love,' Frank said brokenly, pulling a chair away from the table and sitting next to her. Then he reached for her hand and patted it. '*Is* there any TB in your family?'

'Not that I know. Anyway, don't let's worry about it,' Cathy said briskly, looking at the kitchen clock. 'You best hurry and pick up Jenny. I think I'll go and have a little rest.'

'Geraldine keeps asking after you,' Philip said with a worried frown. 'I think you'd better go and see her.'

Verity knew it would have to come, but it was something she dreaded.

'How can I?' she asked. 'I feel such a hypocrite. So guilty.'

'There is no need for guilt,' he said a little sharply. 'If a woman denies her husband love and affection, what else can she expect but that he will be unfaithful to her?'

'Have you ever been unfaithful before, Philip?' She turned and looked at him and he shook his head.

'You mean I was the first, even though you and Geraldine didn't sleep together?'

'I'm not the sort of man to lightly engage in an affair, Verity. Besides' – his voice grew tender – 'I love you.'

'I love you too.'

She lay back in his arms with a deep sigh and his hand lightly caressed her breast.

After a while he stirred, kissed her gently and got out of bed. 'You'll have to go and see her. I know it's awkward, but –' He sat on the side of the bed, rubbing his chin uneasily with his hands. Then he leaned back, kissed her again and began putting on his clothes.

'I wish you could stay the night,' she said.

'Well, that, alas, is not possible.' He was looking at himself in the mirror, tying his tie. 'But I thought we might have a weekend away. I'll manufacture some conference or the other.'

'That would be wonderful.'

He finished dressing and leaned over her.

'Meanwhile, darling, drop Geraldine a note. The situation could be awkward. You were such friends.'

And then he was gone.

The emptiness Verity felt after Philip left was the worst part of a relationship which, despite her guilt, gave her nothing but joy. It was the joy that she knew she would have felt if she'd gone to bed with Rex, but she had been too inhibited, too afraid of losing his respect. There had been something very strait-laced about Rex. Philip was quite different: a passionate man who had released a store of equally passionate feelings in herself. She had known magic in the arms of her lover and she would never regret it, whatever happened.

Philip would be speeding back to his family. There would be a romp with the children, who would be taken off to bed by their nursemaid, and then dinner. What did he and Geraldine talk about? Was dinner eaten in silence? Verity never asked him, but she envied him his family life, from which she was cut off, the normality she might have had if she and Rex had married, above all the respectability.

She often tried to warn herself against dwelling on what might have been, but it was not only the physical side of marriage that she had been denied but all that went with it: the home, the family, the children.

Respectability was very important to Verity. Jack Hallam, her stepfather, had been a rogue and she was ashamed of him. To counteract this her adoptive parents had been eminently respectable, sent her to a good school and brought her up as a lady.

Her marriage to a doctor, also from a respectable family, had seemed just right. And now she was not respectable at all, but the mistress of a married man, engaged in a clandestine affair that some people might have thought rather sordid. Aunt Maude and Uncle Stanley would have a fit if they knew.

Restlessly Verity got up and made herself a cup of tea, but she was not hungry. For some time after Philip left her she could still feel the warmth of his love as if she was on a cloud from which she only slowly descended. Sometimes she felt she fed on love, which was a silly notion, but her affair had released a lot of sentimental ideas which in the old days she would have had no time for.

Some at the hospital had commented on her weight loss, but it didn't worry her because she knew the cause.

Now she got through each day knowing that in all probability, if their shifts worked out that way, she would see Philip in the early hours of the evening. He would stop for an hour or so on his way home and they would make love. Sometimes it was possible during the afternoon, or on her day off.

It was extremely liberating for a woman whose life had been one of restraint and rigidly imposed self-control. This sense of euphoria, always with her, had also enabled her to deal with the arrival of the new sister in charge, Miss Frobisher, who turned out to be a rather pleasant woman a few years older than Verity.

However, despite the ecstasy there was also sadness: the knowledge that, however much she loved Philip, he never would, never could leave Geraldine. Divorce would seriously jeopardise his career.

Verity stood for a long time by the window sipping her tea, that staple of a nurse's life. She felt restless, part happy but part sad because when, eventually, one came down from the cloud there was always a sense of despondency.

Then, finishing her tea, she got out some writing paper and, sitting at the table, began a letter.

'Dear Geraldine . . .'

She stopped, thought for a moment and, drawing another sheet of paper towards her, started again.

'Dearest Geraldine . . .'

Geraldine herself opened the door, rather breathlessly, as if she had flown towards it at the sound of the bell. Verity stood smiling at her, clutching a large bunch of flowers in her arms which she thrust towards her.

'Oh dear, you *shouldn't!*' Geraldine pressed the flowers enthusiastically to her nose. Then she kissed Verity on both cheeks, stood gazing at her for a moment with shining eyes, and then stood aside. Verity stepped cautiously into the hall, aware of a nervous flutter in her heart, anxiously looking round in case Philip should somehow be there, though she knew he couldn't, or shouldn't, because he was on duty at the hospital.

'Take off your hat and coat,' Geraldine commanded, putting the flowers on the hall table, 'and come in by the fire. Isn't it freezing?'

'Freezing,' Verity agreed, and as she went into the drawing room she was aware of Geraldine's arm round her waist, solicitously ushering her towards the fireplace.

'It was so lovely to get your letter,' she said, letting go of Verity and taking a poker to attack the fire, thus engendering a fierce blaze that roared up the chimney. She turned towards Verity with a quizzical expression and touched her cheek, leaving her soft white hand with its long bejewelled fingers resting there.

'I missed you, you know.'

'I missed you too.' Verity gulped, disconcerted by Geraldine's emotional welcome.

'Was it something that happened in Florence?'

'Oh no!' Verity replied with a guilty start. 'Whatever made you think that?'

'I thought perhaps it was. I know you didn't have a very nice room, and maybe we overdid the sightseeing, and then I was ill. Also it was so *hot*. The wrong time to go.'

'No, no,' Verity interrupted her, 'it was nothing like that.'

'And I do think we shouldn't have taken Philip.' Geraldine withdrew her hand with an expression of annoyance. 'I knew he'd spoil everything.'

'Oh, but he *didn't*.'

'He has no interest in cultural things at all.' Geraldine turned to Verity with a conspiratorial smile. 'Next time we go away we'll leave him at home.'

Inwardly floundering, as she knew she would, Verity flopped into a chair.

'It was *nothing* to do with the holiday, nothing at all. I thought we had a wonderful time and I enjoyed every moment. The truth is that as soon as I got back I was plunged into a crisis at the hospital.'

Geraldine grimaced sympathetically. 'Philip told me you were passed over. I thought it disgraceful; so did he. I wanted to write you a note but felt it might be misconstrued.' She interlaced her fingers, her head on one side. 'I decided you might think it tactless.'

'Not at all,' Verity replied. 'It was kind of you to think of it. I have been busy inducting the new sister in charge, Miss Frobisher. She is very good. I like her.'

'*So* magnanimous,' Geraldine murmured admiringly. 'Oh Verity, I *have* so missed you.'

She leapt up and, rushing across, took Verity's face firmly between her hands and kissed her on both cheeks. She stood for a few seconds looking into her eyes and then said breathlessly: 'I think maybe Spain for our next little jaunt. Have you ever been to Santiago de Compostella? The cathedral there is one of the finest in the world.'

'No' – Verity stifled a sinking feeling – 'but my sister was there for part of her honeymoon and she said it was lovely. But hot,' she added, thinking of Florence. 'She was there in the summer too.'

'*We* shall avoid the summer,' Geraldine said firmly and got up to ring the bell for tea.

On the way home a bemused and bewildered Verity tried to make what she could of the visit; a strange, strange event, with Geraldine's behaviour at times almost coquettish.

Verity realised that her attitude towards her friend had changed in a way she couldn't properly explain. It wasn't only the guilt she felt, the deceit, there was plenty of that, but Geraldine's unique charm seemed to have disappeared, and she failed to find her as fascinating and enigmatic as she had before.

Was the reason, the real reason, that she had now fallen out of love with Geraldine and in love with her husband? Had her complicated emotional involvement with both somehow been turned on its head?

She was glad she had made the visit. Geraldine obviously suspected nothing. There was almost a childlike quality about her that made Verity feel not quite as guilty as she might have done, as if such naiveté didn't deserve respect.

But as she reached the house she felt her attitude had been unfair: after all, it was she who had changed, not Geraldine. Geraldine still looked the same, behaved the same and obviously felt the same. It was she, Verity, who was different.

As she walked up the road she saw a red postman's bike outside the house, and a postman coming as she approached the gate. It was very late for the post, but she was about to pass him when he stopped and held out a buff envelope.

'Are you any chance by the name of Carter-Barnes, miss?'

'Yes.'

'I have a telegram for you.'

'Why, thank you.' Verity took the envelope and studied it. It told her nothing but her name and address. Then as the postman rode away her curiosity got the better of her and she tore through the flap and opened it.

'PLEASE CALL HOME URGENTLY', it said. 'MOTHER SERIOUSLY ILL. LOVE FRANK.'

Sarah Swayle was in her eighty-first year, a strong-minded woman who for most of her life had led the hard life of a farmer's wife. Her husband Joseph had died in 1921 and she lived alone, mostly seeing her late husband's relations and very seldom hers, even though her daughter Maude only lived a few miles away in Bournemouth.

Sarah had been a strict rather than affectionate mother. For one thing, she was always critical of Cathy and the number of marriages she'd made, the number of children she'd had, the general chaotic nature of her life. In Sarah's opinion that had weakened her, but nothing prepared them for the dreadful news that Cathy had been sent to a sanatorium near Bournemouth with advanced TB.

'We've never had TB in the family,' she said, as if there was something shameful about it, like murder or illegitimacy. Her three granddaughters sat around her in a solemn circle, rather as though there had already been a bereavement. 'Your mother did too much. She worked too hard and it did her no good.'

'TB is not caused by hard work, Gran.' Verity said, a little irritated by the diatribe they had been forced to listen to about their mother's deficiencies, especially as she was now so ill.

She and Peg had travelled down from London together and Addie had joined them at their grandmother's.

'Mother must have had a predisposition to it. Besides, for the last few years, since she married Frank, she has been well looked after and enjoyed a happy life.'

'Well, whatever it is she's paid for it,' Sarah Swayle said grumpily. 'She would never listen to my advice. Always knew best.'

'Gran, she's not *dying*,' Peg protested. 'Verity said the doctor thinks she has a very good chance of recovery. The hospital overlooks the coast with plenty of strong sea air.'

'Well, I hope he's right,' Sarah said grudgingly. Then she crossed her arms and looked about her. 'I would like to know what is going to happen to little Jenny. Is Addie going to have her?'

Addie tried to avert her eyes from that grandmotherly inquisition. It was a matter that had been tormenting her ever since she heard of her mother's illness.

'I can't, Gran, you know that. Harold won't have her.'

'Jenny is very well looked after by Frank, and Stella is there as well.' Verity felt a sympathy for her sister in her dilemma. Granny Swayle could be so very unbending.

'That's all very well, but she can't stay there. It's no way for a child to be brought up and, besides, Stella has her schooling to see to. How long will your mother be in hospital? No one knows. Weeks, months?'

Verity shook her head, knowing that Granny was quite right. Jenny was a problem and it was no use denying it.

'I'll make the tea,' Verity said, getting up. 'I'm dying for a cup.'

'I'll come with you.' Peg rose too.

'No, you stay and talk to Gran.' Verity jerked her head at Addie. 'Addie will help me with the tea.' Addie got up willingly, grateful to be away from the accusatory stare of her grandmother.

Verity carefully shut the door of the kitchen and went over to the hob, on which a large black kettle was already boiling.

'Have you thought about this, Addie?'

'I've thought of nothing else.'

'You *are* her mother.'

'I know, and don't think I don't want her. But Harold . . . well, he won't hear of it.'

'You've already asked him?'

'When I heard about Mum I told him my first thought was what would happen to Jenny. He said she was quite well off where she was. He flew into a temper and wouldn't discuss it.'

'Well, I don't know what we're going to do. I feel it's a problem we all must share.'

Verity finished making the tea. She was tired. This, added to all her other problems, had been a terrible strain. Her mother's appearance had shocked her. In the short time since she'd seen her she had deteriorated. The prognosis looked poor, despite what the doctor said. The thought of life without Mum could scarcely be tolerated. Even if she was only at the end of a railway line, at least she was there.

Verity poured the boiling water on to the tea leaves while Addie got out cups and saucers and put some biscuits on a plate.

When they returned to the sitting room Granny Swayle was listening to Peg, with an indulgent smile on her face, for a change.

Peg had tried to deflect her grandmother's wrath by entertaining her with an account of her activities in London.

Following the general election and the return of a Tory government with a massive majority, Peg had turned to writing feature articles and one, 'How Long Must We Say Goodbye To Labour?', had been much praised, as it included an interview with the defeated leader Ramsay Macdonald.

She smiled up at her granddaughters as they entered the room.

'I don't really know that I approve of young women doing a man's job, but I can't help admiring Peg.'

'We all admire her.' Verity poured the tea and handed the cups round. Then she addressed her grandmother. 'Gran, Addie *can't* have Jenny. Harold won't tolerate it.'

'Then she shouldn't have married him.'

'Well, she did. I wondered about Aunt Maude.'

'Oh no!' Addie exclaimed. 'She is much too old. I mean,' she corrected herself, 'she is sweet and was very good to you. But she's older than Mum and, anyway, doesn't have Mum's way with children.'

'Then I don't know what else we can do, except leave her with Frank. Stella will be there in the evenings and at weekends, but only until she goes to college.'

'But surely Mum won't be in hospital all *that* time, will she?' Addie looked aghast.

'We don't know. That is the truth, we don't know. Also Frank has his job. I have my job, Peg has hers. I think neither of us can be expected to give them up to look after the family. If Lord Ryland wants Frank, and there are times when he will, it is possible there will be nobody to look after Jenny at all. The very idea will kill Mum, if the disease doesn't. You know how she adores Jenny.'

There was a silence in the room while they all considered the dreadful implications of what Verity had just said.

Eleven

M any people would have thought that Addie had everything a woman could want in life: a nice house, a car, security, respectability, a husband with a responsible job as a headmaster at a flourishing infants' school in a good part of the town. To all appearances they were a happy and united couple.

Yet it was not so, and Addie felt she lived a cocoonlike existence, protected from the world, yet unreal.

She was able to hide her unhappiness from everyone but her two elder sisters because she threw herself into good works, which Harold approved of. He did not approve of her taking paid employment, such as teaching, which she would have enjoyed, so he didn't allow it. To Harold appearances were all important and his wife must not appear to have to work, even if she wanted to and found it fulfilling to do so.

It was very different from her upbringing, and she knew her marriage had been important to her mother, who wanted so much to enhance the status of her daughters in life. To Cathy the teaching profession was the highest goal to which one could aspire, and Addie had married a headmaster. What could be higher than that?

It was therefore not to let her mother down, as much as for any other reason, that Addie tried not to let the obvious cracks in her marriage show.

She had a maid, so there was no need to do housework, but despite the multiplicity of good works, she had time on her hands, too much time to brood on the greatest misfortune she felt any woman could have: her husband had not made love to her since their honeymoon because, he said, she had kept from him the fact that before their marriage she had had an illicit relationship with another man with whom she had had a child. The effect of this news on Harold had been enormous, yet it could have been largely foreseen because, even from their early courting days, it was clear what sort of person he was: conventional, unimaginative, rigid. Yet to her it was better to have a husband than not to have one and, after all, one always imagines, or hopes, that things might change.

It was of course a heinous thing to have kept this information from him. Addie only realised that in retrospect, and had ample time to regret it.

Harold wished to make it seem that they had a normal marriage because he had been about to take up his new position as headmaster, and to dump a wife one had just married would have caused raised eyebrows. In order to fulfil what was expected of him, he had to arrive with a wife, an intelligent and attractive woman, very much younger than he was, and give the impression that all was well with their life – because why, people would ask, should it not be?

So far he had succeeded. Everybody was fooled and Mr and Mrs Harold Smith were an admired and respected couple, considered assets to the community and much sought after for social invitations in their locality.

Addie got a taxi from the station the day after she and her sisters had met with their grandmother. It was late afternoon and Harold might be home. Now that she had succeeded in escaping from him for a day or two, she realised how much she hated to be back, and how much she loathed her home and the sham of a marriage that she was forced to live. But to escape from it was impossible. She had no money, no means of support, no life, really, away from her husband. Besides, there was the shame of failure, the hurt it would cause her mother, now possibly mortally sick.

145

Harold was fifteen years her senior and as far as she was aware she had been his first girlfriend. His only sexual experience had been with her and, at the start of the honeymoon, their physical relationship had not been satisfactory due to his inexperience and her natural shyness. But there was one hot day in Santiago de Compostella when everything had gone right, fusion and harmony were finally achieved, and she was rash enough to tell him about her past, wishing to bring her spouse into her confidence.

What a disaster that had been. But she had often thought that, even supposing this had not happened, Harold was not a very passionate man: austere, precise, scholarly and devoted to his work, but not sensuous.

As a schoolmaster he had an excellent reputation. He was liked by his small charges and they did well. His was the model of a well-run school and to have deserted Harold would have been unthinkable.

But all the way back on the train Addie had been haunted by the thought of Jenny and what would happen to her without the woman she had been brought up to think of as her mother.

Harold was not yet home after all when Addie arrived, something she was grateful for. Their maid Dorothy greeted her politely, carried her case to her bedroom and asked if she would like tea.

Addie said she would and started to unpack in the room she shared with Harold, in which there were twin beds, not too close together.

She sat in front of the mirror brushing her hair, applying some make-up – though Harold didn't like too much of it – to give her face colour; a little powder, a dab of rouge and a light application of lipstick.

After she had finished she examined herself carefully and thought that, despite her efforts, she looked drab and uninteresting, a colourless suburban housewife with nowhere to go and not much to do. She had none of the vivacity of Peg, the serenity and self-assurance of Verity. Sometimes she felt she was like a little mouse, timid and uncertain, who'd had a brief moment of a love that was doomed to fail. Even if he hadn't been killed, her affair with Lydney Ryland would surely have ended in disaster.

She had often said she married so as not to be a spinster like Verity, and yet Verity had a responsible job which gave her security and also status in life, and Peg had branched into a field of work which was still almost uniformly closed to women.

Addie felt at that moment terribly alone and so depressed that, had she not heard the sound of the door closing downstairs and Harold calling for Dorothy, she felt she would have burst into tears.

Instead she tried to pull herself together, force herself to smile and summon an inner source of strength before she went downstairs to greet her husband, who was standing in front of the fire, pipe in his mouth, reading the evening paper. As she entered he put the paper aside and went up to give her a perfunctory kiss on the cheek. 'How is your mother?' he enquired solicitously.

'I didn't see her. Strictly it isn't allowed because her disease is so contagious. But Verity saw her and is very worried about her.'

'I'm sorry, dear. Have some tea.' Harold crossed to the table on which Dorothy had left a tray and poured her a cup. 'How very worrying for you.'

He then went back to the fireside and resumed his perusal of the evening paper.

Drinking her tea, looking at him, this seemed to Addie the summation of their married life: Harold's total lack of interest in her or anything to do with her, or her family. Having gone through the motions of expressing concern, he now had no more to say.

'How was *your* day, Harold?' she asked at last.

'As usual,' he said without looking up.

'I'll go and talk to Dorothy about dinner,' Addie said.

'Good idea,' Harold replied and she left the room.

*　　*　　*

That night she lay in bed listening to the sound of Harold breathing and thinking about the dismal life she led, and about Jenny.

It would have been so different if they had had their own children, as Harold said he had wanted. He liked small children and was good with them, just about the last thing you would have expected from someone of Harold's rather withdrawn, repressed nature, but it was so. This was the reason he had given for not making a home for Jenny, apart from his natural revulsion at her being the result of an illicit union. But the chance to have their own children never came, as he made it clear he didn't want to make love to her. Possibly he couldn't.

Because of the sort of person he was and the sort of person she was, shy, rather inhibited, the least confident and outgoing of the three elder sisters, it had never been something she could manage to talk to Harold about. She had made some feeble attempts but failed, both through timidity and lack of encouragement. Knowing what was coming he would fix her with a glassy stare and she would stop, lacking the courage to continue.

The next day was a routine kind of day. Harold went off to work bang on the dot of ten minutes to eight as always. It was a short walk to the school and he timed it so that he was never a minute early or a minute late, but arrived just as eight was striking on the school tower.

Dorothy cleared the breakfast dishes and Addie wondered what she should do to occupy herself. Her depression had continued and she had had very little sleep.

After Dorothy had made the beds and cleaned the bedroom and bathroom, Addie went upstairs and began to sort through some clothes for a jumble sale. They each had a chest of drawers and the wardrobe was scrupulously divided into two. Harold also had a wardrobe and chest of drawers to himself in the spare room, which he used as a dressing room. Addie thought that he preferred this so that they should avoid the sight of each other dressing and undressing. However, it suited her too.

This took up most of the morning, and at lunchtime Addie took the clothes downstairs and sought Dorothy's help in sorting them into bundles: male and female.

'Are you going to throw *all* these things out, madam?' the servant asked incredulously.

'They're for the jumble sale.'

'Some of the things are so *good*, madam. This suit of the master's –' Lost in admiration, Dorothy held up a perfectly good suit, which Harold seemed to have outgrown over the years. 'It would fit my brother a treat,' she added enviously. 'He never had a suit in his life.'

'Well –' Addie looked from her to the garment. 'You're very welcome to it.'

'Oh no, madam, I couldn't!'

Addie didn't really know much about Dorothy's circumstances, except that she was a country girl and her family a large one.

'What does your brother do, Dorothy?'

'He works on the farm, madam, like my father, labourers, you know. We don't own the farm. Wages are very bad and there is little money to spare for new clothes. My brother is getting married soon, and it would be so nice if he had something decent to wear for his wedding.'

'Then he must definitely have it, and look' – Addie gestured towards the clothes – 'take anything else you'd like for your family. Take it *all!*'

Dorothy stared at her mistress, blushing to the roots of her hair.

'Oh no, madam, I couldn't.'

'They will only go to the school jumble sale and I'm sure your needs are much greater. Look, the next time you go home I'll take you in the car and you shall give your family what items of clothes you choose.'

To Addie's consternation Dorothy went even more scarlet and then burst into tears, kneading her fingers in her eyes to try and stop the weeping. Finally she dabbed at them with the hem of her white apron while Addie looked helplessly on at the stricken, tearstained face. Eventually she went up to her maid and put her arms around her.

'I'm sorry, Dorothy. I didn't mean to distress you. Are things *so* bad at home, then?'

'They're terrible, madam.' Dorothy screwed up her apron into a tight little ball. 'There's no work to be had in the country. So many men have come back from the war without jobs. There are seven in our family – four boys and three girls – and two of the men have no work. My father served in the army and was gassed. He's not fit but he's so terrified of losing his job he turns out at all hours. He's racked with rheumatism but won't say anything for fear of the sack.'

'I'm very distressed to hear this, Dorothy,' Addie said with real concern. 'I had no idea, and if I can help in any way with food or' – she paused, thinking of Harold's stinginess – 'even money.'

'Oh, you're too good, madam.' Dorothy grasped her hand and looked as though she was on the point of kissing it. Then, changing her mind, she hurried out of the room before a fresh wave of tears engulfed her.

Addie was very distressed about what she had heard from Dorothy. It was true that the girl had not worked for them for very long and she knew little about her or her family. They had taken up references which were satisfactory. They knew how old she was – sixteen – and that was about all. She was clean, neat and diligent, but apart from that they knew nothing.

After lunch Addie took herself for a walk round the town, gazing in the shop windows, noticing with a fresh eye all the good things that were on offer, but observing also the number of ex-servicemen on the street selling boxes of matches, hunched up in threadbare overcoats, or sometimes no overcoat at all.

Really Dorothy was comparatively well off. She had a good job with full uniform and her own room, all found, and a small wage as well. She had a day off a week, which was more than a lot of domestic workers had, but she was obviously and understandably concerned about her family. However, there was, Addie felt as she ruminated on the day's events, something very wrong about a society which enabled people like her and Harold to have such a good standard of living while others were so poor.

Compared to many in society, her own family were comparatively well off, and this train of thought led her to think once again about Jenny, deprived of the one person who had given her love and security.

Her eyes suddenly filled with tears. She really didn't know what to do or where to go for advice or support. Her sisters were far away, she had not yet made any new friends and her husband was the last person she could turn to.

When she got home it was nearly dark and yet it was not yet four o'clock. December was such a depressing month, and soon it would be Christmas. Addie went into the kitchen where Dorothy was taking a cake she had baked out of the oven.

'I thought it would be nice for tea, madam,' she said, looking gratefully at Addie. She was much more cheerful now, her tears quite dry, and had put a fresh white apron on. 'You were so good to me this morning. I never had such kindness.'

'Oh, Dorothy!' Impulsively Addie squeezed her arm. 'I want you to think of me and the master as friends. Do you know I have a sister your age?'

'Oh!' Dorothy's face brightened. 'And what is she called, madam?'

'Stella. She wants to be a schoolteacher.'

'And have you other sisters, madam?'

'Two. Verity, who is a nurse, quite a senior one, and Peg, who is a journalist on a newspaper.'

'Oh, how interesting.' Dorothy looked impressed.

'And I have a younger brother, Ed,' Addie went on, 'who started at university in October. We're very proud of him. He is very bright and got a scholarship. No one in the family has even been to university before, though my sister Verity, the nurse, is very highly trained.'

'You see, madam, none of us had much education,' Dorothy said soulfully. 'None of my brothers really had a chance. My eldest brother was in the war and he has never been able to get work because he was shell-shocked. He has terrible blackouts and fits of weeping. Can't seem to get the sights he saw out of his mind. My father says he's useless and should pull himself together, but I feel sorry for him. I really do.'

'Let's have a cup of tea,' Addie said, going to the stove, 'and a piece of your cake.'

They were sitting chatting at the kitchen table drinking tea and eating cake when they heard the front door open and Harold called out: 'Addie, are you there? I'm home.'

Addie, feeling much more cheerful now, rose and opened the kitchen door. 'In here, dear, just having a cup of tea.'

Harold came to the door and stood on the threshold, looking at them.

'Oh!' he said.

'Come and join us.' Addie beckoned to him.

'I would prefer my tea in the drawing room,' Harold said coldly, 'and I would like you to join me there too, please, Adelaide.'

He then firmly shut the door and they could hear his heavy footsteps echo down the corridor with an ominous tread.

Addie grimaced. He only called her Adelaide when he was annoyed.

'What was all that about?' she murmured almost to herself.

'Oh dear, I'm ever so sorry, madam.' Dorothy nervously touched her bare head. 'And me with my cap off. I don't think the master was very pleased.'

'Don't let it worry you, Dorothy,' Addie said, stiffly getting to her feet. 'You know the master has his moments. I will take him a tray and soothe him down.'

She made a fresh pot of tea, put it with two cups, milk and sugar on a tray and added some of Dorothy's freshly made jam sponge cake. Then, with a sense of trepidation, she carried it along the hall to the drawing room where, as usual, Harold stood by the fire looking at the evening paper.

'Don't you think it's a little unwise to fraternise with the servant?' he said, putting the paper aside and sternly watching Addie pouring out the tea. 'We'll have her eating in the dining room with us next.'

'Don't be absurd, Harold.'

She passed him his cup, her expression stony. He began thoughtfully to stir his tea, as though he was brooding over his next remark.

'I suppose you feel more comfortable mixing with people of your own class?' he said at last, a smirk on his face as though he was rather pleased with himself.

'And what do you mean by that?'

'Don't pretend you don't know.' He lifted his cup to his lips, pausing to say: 'I believe your father was a butcher.'

'You *know* my father was a butcher. I have never tried to pretend anything else. I'm proud of my family and proud of my heritage.'

Harold finished his tea, put down his cup and took up the paper again, but before reading it he glanced at her.

'What are all those bundles of clothes doing in the hall?'

'They were for the school jumble sale. But I'm giving them to Dorothy.'

'You are *what*?' He threw down his paper in a renewed gesture of exasperation.

'Giving them to Dorothy,' Addie repeated in a calm voice. 'Her family is very poor, some are out of work and she needs them.'

'Is she paying for them?'

'Of course not,' Addie said contemptuously. 'I said she was poor.'

'Then what about the money that might have gone to the school?'

153

'I think the school with its well-off parents can easily do without the money. I haven't seen any children there in rags or with no shoes. I didn't realise in what desperate straits Dorothy's family lived, and it made me deeply ashamed of myself.'

As she returned his hostile stare a very strange thing happened: Addie felt a surge of confidence in herself and realised that she was no longer afraid of Harold. She could meet him on his own ground. Look him in the eyes. She took a deep breath and said: 'And while we're being honest and truthful with each other, Harold, I think I should tell you that I must insist that Jenny comes to live with us. She is my daughter. She is only six, and for the time being she has lost the woman she thinks of as her mother and who is all the world to her. Jenny needs me.'

'Well, she's done quite well without you for the past few years,' Harold retorted.

'That's as maybe, but now Mother is ill and Jenny needs looking after. Well, I am her mother and I want her here.'

Harold, whose anger had been visibly mounting, raised his hand and shook a finger violently at her. 'And *I'm* telling *you* that as the master of this house I absolutely forbid it. I refuse to have that bastard here. How shall I explain it? What will parents think, to say nothing of members of the board of governors of the school? What shall I tell them?'

'You'd better think about what to tell them, Harold, because she's coming here whether you like it or not.'

'If that child comes into my house I shall throw her out into the street, and that's a promise.'

'You once told me you wouldn't have her because you wanted our own family,' Addie shouted back, almost beside herself. 'Well, when is that going to happen? I'd like to know, as you never come near me.'

'Because you disgust me. A woman who can give herself to a man who just uses her.'

'I was *not* used. I was in love. And so was he. He—'

'I refuse to hear another word on this subject,' Harold cried and brushed past her towards the door. She caught at his wrist and held him back.

'This can't go on, Harold, this sham, this pretence. If it does I shall leave you.'

He turned to her with a withering, mocking glance.

'You wouldn't *dare*,' he said, and left the room, banging the door behind him.

Addie gazed at the closed door, her breathing heavy, almost forced, as though she'd completed a steep, difficult climb. But to her surprise there were no tears. She felt nothing but rage against Harold, and with it a sense of despair that she'd let this impossible situation continue for so long because she'd been too timid to stand up to him.

Well, she would be timid no more.

Addie remained in the drawing room for some time sitting quietly in front of the fire. After a while she heard the front door close and a few minutes after that there was a knock at the door and Dorothy popped her head round.

'Do you need any more coal for the fire, madam?'

'I don't think so, thanks,' Addie said, forcing a smile. 'Did I hear Mr Smith leave?'

'Yes, madam. He said he would not be having dinner.'

'In that case, I'll have it by myself at the usual time.'

'Yes, madam.' Dorothy gave an awkward bob and withdrew.

Addie had her meal sitting by herself at the dining table, and then she sat for some time in the drawing room staring at the fire.

Her mood was a strange one. She felt restless, afraid but also resolute, as if she knew now with certainty what she must do.

At about ten she went up to the bedroom, undressed, performed her ablutions and got into bed. She knew she wouldn't be able to read, so she put the light out and lay listening for the front door, wondering if Harold might have decided to stay the night at a hotel, as he had when he'd walked out on her on their honeymoon.

155

Then he'd returned and laid down the law about her future behaviour and conduct and she'd accepted it all, terrified of the consequences, grateful still to have a husband after confessing her misdeeds.

She was feeling drowsy when she heard the bedroom door open and the light go on. She lay still with her eyes shut, listening to Harold moving about, making no effort to be quiet, first in their bedroom, then in his dressing room. Finally he got into bed and put out the light.

Addie didn't think she would sleep but she did, maybe from exhaustion. When she awoke the following morning Harold was already in the bathroom, and she waited for him to come out and go into his dressing room before getting out of bed. She stayed for a long time in the bath and when she had dressed and come downstairs it was after eight and Harold, with his usual precision, had gone. So they had missed seeing each other completely, and not a word had been spoken.

After breakfast she went upstairs and took everything out of her wardrobe, laying the clothes neatly on the bed. She emptied her drawers and a cupboard and packed some things, discarding others. That done, she summoned Dorothy, who came nervously into the room and stared at the clothes on the bed, at the open wardrobe and empty drawers.

'Dorothy, I am leaving my husband,' Addie said matter-of-factly. 'My mother is seriously ill and I am going back to look after my family. You are an intelligent girl and you probably realise Mr Smith and I do not get on, have not got on for many months. No doubt you heard the row yesterday. The reasons for this need not concern you.'

She saw tears well up in the young girl's eyes and the hem of her apron once more act as a handkerchief as Dorothy dabbed at her eyes. 'Oh, madam,' she sniffed, 'I shall miss you.'

'And I shall miss you, but I am sure Mr Smith will need you and want you to stay on. In the meantime, before you help me pack, I have put out some things on the bed and would like you to take what you want. There, help yourself!' she said, standing back.

Still snivelling, Dorothy crept cautiously forward and peered at the garments displayed like wares on a market stall. With a little more encouragement from Addie she selected three dresses and a costume, two jerseys, four blouses, three pairs of shoes and a hat, which she perhaps hoped to wear to her brother's wedding. Then, by this time greatly cheered, she helped Addie to pack and secure the suitcases which they both took downstairs.

Addie took a last look round the house where she had lived for such a short time. But her marriage had only lasted eighteen months, surely some sort of record? There was nothing she really wanted in the house. It had never been a love nest. There were no sentimental items reminding her of good times shared, of things lovingly done together. There were really no good memories at all since, she realised now, Harold had found her repulsive and unclean because she had slept with another man before him. Such was his own warped nature, his lack of understanding about the nature of love, his inability to forgive.

The inspection completed, she rang for a cab and then handed Dorothy a sealed envelope.

'I want you to give this to your master. You need say nothing else. He is bound to ask you questions, to be very angry, but everything is explained in the letter, and he is a man too concerned with his reputation to do anything rash.' Then, as they heard the cab draw up in the road outside, she leaned towards Dorothy and hugged her. 'I hope we shall see each other again. Here is my address; keep in touch.' She pressed a piece of paper and a five-pound note into the young woman's hand.

Then, followed by Dorothy struggling with the suitcases, she flew towards the cab such as might a caged bird regaining its freedom.

Dusk was falling and the house seemed very still. The driver of the cab that had brought her from the station unloaded her cases, put them by the front door and she paid him and gave him a generous tip.

'I'm not sure if anybody is at home,' she said. 'It doesn't seem like it.'

'Will you be all right, miss?' the driver asked.

'I'll be fine.'

Addie stood by the front door feeling, now, a little unsure of herself. She had acted very impulsively. Twenty-four hours previously it had never entered her head that, much as she would want to, she might one day actually leave Harold.

Now she had and the die was cast.

The front door was never locked. She pushed it open and a light fell on the hallway from the kitchen. Leaving her cases, she shut the door gently and listened to the voice coming from the kitchen.

'And Little Red Riding Hood said, "But Granny, what big *eyes* you have . . ." ' There was a squeal of childish terror as the voice went on, ' "All the better to *see* you with, my dear." '

Addie walked along the corridor and stood for a moment at the open kitchen door. Frank was sitting at the table, a book propped in front of him, and opposite sat Jenny, her head held in her hands, staring at him open-mouthed. She looked so innocent, so beautiful that Addie's heart turned over and her eyes filled with tears. How *could* she ever have given her up?

' "But Grandmother," said Little Red Riding Hood, "what big *ears* you have." "All the better to HEAR you with," ' Frank growled and once again Jenny squealed with terror. At that moment Addie decided to make her presence known and walked into the room.

They both stared at her in silence for a moment and then Frank put the book down and got up.

'Is everything all right?' he asked anxiously. 'Cathy . . .'

'Oh, it's nothing about Mother,' Addie said embracing him. She turned to Jenny, but the child shyly held back.

'Hello, Jenny,' she said, feeling, now that the moment had

come, a little shy herself. For it was a very big moment, reclaiming the daughter she thought she had given up.

'Hello, Aunt Addie,' Jenny said politely.

'Are you going to give me a kiss?'

Jenny still held back as Addie went over to her and bent down.

'Go on, give me a kiss.' Addie drew the warm little body towards her, but Jenny remained, as she always had with Addie, stiff and unresponsive, as though she was somehow afraid of her.

'Is Mum with you?' she asked, looking hopefully towards the door.

'I'm afraid not.' Addie got up. 'But I'm going to see her tomorrow, or the day after' – she looked at Frank – 'if Frank can take me.'

'I would like to see Mummy too,' Jenny piped up.

'I'll ask if it's allowed at the hospital,' Addie promised her.

Then she took off her hat and put it on the table, removed her coat and hung it over the back of a chair.

'I've come to stay for a while, Frank,' she said. 'I want to help look after you, Stella and Jenny.'

'Oh, that's *marvellous* news.' Frank's anxious face immediately became wreathed in smiles. 'For how long?'

'It depends. Is Stella in?'

'She's helping up at the castle. A lot of staff are down with the flu. Jenny, would you run up to the castle, find Stella and tell her Addie is here? Put a coat on so that you don't catch cold.'

Jenny nodded obediently and immediately ran off. 'Oh Addie, it *is* good to see you.' Frank again threw his arms round her. 'I hope you can stay for a little while.'

Addie freed herself from his embrace and suddenly, over-whelmed with exhaustion, flopped down on one of the kitchen chairs.

'I've left Harold. The details needn't concern you now, but I am never going back to him. I am here to stay and look after you and the family, and be a proper mother to Jenny.'

Frank went across to her and hugged her. With the tears

159

streaming down his face, he said: 'Oh, Addie, I've been a lonely man all my life and then I find a wonderful woman who makes me very happy, and now she's going to die. I love little Jenny and I love Stella, but on my own –' He shook his head. 'I can't cope, Addie, I really can't.'

'Mum's not going to die,' Addie said bravely, patting his tearstained cheek. 'And in the meantime you've got me and now I'm here to stay.'

Twelve

A rm in arm Verity and Philip took advantage of the late
afternoon sunshine to stroll through the lovely grounds
surrounding the hotel. The venue and the circumstances, but not
the weather, reminded her so much of that hot afternoon in
Florence when they had first kissed. If she had been told then
that within six months they would be lovers and she would be
spending the weekend away with him, she would not have
believed it.

Philip tossed his cigarette away and squeezed her arm.

'Happy?'

'Very, very happy.'

She stopped and raised her mouth to his and they kissed. From
somewhere in the branches above them came the piercing whistle
of a nuthatch for, though it was still the depth of winter, birds
had begun to call for their mates. They broke away and resumed
their walk, Philip putting an arm round her waist.

'I've got something to tell you.' His expression was grave and
Verity's heart skipped a beat.

'What is it?' she asked, always fearful because of the fragile
nature of their relationship.

'Nothing to worry about, darling' – he touched the tip of her
nose – 'it's something nice. I have applied for a post at St Mary's
and believe I am in with a good chance.'

Verity leaned her head against Philip's chest but her feelings
were mixed.

'Oh Philip!'

He looked at her in surprise. 'Aren't you pleased?'

'Very pleased for you, darling; but . . .'

'But what?'

'Will it make a difference to us?'

'Of course not. How can it?'

'I see you at the hospital.'

'Well, I won't be so very far away, and in many ways it might be better. No chance for gossip.'

'But there hasn't been much of that lately, ever since Miss Frobisher came.'

They recommenced their walk and he lit a fresh cigarette.

'You like her, don't you?'

'Very much. She is both capable and fair. She realises my nose was put out and has gone out of her way to give me more responsibility and take my feelings and opinions into account. I respect her.' Verity sighed deeply and pushed her hair away from her forehead. 'I still feel I should make a change and yet I can't.'

'Why not?'

'Because it will inevitably mean moving out of London. I'll miss you too much.'

'Oh, my darling,' he said and kissed her again.

They came to the edge of the hotel grounds. The sun had gone in and it was getting colder and darker. Verity pulled her warm coat tightly around her and shivered.

'Let's get back and have some tea,' Philip murmured. 'Then maybe a little rest before we change for dinner?'

He looked at her slyly, and she knew what he meant.

'Perfect,' she said happily. Then: 'I think this is one of the best times in my life, being here with you all to myself.'

And indeed it was a very happy time, and yet . . . being with Philip, sleeping with him all through the night, was almost more torment than pleasure. The more she had of him the more she wanted him.

Driving from London to the hotel deep in the Sussex countryside, being greeted by the deferential staff as they registered as husband and wife, made her wish so much that it was real, that they were a married couple, not deceiving anybody, and that there was nothing illicit or potentially scandalous in their relationship.

It was true that it probably added spice to their lovemaking. People said that such a situation often did. The hours that were snatched and stolen, the hasty assignations made in the hospital corridors, the secret smiles and furtive encounters as their bodies casually touched, all this added a frisson of danger to what was, after all, an adventure.

But Verity wanted it to be so much more, to be the real Mrs Beaumaurice, and she had begun to wonder if somehow, one day, it might not come to pass? But how could it? And how could she square her happiness with deceiving a woman who thought of her as a friend and whom she continued to see, though not as frequently as before?

That was the tormenting part.

It was almost dark when they reached the drive. In front of them baggage was being unloaded from a car and a tall man was talking to the porter, while on the other side a woman dressed in furs began to make her way into the hotel.

Philip suddenly came to a halt and so did Verity, her arm linked to his.

'What is it, Philip?'

'Shh.' He put a forefinger to his lips. 'Don't move.'

'Is it someone you know?'

He nodded and the joy in her heart was abruptly replaced by a feeling of foreboding as they took shelter in the trees. Finally, after more discussion, the couple, preceded by ample baggage, disappeared into the hotel lobby and their car was driven by a flunky to the garage at the rear.

'Arnold Thompson,' Philip murmured, 'a member of the Royal College of Surgeons.'

'Who knows you, of course.'

Philip nodded. 'Also his wife and Geraldine are friendly.'
Philip pressed her arm. 'My darling, I am so sorry.'

'We must go?'

'At once.'

'But what will you say?'

'I'll think of something. Let's try and find a back way into the hotel and then go and pack.'

But alas, there was no obvious back way into the hotel except through the kitchens, which was out of the question, so, after lurking outside, feeling extremely foolish, Philip and Verity finally managed to enter and find their way to their room without being seen.

They made a similarly furtive escape, Philip carrying their luggage which, for a weekend, wasn't too extensive and which he put into the car, leaving Verity sitting miserably in the hall, her coat pulled up to her face. Philip returned after a few minutes and went over to the reception to pay his bill.

'Unfortunately I have to return to London,' he told the receptionist who, apparently concerned, asked if anything had been wrong with his stay.

'Not at all,' Philip said reassuringly. 'I am a doctor and have been recalled to London on a medical matter. The stay was most enjoyable and my wife and I shall be returning.'

The clerk produced the bill and Philip was in the act of producing his wallet when Mrs Thompson emerged from a side room and walked straight into him.

'Philip Beaumaurice!' she cried in obvious delight. 'How lovely to see you.' She turned to her husband, who now joined her.

'Darling, Philip Beaumaurice is here.'

'So I can see,' Dr Thompson replied, pumping his hand. 'Nice to see you, Philip.'

'And you,' Philip replied.

'Are you staying?'

'Just going, unfortunately.'

'Oh what a pity.' Mrs Thompson looked around, her eyes

lingering for a second on Verity, who sat as though she had been turned to marble, clutching her coat to her chin. 'Is Geraldine with you?'

'She's in the car,' Philip replied, handing the clerk some notes.

'Oh, I must just pop out and say hello.'

'Oh no, please don't.' Philip caught her arm, smiling apologetically. 'I mean, forgive me, but we are in a dreadful hurry. There is an emergency at the hospital.'

'Give her my love.'

'Don't worry, I shall.' Philip hastily shook hands and then hurried out of the vestibule. After watching the Thompsons go into the main lounge, Verity followed him in as dignified a fashion as possible.

It was, however, hard to be dignified when suffering from shock and humiliation.

'He recently got his consultancy.' Philip turned to her as he negotiated the car out of the drive. 'St Thomas's. We trained together.' He sounded perfunctory, matter of fact, not at all as though he'd just escaped an embarrassing exposure.

'So you know each other very well?'

'We were never great friends. He went on to specialise in orthopaedics, but by extreme coincidence our wives were at school together.'

'So they are close friends?'

'I wouldn't say close, not at all, but they keep in touch, school reunions, that kind of thing. He had a brother who was killed in the war.'

Verity felt that Philip was playing for time because he did not want to face the possibility of which both of them were aware, and which one did not have to be a fortune teller to predict: that this unhappy incident might mark the end of their relationship.

Verity was still suffering from the humiliation of their abrupt departure from the hotel, the shattering of what had been a dream.

Philip put a hand on her knee.

165

'Sorry.'

'It wasn't your fault.'

'How on earth were we to know we would bump into someone one or other of us knew?'

'We weren't. We couldn't. Yet it could happen and did and might happen again anywhere.'

'Would you like to go somewhere else? We have a day, and there are plenty of hotels. Two nights,' he added rather half-heartedly.

Verity shook her head. 'At this time of night? No.'

'At least let's have a meal.'

'I'm really not hungry.'

'No, neither am I.'

They travelled through the night, mostly in silence, both of them occasionally smoking, each quite obviously locked in their respective thoughts.

Finally Philip drew up outside the house and looked at her.

'Do you want to come in?' Verity asked.

'Of course. Do you mind?'

'Of course not.'

Geraldine had gone to visit her parents with the children and was not due back until Monday. The household staff, a maid, nanny and the cook, had been given the weekend off and Philip had told his wife he had work to do at the hospital and then would probably stay at his club.

Verity thought how drab and how unlived-in the flat looked after the luxury of the hotel with its plush interior, the private bathroom, the servants who could be summoned at the touch of a bell. What a contrast too was this student-like abode to the elegant surroundings of the Highgate home of the Beaumaurices.

'I must either do something about this place or move,' she murmured. 'Suddenly I feel unhappy and discontented.'

Philip sat down and lit a cigarette, extending his cigarette case to her.

'Don't let it discourage you, Ver.'

'How can I not let it discourage me, Philip?' she said sharply, accepting a cigarette. 'Today I felt second class, a mistress.'

'You are not a mistress. I don't keep you.'

'No, I mean someone whose emotional life has to be lived in secret. I felt shocked and humiliated.'

'Well, so did I, if you want to know.' Philip began to remove his tie. 'You don't mind if I stay the night, do you?'

'Of course I don't. I want you to stay the night. I love you staying the night, trying to weave this whole sordid business into something normal and ordinary, which it is not.'

Philip got up and started to pace restlessly round the room.

'Verity, darling, I know you're upset and I can see why. So am I. It was horrible, furtive and worse because we'd had such a wonderful time. Hadn't we?' He looked anxiously at her and she nodded, her expression abject and haunted. 'Well, this, this state of affairs, this hole-and-corner business, shall we call it, is not satisfactory for me either.'

'But do you love Geraldine?' Verity demanded, her voice rising. 'Do you still love her?'

Philip scratched his head.

'You know Geraldine is my wife, the mother of my daughters. She has done nothing wrong.'

'That doesn't answer my question, Philip.'

'Well, I find it very hard to answer.' He scratched his head again.

'You said she didn't sleep with you.'

'Well –' Philip stroked his chin and Verity began to find his procrastination infuriating.

'Does she or does she not? You must know.'

'I told you, no.' He looked at her angrily. 'But you must realise, Verity, that Geraldine has been a loyal wife and that counts for much. She has been lonely too during all my years of study, sacrificed a lot, spent countless hours on her own while I was working away to pass my exams. And not only has she supported me emotionally during all those years, but her money has helped pay for my career. She inherited a small fortune from her father and this enabled me to live well and in some comfort at a time when many newly qualified medical men are very strapped for cash. Professional competence, rather than the need to make a living, helped me to succeed. I can't throw it all in her face.'

'I'm not asking you to.'

'No, but you asked me if I loved her and I wondered why you asked me that.' He looked long and hard at Verity but she didn't reply. 'You must understand now,' he went on, 'that all these years of work are about to pay off and I shall achieve my consultancy, a position in a teaching hospital, a brass plaque in Harley Street. I don't want to blow it.'

'And I don't want you to blow it either.' Verity felt suddenly deflated, her anger gone. 'Of course I don't, and I don't want to make Geraldine suffer. You don't know how dreadful I feel that she is always so terribly nice to me. I feel she must see through me, but she doesn't.'

'She's extremely fond of you,' Philip agreed, but despite his words it didn't seem to make him feel guilty, as it did Verity. Maybe he was relieved, or even pleased, that his wife and his mistress got on.

'If I wanted a divorce now it would finish me. I wouldn't get my consultancy if Geraldine found out and sued me. I'd end up in the country in some second-rate hospital, with a mark against my name even then.'

'But Philip,' Verity said gently, 'have you thought about the possibility that Geraldine will get to hear about this weekend through Mrs Thompson?'

'Yes, I have. I have thought about little else.'

'So what are you going to do about it?'

'Well' – Philip resumed his pacing of the room – 'I don't think I am going to do anything until Geraldine forces my hand. For one thing, they are not very close friends. The Thompsons don't live in London but somewhere in the Home Counties – Surrey, I think. I don't see why Abigail Thompson should telephone

Geraldine about the meeting in the country. I don't *know* she won't, but this is one of the imponderables in this situation. They are not close, they don't meet very often. When they do Abigail might have forgotten the whole thing. That's the chance I have to take. Anyway, by that time I might have my consultancy, and that is what matters most to me.'

He went over to Verity and attempted to take her in his arms, but she resisted him, stung by the implication of his last words.

His consultancy was really all that mattered to him, not her. Certainly not her.

He spread his arms wide in a gesture of helplessness. 'Now, my darling, we're both very tired and a bit out of sorts. Shall we have a cup of cocoa or something and go to bed?'

But they did not make love. Unusually, when they had so much time and the opportunity, they didn't take advantage of it. The atmosphere between them was strained, the situation too tense. It was as though they both knew that, however much they might try and talk their way round the issue, the unfortunate meeting with the Thompsons lay between them, and its potential repercussions could shatter their lives.

It would always be a possibility that one day, perhaps the following week, or maybe not for months or even a year, Geraldine Beaumaurice and Abigail Thompson would meet up and Abigail would tell Geraldine how sorry she was she and her husband had missed them at the Sussex hotel, and Geraldine would ask what hotel and that would be that.

Eventually Verity fell asleep and she supposed Philip did too. They woke quite late, but did not feel refreshed. While Philip had a bath Verity got breakfast and, although she was still in her gown, Philip appeared in the kitchen dressed and looking as though he was ready to go.

'Are you going already?' she asked him.

'I thought I'd look in at the hospital and then I'd go to my club.' He sat down at the kitchen table. 'Then that part of the weekend can be true when Geraldine asks me what I did.'

'Right, if that's what you want.' Lips pursed, Verity put the slices of bread she had toasted under the grill on a plate.

'Marmalade all right for you?'

'Marmalade is fine.'

It was not quite the sort of breakfast they had had at the hotel: an assortment of hot dishes, toast wrapped in a napkin, tea or coffee served from a silver pot, and a bevy of waiters attentive to their every whim. Philip had eaten a hearty cooked breakfast. Verity, still too excited by the occasion, had hardly touched a thing.

How very different was today.

She knew now that Philip was restless and eager to be gone; perhaps to think the whole thing through, to worry about the possibility that Geraldine and either Arnold or Abigail Thompson might meet up sooner rather than later, or that Abigail just might make that telephone call and an affair would be revealed that would scupper once and for all Philip's chances of a consultancy at a major London teaching hospital.

After breakfast he lit a cigarette and pushed back his chair.

'Thank you, dear. That was very nice.'

Verity also lit a cigarette. She could think of nothing to say, but she was already anticipating the loneliness she would feel after he'd gone; the sense of isolation, and also of rejection.

The silence in the room was suddenly broken by the sound of the key in the lock. They both stared at each other as the door of the flat opened and Peg appeared and, without seeing them, shut the door behind her.

Then she turned.

It was another moment to remember, rather like the one when Philip had seen the Thompsons and that particular idyll had come to an end. Unfortunately this weekend seemed full of disastrous occurrences.

As if to forestall her, Philip said: 'Hello, Peg. I was just about to go.'

Peg looked from Verity to Philip and then back to her sister again.

'I just came for a few of my things,' she said awkwardly. 'I didn't know you'd be here. You said you were going away.'

'That's all right.' Verity stood up, pulling her dressing gown tightly around her. 'Philip was just leaving.'

'I shan't be a minute.' Peg started for the room she used to occupy.

'No, really. I am going.' Philip looked towards the door and then remembered that his overnight suitcase was in Verity's bedroom.

'Your hat's in the hall,' she said rather pointedly.

'I'll see you later, then.'

He nodded to Peg and then to Verity, who saw him to the door. There was no lingering kiss, or even a peck on the cheek, their hands didn't touch. Verity felt slightly sick as she closed the door behind her and came slowly back into the kitchen.

Peg had gone into her bedroom and after a while Verity followed her and stood in the doorway watching her go through some drawers where she had left clothes.

Peg closed the drawers, stood up and went over to the wardrobe.

'Can I help?' Verity asked, but Peg shook her head.

Verity went back into the kitchen, passing her open bedroom door with the unmade bed, which Peg could hardly have failed to see. She poured herself a fresh cup of tea and lit a cigarette. She appeared relaxed when Peg returned with a small suitcase.

'Well, that's that, then,' Peg said and sat down. Then looked gravely at her sister. 'Quite honestly I don't really know what to say.'

'Neither do I.' Verity stubbed out her cigarette and stared in front of her.

'I suppose Philip stayed the night—' she began.

'It started after the summer holiday. This was our first weekend away.'

Verity stared abjectly at her younger sister, who had always looked up to her, and tried to fathom the expression on her face: shock, amazement, disgust? Hard to tell.

'I'm not at all *proud* of it, Peg,' she went on. 'I wish it hadn't happened, yet it did and I can't say I regret it.'

'But you've always been . . .' Peg appeared lost for words. 'So *proper*. This is the last thing I'd ever have expected of you.'

'I know. I was always telling you how careful you must be, didn't want you to be alone with Alan. It must seem hypocritical.'

She lit a fresh cigarette, her hands shaking. 'I think I told you I didn't go to bed with Rex. You remember you asked me that day we—'

'Yes, I remember, when I asked you about how Addie could have a baby without being married.'

Both smiled at the memory of something that had happened a long time ago, when Peg had still been a schoolgirl.

'I always regretted it,' Verity said. 'He was going to the war. He might not have come back. But I had this idea it was wrong and that he wouldn't respect me if I had. Well, it didn't help me keep him, and whether I did the right thing or not I shall never know. But at least at the time I thought it was right. My philosophy, my yardstick has always been to do what is right or seems to be right.'

'But how long can you keep that up?'

'Now things have moved on. I am thirty years of age. I don't think I will ever marry or have children. I have led a blameless, virtuous life and Philip Beaumaurice seemed to bring some excitement into it.'

'But you were his wife's *friend*,' Peg exclaimed, and this time her tone was censorious.

'I know, that's what's so awful. I'm ashamed, Peg, and telling you makes it worse. It *is* sordid, and just how sordid came home to me yesterday . . .' And she told her sister about the chance encounter that had ruined the weekend.

'I felt so isolated, left sitting in the hotel lobby, the mistress who could never declare herself or be acknowledged in public.'

'But what if these people tell his wife?'

'That's the point. Philip is on the verge of promotion to the consultancy he has worked so hard for and which we both want, because he deserves it.' She lowered her head. 'We've had a miserable time since we got back. It seemed to bring it home to us, and Philip was just leaving to spend the rest of the weekend we planned to have together in his club. It's as though he no longer wanted to be with me.'

Peg got up and came over to her sister, whose shoulders had started to heave. She put her arm tightly round her and her cheek close to the one wet with tears. 'Poor Ver,' she said sadly. 'Poor, poor Ver.'

Thirteen

Although Peg was shocked by Verity's affair she was, in a strange way, rather comforted by it. She had always looked up to Verity, regarded her with awe as someone who was not like other people: remote, powerful, above all virtuous. Now she knew she was human like everyone else, like her, perhaps more so because Peg had never been tempted to go to bed with Alan, or with anyone.

Peg, who was just twenty-two, often felt there was something missing from her life. She was passionate about certain things: war, injustice, the plight of the poor, but not about Alan. Yet she regarded him as her man; they went everywhere, did everything together, and she would be devastated if, for any reason, Alan stopped loving her or wanting to be with her as he undoubtedly did.

She knew she would never find anyone else like Alan: steadfast, loyal, true, sharing her beliefs, her ideals. When her mother became ill it was Alan rather than her sisters she turned to for comfort, and he gave it. No one understood her as well as Alan or, she thought, ever would. But it was not only Alan, it was something about her life that seemed lacking in direction.

Peg had expected that living on her own, the independent life of a reporter would be exciting, but it had become humdrum. With the return of a Conservative government there was little excitement at home; everything seemed to be happening abroad, with unrest throughout the continent and in Russia. The release of Adolf Hitler from prison, and the possible resurrection of his National Socialist party, sent a frisson through the socialist world. For Hitler was not a socialist as Peg and Alan were; the emphasis was on nationalism, zenophobia and the resurgence of German aggression through resentment stoked by poverty and the post-war reparations insisted on by the Allies.

Peg, after filing her copy on a routine event, was making her way back to the newsroom when the tall, elegant figure of the proprietor, accompanied by a member of staff, sauntered towards her. She flattened herself against the wall, not expecting to be noticed by him, but he stopped with a smile.

'It is Miss Hallam, isn't it?'

'Yes, Mr Moodie.'

'I've been following your progress. Don't think I've forgotten you. You have done very well, my dear.'

'Thank you, sir.'

He seemed suddenly struck by a thought. 'Why don't you come and have a little chat with me?'

'When, sir?'

'Now. Is it convenient? I have a few moments.' He murmured to his companion: 'We have nothing else to talk about, have we, Gerald?'

'No, Mr Moodie.'

'See you later, then.' Mr Moodie made a dismissive gesture, the minion trotted off, and he beckoned to Peg who followed him to his office on the third floor.

Oliver Moodie went immediately to his desk, sat behind it and pointed to a chair.

'Do sit down. I am glad to have this chance of a little chat. As I said a moment ago, I have been following your progress. You have done exceptionally well. You get yourself talked about, which is good for a journalist.'

'Thank you, sir.' Peg endeavoured to sound modest. 'Thank you for giving me the chance.'

175

'No, I mean it. And I hear you're doing more features.'

Peg nodded.

'Excellent. Good. Do you like features?'

'If there's not a good news story, yes.'

Moodie sat back, drumming his fingers on his desk. 'Well, then, I have something that might interest you. I thought of starting a page devoted to women's issues: you know, cookery recipes, good housekeeping, emphasis on the home, that kind of thing. Knitting patterns,' he added, as if that made the prospect even more enticing. 'I will need an editor for it. Is that something that might appeal?' Head on one side, he looked at her as though anticipating an immediate and gratified response.

But without giving the suggestion a moment's thought Peg shook her head.

'I am a feminist, Mr Moodie. I'm afraid I think a woman's page would be much too trivial to interest me. I am not a bit interested in the subjects you mention. I am not at all domesticated. I'm useless at knitting, though my mother taught us all to cook.'

'Oh!' Mr Moodie appeared disconcerted, and swept back his splendid mane of white hair, which contrasted so incongruously with his unlined face. As usual he was immaculately dressed in grey pinstripes with a violet tie and a matching handkerchief in his breast pocket. He wore grey spats over highly polished black shoes.

'I hope I haven't offended you, Mr Moodie' – Peg sat forward on her seat – 'and I thank you for your kind offer, but I do wish to be honest with you.'

The proprietor agreed at once. 'Oh, I'd much rather you were honest,' he said. 'I appreciate your frankness. Tell me what other aspect of the paper interests you?'

'Politics and foreign affairs,' Peg said immediately. 'You have a very good lobby correspondent, so not much chance for me there. But the paper's coverage of foreign affairs is weak. There has, for instance, been no good appraisal in your newspaper of the menace of Herr Hitler.'

'Oh, he is no menace.' Mr Moodie relaxed and folded his arms. 'Why, he is scarcely known.'

'He will be. The German people are simmering with resentment about reparations, and he will fan the flames of unrest. For someone as insignificant as he is, he has already made an impact. Recently four thousand people attended one of his meetings. He is a fiery, hypnotic speaker. In Italy Mussolini is disposing of all his opponents. And in Russia –' Peg stopped to draw breath. 'In short, I would like to be a foreign correspondent and have the chance to travel abroad.'

Mr Moodie, looking surprised, tapped the top of his desk with a silver pencil.

'Do you think that is a good idea for a woman? Also, we rely a good deal on news agencies, such as Reuters, for our foreign news.'

'That's what I think is wrong with the paper.' Peg grew more and more animated as she spoke, the colour rising to her cheeks.

'Is that so?' Mr Moodie mused, crossing one elegant leg over the other, his shoes gleaming beneath his grey spats. 'Well, naturally, I am interested to hear your views on the matter and appreciate your frankness. But I really think it is too early and, besides, you are far too young to be made a foreign correspondent. In any case' – his expression grew avuncular – 'can you please tell me why a nice, pretty young woman like you isn't married? I should have thought there were any number of young men anxious to snap you up.'

Peg's colour heightened. 'I hope you don't think I speak out of turn, and I know you mean it as a compliment, but to me views like that are rather outdated. Women found their place in the war, you know. Some regard a career as important as marriage and a family, and I am one of them.'

Mr Moodie tried to make up for his faux pas by a subtle change of tone. 'But I am *sure* a young lady as charming and attractive as you does not lack for admirers?'

'There is someone I see regularly, but we are not in any way attached. His name is Alan Walker and he works for the *Telegraph*.'

Mr Moodie made a note on a pad by his elbow just as the telephone rang, and he answered it.

'Moodie here.' Then: 'This is from Whitehall and will take rather a long time,' he said to Peg, his hand over the mouthpiece. 'Why don't you bring your young man to dinner and we can discuss the matter further? I'll ask my secretary to call you.'

Then he gave her a friendly wave of dismissal. It seemed that a member of the Cabinet was on the line.

And she had been telling him how to run his newspaper. Peg crept out of the office, feeling rather foolish.

'Come and get your tea, Jenny,' Addie called from the kitchen door and, obedient as always, Jenny stopped what she was doing in the garden – feeding her pet rabbit – and came in, scrambling up to the table while Addie served her from the stove. Then she made herself a cup of tea and sat next to her.

'Well, what did you do at school today?'

'Sums,' Jenny said, pulling a face.

'Don't you like sums?' Addie leaned across the table and pushed her blonde curls out of her eyes.

Jenny shook her head.

'They're very important.'

Jenny nodded.

She was a bright, intelligent, articulate child, already doing well at her little infants' school. Addie took her to school and picked her up again, or sometimes Frank did if he was going that way.

It was a happy, harmonious household, an ideal life, and Addie felt that she had at last found peace. She much preferred the role of mother to that of neglected wife. She felt that finally her life was useful and rewarding; that she was doing what she should have been doing all along. The guilt of disowning her own daughter had been always there, just below the surface of her life.

The only continuing sadness and worry was about her mother, who seemed to benefit little from the Bournemouth air. Every week, sometimes more often, someone went to visit Cathy. Frank tried to go twice, her mother went, her sister, cousins went and one of her daughters went every week, usually Addie because it was easier for her. They had never yet taken Jenny. The hospital staff thought she was a bit young; she also might be more susceptible to infection on account of her youth.

It seemed to Addie that she and Jenny grew daily closer. The strange thing was that she had connected so badly with her while her mother had been at home, rather as though she unwittingly proved a barrier. Or maybe it was Addie who had been the strange one: awkward, guilty, never her natural self in front of her daughter, always trying to please her and getting little thanks for it.

Since she had been back, she had tactfully and very gradually tried to win Jenny's affection. She talked a lot about Cathy and about her coming home and carefully reported details after each visit. Jenny was a credit to Cathy, well brought up, a shy child, but cheerful and obedient. She wasn't subservient, she had plenty of character, above all she had charm. This, added to her considerable Ryland good looks, was an asset that made her acceptable and successful wherever she went, so that she seemed to have an easy path through life.

Whether it would always be like this no one could say.

Now she prattled on about her day, about a new friend she had in class, and Addie listened with fascination, marvelling at the miracle of the transformation that had taken place in a few short weeks, the trust that had grown up between them, the love she hoped would develop on Jenny's part.

Jenny finished her rice pudding and Addie got up to take the bowl to the sink when there was a knock on the front door. Wiping her hands on her apron, she hurried out and then froze as she recognised a familiar silhouette through the frosted glass.

179

For a moment she stood where she was, reluctant to open it; and then he knocked again.

Tidying her hair, taking off her apron and hiding it away behind a chair in the hall, she took a deep breath and opened the door.

Harold, without smiling, removed his hat. 'Good afternoon, Adelaide. May I come in?'

Addie looked at him and then stood back.

'I can hardly say no, can I?'

'You don't answer my letters.'

At the end of the hall Jenny stood looking gravely at him.

'Hello, Jenny,' Harold called out in a kindly tone. 'How are you?'

'You remember Uncle Harold, don't you, Jenny?' Addie prompted and Jenny nodded and went a little reluctantly up to Harold, who bent to her level and gave her a kiss, to which Jenny did not seem responsive.

'Now you run up to the castle and see Mrs Capstick,' Addie said, getting Jenny's coat from a hook in the hall. 'Uncle Harold and I want to talk.'

Obedient as always, Jenny allowed Addie to fasten her buttons and wrap a muffler round her neck. Addie went with Jenny to the door to see her off, returning to the hall only when she saw the little girl go round to the back door of the castle where Mrs Capstick presided over the kitchens.

Addie shut the front door.

'Well,' she said to Harold, 'what is it you want to say?'

'Could we sit down, do you think?' Harold fiddled with the brim of his hat, turning it round and round between his fingers.

Addie pointed the way to the parlour, which was seldom used, and cold at this time of the year, being without heating.

'Frank will be here any minute,' she said as if in warning. 'He'll be back for his tea. He's gone to see Mother.'

They went into the parlour and Harold, who had been about

to remove his coat, decided to keep it on after all. He sat down but Addie remained standing.

'Won't you sit down?' he said, pointing to a chair.

'I prefer to stand. You won't be long, will you? I have Frank's tea to get.'

Harold gnawed awkwardly at a fingernail. 'How is your mother?'

'Not very well.'

'I'm sorry.' He paused. 'No indication, then, when you will be back?'

'I am not coming back, Harold. I thought that I made that plain in the note I left?'

'But I can't understand you, Addie. I thought we had quite a happy marriage.'

'How could you *possibly* think that?' She looked at him in astonishment. 'After what you said.'

'What did I say?'

'That I repulsed you. You couldn't bring yourself to make love to me.'

'Well, I was a bit hasty. I was angry.'

'But it was true, wasn't it, Harold?' All her resentment brimming over, Addie pointed a finger at him. 'It was all true.'

'Not really.' He fiddled about with the brim of his hat again, his expression contrite. 'I really am sorry. I do miss you and it's awkward without you. I keep getting invitations and don't know how to say where you are. Of course I have a good excuse, your mother, but it does sound a bit feeble to explain such a long absence. Most women wouldn't leave their husbands for weeks on end. People will think something is wrong.'

The naivety of such a statement brought a wry smile to Addie's face.

'Tell them, Harold, tell them the truth. Something *is* wrong. Say I've left you because our marriage wasn't working out.'

'But I *can't* do *that!* What will people say? Besides, Addie, I don't think it's fair. You're not being fair. I don't think that I did

or said anything to justify this behaviour on your part. I thought
we were reasonably happy. You seemed to find things to do.' His
expression changed and his tone grew petulant. 'You made vows,
you know. You promised to love and obey.'

'And *you* promised to cherish me. There was something in the
marriage ceremony about honouring me with your body. That
hasn't happened much, has it, Harold? Then there is the question
of Jenny.'

'Jenny is a very sweet child,' Harold faltered, 'but I can't
explain the feeling I have about giving her a home. I simply can't
seem to do it. Oh, Addie' – he extended his hand towards her in
the gesture of a supplicant – 'I do wish you'd put this whole thing
behind you and come back again. I promise I will try and make
amends. I promise I will . . .' He trailed off, as if afraid of making
too binding a commitment.

Addie leaned forward and shook her fist at him. 'Will you take
Jenny? That is the question. What if my mother dies?'

Harold looked shocked.

'Is she expected to die?'

'She's not getting any better.'

'Oh, I'm very sorry about that. Then it might take a long time.'

'Or a short time if she doesn't get better. Then what will you do
about Jenny?'

'I'll have to think,' Harold said solemnly. 'I will think about it
very hard if you will agree to return to me as soon as is
reasonable. I won't make any commitment, but I promise to
think about it seriously. I don't dislike Jenny, as you know.
Indeed, I think she is a very appealing child. You know my
reasons, and they are all to do with the past . . . that man you . . .
There is also the question of what to tell people. At least in the
meantime won't you come back just for a few days, so that
people won't think there's anything wrong? It really damages my
position as headmaster.'

'Anyone at home?' Frank called from the hall and Addie went
to the door and opened it.

'Harold is here, Frank.'

'Oh, Harold,' Frank said in surprise coming over and shaking his hand. 'How are you?'

'I'm quite well, thanks, Frank, and you?'

'Can't grumble, especially with Addie taking such good care of us all. Are you –' He looked from one to the other, as if wondering why Harold was here.

'Harold's just going, Frank,' Addie said brusquely. 'Could you show him to the door while I get your tea?'

Without saying goodbye, Addie went into the kitchen and began preparations for Frank's tea, which was what Jenny had had: shepherd's pie followed by rice pudding.

After quite a long time Frank came into the kitchen and sat down heavily at the table.

'Harold is very upset,' he said. 'He wants you back. Said you didn't give him a chance.'

'Didn't give him a chance!' Addie snorted. 'He had several chances. I have no intention of returning to him.' She stood by the stove shaking her head. 'Too much has passed between us. Too many bitter words. Things you can't unsay.'

She turned and looked at Frank, who sat with his shoulders hunched.

'How was Mum?'

Frank shook his head and then suddenly crumpled and began to weep.

'Oh Frank, Frank . . .' Addie rushed over to him and put her hand on his shoulder. 'What is it?'

'Mum wants to see you. She wants to see Jenny too, and the doctor said you shouldn't leave it too long.'

Peg had never been to such a smart dinner party in her life. The house in Welbeck Street had belonged to the Moodie family for over a hundred years, since Oliver Moodie's grandfather, a master printer, had started a newspaper in Marylebone and sowed the beginnings of the family fortune.

With increasing prosperity, the Moodies had also dabbled in politics, and a number of MPs figured in the family archives well into the end of the nineteenth century.

Peg had to buy a dress specially for the dinner. It was ankle length, of pale blue chiffon over a taffeta sheath with a halter neckline and a straight bodice that made her look fashionably flat-chested and, with her newly shingled hair, emphasised the boyish look for women which was all the rage. She wore little make-up, a trace of powder to take off the shine and a splash of pink lipstick that complemented the striking effect of her pale complexion and violet blue eyes. Despite her serious views, Peg had a liking for fashion and being fashionable.

Alan complemented her. Having moved swiftly and inexorably up the hierarchy of his paper, he already owned a dinner jacket. His hair was sleeked back and well greased, and with his horn-rimmed spectacles and grave demeanour he looked about ten years older than he was, a person in a position of responsibility.

They had arrived at eight and the first thing Peg saw was the back of Philip Beaumaurice, who was just ushering his wife into the first-floor drawing room. There Oliver warmly shook hands with them before greeting Peg and Alan and introducing them to the other guests. Besides Philip and Geraldine, these included a beautiful young man called Sir Magnus Livingston – whom Oliver, with a fond look in his eyes, described as a 'house guest' – and an affluent-looking couple in their thirties, Clive and Margaret Fookes-Pearson. Apart from cordial greetings – Geraldine had embraced her – Peg and the Beaumaurices had not exchanged a word, and Philip took care to keep to the opposite side of the room from her. She didn't want to talk to him much either, remembering the way he had compromised her sister.

Now they were halfway through dinner, served on exquisite china by two manservants. Tall candles guttered in silver candle-sticks which enhanced the Georgian elegance of the long room with its well-polished mahogany table, heavily embossed green and gold wallpaper, and family portraits. There was a strong family resemblance and white hair, contrasting with the youthful appearance of the sitters, seemed to predominate.

Oliver sat at one end of the table and the other end was occupied by the elegant Sir Marcus, his blond wavy hair almost down to his shoulders, the jewels on his fingers glittering as he gesticulated, which he did extravagantly almost all the time. He had luminous pale blue eyes, a pale complexion, a little beard and a manner that was flirtatious, almost feminine, whether directed towards men or women. He wore a purple velvet dinner jacket with a yellow cravat and looked like some exotic bird, a little out of place in its surroundings. Next to him Geraldine, who seemed to know him well and find him a delightful and amusing companion, sparkled too and kept on clasping his hand as they embarked on a fresh gale of laughter.

Nothing appeared to amuse Philip, who remained taciturn and morose. One could see that he and Sir Marcus were diametrically opposite personalities, though he obviously felt it incumbent on him at least to be civilised to his brother-in-law's rather strange and camp friend.

In contrast to Marcus, Oliver seemed quite reserved and dignified in a conventional dinner jacket and black tie with his white hair forming a kind of halo round his noble-looking head.

Peg sat between Oliver and Clive Fookes-Pearson, who was an industrialist and had been at school with Oliver. They all knew one another, but Oliver was an excellent host and put Alan on his other side so that he was not left out of the conversation. In fact he seemed deeply interested in Alan and his views. Peg, keeping an anxious eye on him, was relieved to see Alan relaxed and expansive as he earnestly emphasised some point he was making, possibly on the subject of politics or international relations, to his host.

Peg felt proud of him, holding his own in this rather exalted company, not awed by it but at ease as, strangely, so was she. Oliver courteously divided his time between Alan and herself, first turning to one then the other, and when Oliver wasn't occupying her attention Clive Fookes-Pearson seemed anxious to take over. He was clearly fascinated by his emancipated young companion and the fact that she was a working journalist; also, perhaps, by her vivacity and beauty, which were a marked contrast to his rather plain and bitter-looking wife who engaged for most of the meal in platitudes with Philip.

Clive Fookes-Pearson was in ball-bearings. He said they were used in the manufacture of munitions and his family had made a fortune during the war. In the interests of harmony Peg managed to prevent herself from criticising him outright, though she did not conceal her disapproval. Someone had to make them, Mr Fookes-Pearson pointed out and, besides, his real ambition was to stand for Parliament as a Conservative. He was seeking a safe seat.

At this stage Peg felt she had to declare her political colours and for the rest of the meal they engaged in semi-serious banter in order to avoid getting involved in a furious row.

'Alan thinks that Herr Hitler is a real threat,' Oliver said as the dessert was served, accompanied by a fine Sauternes. 'You agree, don't you, Peg?'

Peg nodded. 'He says he has foresworn the use of force, but I don't believe him.'

Clive leaned back in his chair looking replete, glass in hand, the knowledgeable man of affairs. 'Hitler will *never* be a threat. He is of no importance, and as long as Germany is not allowed to rearm—'

'You'll be all the poorer.' Sir Magnus shrieked from the end of the table and there was a chorus of well-bred laughter.

'I am *much* more interested in what is happening in Russia,' Clive continued once the laughter had subsided. 'The ruthlessness with which Stalin has got rid of Trotsky is disturbing.'

'I thought you welcomed disturbances,' Oliver said, 'so that you could sell more ball-bearings?'

'Not so,' Clive corrected him. 'I am a man of peace. I am more interested in politics than selling more weapons.'

'Stalin is more interested in peace than Trotsky,' Alan intervened smoothly. 'Trotsky wanted a state of permanent revolution. Stalin wants to concentrate on reform in Russia. Personally I am for him. I hope one day to visit Russia and see for myself.'

Peg was about to add a comment but Oliver raised a hand. 'I think this interesting conversation could go on for ever, but now it is time for the sexes to separate.' He looked over at his sister. 'Would you take the ladies out, my dear, and we'll join you after a cigar and a glass or two of port.'

Geraldine rose and led the two other women to the drawing room which was large, exquisitely proportioned with cream walls, a high ceiling, its cornice picked out in gold, and a magnificent central chandelier from which a thousand tiny pieces of glass sparkled like diamonds. Here the pictures were old masters: a Hobbema, two Constables, several hunting scenes by Benjamin Marshall and a Goya which dominated the room.

In the corner was a wind-up gramophone, and a servant was laying out coffee cups on a table laden with liqueur bottles. Rich brocade curtains were drawn across the tall windows overlooking the quiet London street.

'I must just powder my nose.' Margaret Fookes-Pearson looked enquiringly at the two women who shook their heads.

'You do know the way, don't you, dear?' Geraldine saw her to the door.

'Such a charming couple,' she said, shutting the door. 'Have you met them before?'

Peg shook her head.

'She actually is *very* nice, though a bit overpowered by him. She is the one with the money, whatever he says about ball-bearings. In fact, I think they have oodles of the stuff.'

'How lucky,' Peg said dryly, thinking with what care she husbanded her monthly pay cheque, accounting for every penny since she liked, as did Verity, to send something home.

Bright, carefully made up, with feathers in her bobbed hair, a knee-length draped frock of pale grey crêpe de chine and high-heeled embroidered grey shoes, Geraldine appeared a little over-excited, as though she were slightly drunk.

She looked knowingly at Peg, who felt decidedly awkward being alone with her, wondering what, if anything, she knew about her husband's affair with Verity. 'Such a nice young man, your Alan. So quick and intelligent. I can tell he will go on to great things. Serious, is it?'

Peg shrugged. Geraldine waited for her to reply and, when she didn't, went on. 'He *is* very clever, I imagine?'

'He's certainly very good at what he does,' Peg replied a little stiffly.

'Oh, I can see that. *And* I think Oliver can see it too.'

Geraldine went over to a small table, picked up the silver cigarette box and handed it to Peg.

'No thanks,' Peg said shaking her head.

'Not like your sister.'

'No, not like Verity.'

Geraldine exhaled a long stream of smoke. 'Tell me, I've been *dying* to ask you about your sister. How *is* Verity?'

'She's very well.'

'I do miss her.' Geraldine looked wistful. 'I really do. We are, *were* such friends. But we don't see nearly as much of each other as we used to.' She gazed speculatively for a moment at Peg. 'Tell me, tell me truthfully. Have I offended her in any way? I often wonder. If I have I don't know how. Sometimes I think she's avoiding me.'

'Our mother is very ill,' Peg said guardedly. 'I'm sure it's nothing you've done. Verity spends all her free time going down to see Mother.'

Geraldine put her hand on Peg's arm, her eyes brimming with sympathy.

'I am *so* sorry—' she began when the door opened and the men wandered in, cigars still in their hands, looking rosy-cheeked and jolly, Marcus exchanging some amusing aside with Alan. Philip trailed a little behind the others and stood on the threshold, looking lost, until Geraldine beckoned to him.

'Darling,' she cried, tucking her arm through his as she drew him forward, 'I was just telling Peg how much we miss Verity. Did you know her mother was very ill?'

'Yes, I did,' Philip said stiffly.

'I expect you see her at the hospital, but that explains why she doesn't come and visit us. Oh, we *do* miss her, don't we, Philip? Those little outings. Remember Florence?'

'Yes, I do,' Philip said, carefully avoiding Peg's eyes, 'very well indeed.'

Fourteen

The nursing staff of the maternity unit, with Matron, Sister Frobisher and Verity in the centre, stood in a self-conscious little group facing a bashful-looking Philip Beaumaurice who had seemed quite nonplussed as he entered the room to which he had been summoned to find this reception committee awaiting him.

'Well—' he began as Matron stepped forward.

'Dr Beaumaurice, I am sorry to have given you such a surprise, but I hope you will find it a pleasant one.'

She produced a piece of paper from her pocket, cleared her throat and continued. 'Dr Beaumaurice, we, at this hospital, the nursing staff and, of course, the patients who have passed through your hands, would like to say how very sorry we are that you are going and how much we shall miss you.'

She paused and noisily cleared her throat again. 'We have been very privileged to work with an inspired obstetrician who has undoubtedly eased the pain of childbirth for many women, and often saved the lives of mothers and babies.

'However, we rejoice in your appointment as consultant at a hospital whose excellent maternity practices mirror our own, and we hope that this will not be the end of our relationship with you.'

There was polite applause, after which Matron tucked the paper back into her pocket and turned to Verity. 'I would like to invite Sister Carter-Barnes, with whom you have worked so well, to make a presentation on behalf of all the staff.'

Verity, who had been dreading this moment, for which she had had little warning, stepped forward, firmly clutching a silver salver between her hands, which she held out to Philip amid more applause.

'Thank you, Dr Beaumaurice, for all you have done,' she said in a steady voice. 'We all wish you well.'

Philip gave an awkward little bow as he took it from her, and looked as though he was about to kiss her on the cheek. But Verity took a step backwards and they politely shook hands. Then she rejoined Matron and the senior staff.

'Thank you, sister,' he said and then, addressing the assembly: 'And thank you all for this most generous gift, which I shall treasure all my life. Needless to say it is a great wrench for me to leave a place where I have worked for so long and to which I owe so much. The experience of working with a skilled and dedicated staff has been of enormous assistance to me and, of course, I shall be back to visit you all.'

He then came over to Matron and shook hands with her, with Sister Frobisher, with Verity again and then with all the staff in turn. He turned to talk to Matron and Sister Frobisher as the gathering broke up and the rest, including Verity, drifted out of the room and went back to their respective tasks. Verity had balked at making the presentation, suggesting it should be the function of Sister Frobisher, but Matron had insisted that it should be her, as they had worked together the longest and she knew him much better than Sister Frobisher. Still, it hadn't been too bad an ordeal, Verity decided, entering the office she shared with the senior sister and shutting the door behind her.

In a strange way she felt tearful. In one sense it was the end of an era, with Philip leaving for a new post, but in another sense it had ended already.

Their relationship had simply fizzled out after the abortive weekend and the discovery by Peg, and he had made no attempt to contact her again.

At the hospital they continued their professional relationship, as though they had a tacit agreement that it had never been anything different. They took care never to be alone together, or to be in a position where any kind of confrontation was possible.

But now he was going. There would no longer be even a casual contact that, perhaps, meant something to her.

It was over for good.

Verity took up her pen and started writing her report when there was a tap on the door and Philip put his head round.

'Did you want Sister Frobisher, Dr Beaumaurice?' Verity asked, half rising.

'No, I wanted a quick word with you,' Philip said, closing the door. 'I took care to see that Matron had business with Sister Frobisher and they've gone off to one of the wards together. Verity –'

'Philip –'

He rounded the desk and put his hands firmly on her shoulders. 'I can't let this finish without seeing you and . . . well, saying thanks for being so gracious during the presentation. I know it must have been hard for you.'

'No harder than for you, I imagine. Naturally I was reluctant to do it.'

She moved away from him and his arms fell to his sides.

'I haven't been in touch . . .' he tried again.

'I know, I know.' She nodded several times. 'It's over. I agree.'

He got out a handkerchief and wiped the thin film of perspiration from his brow. She thought, could not help thinking, how attractive he looked: a tall figure with strong features, swept-back black hair, a full moustache, clever, knowing dark eyes, a high, intelligent forehead. He wore a double-breasted dark grey pin-striped suit, a white shirt, stiff collar and his university tie.

He looked the part. Undoubtedly he would go far. She could already see in her mind's eye the sparkling brass plate on a door in Harley Street. She also saw, as if from some place on high, like a disembodied spirit, herself lying in his arms, the thrust of his body as they made love.

Momentarily she shut her eyes, then opened them wide.

'You look the consultant already,' she said with a smile. Then: 'I have no regrets, you know, Philip, about us.'

'No,' he said quickly, 'neither have I. But it had to end, hadn't it, Verity? We never felt *right* about it, did we? About Geraldine?'

'No.' She shook her head. Then: 'Does she know? Did she find out?'

'Oh no. I didn't think she would. People like the Thompsons don't chatter or gossip, you know. But maybe you'll come round and see Geraldine more often? She'd like that.'

Verity returned to her desk and played with the cap of her fountain pen.

'Philip, I shall also probably be leaving soon. I have applied for a position in Bournemouth. I want to be near my mother who, as you know, is seriously ill. I don't think she has very long to live. Besides, I think I have had all from London that it has to offer me. I'm a little tired of it, to tell you the truth.'

'Well, do come and say goodbye, won't you?'

'Of course.'

They walked together to the door and stood there shaking hands, to all appearances like the good colleagues they were and had been, as though they had never been lovers at all.

The scene often came back to Verity in the following days, as she made plans for her own departure from the hospital. Now she stood at the window of the room she had had as a young girl in her uncle and aunt's house, and which was still kept ready for her for whenever she wanted it.

Uncle Stanley had retired from his professional work as an engineer, partly so that he could follow full time his beloved hobby collecting and cataloguing butterflies, of which he had a large collection.

It seemed strange, but in all the years that had passed since she had first come here as a child, both her aunt and uncle appeared hardly to have changed. Aunt Maude was firm, upright, her face scarcely lined. She walked daily into the town to see friends or do her shopping and Uncle Stanley, still youthful-looking, with a full head of thick white hair, walked miles every day in pursuit of his hobby. Of course to the eight-year-old Verity they had both seemed quite old, but they would only have been in their thirties, Maude being a few years older than Cathy. Now thirty herself, Verity seemed to have caught up with them and it was she, not they, who had changed. It seemed very cruel to compare the healthy, young-looking but older Maude to her younger sister wasting away from tuberculosis in hospital.

They still had the same maid, Doris, and the smell of baking cake assailed Verity's nostrils as she opened the door and descended the stairs for tea, which awaited her in the drawing room. The faces of Aunt Maude and Uncle Stanley, sitting on either side of the fire, lit up as she entered and Aunt Maude pointed to the tea table.

'Do help yourself, dear. We started without you. Doris has made your special sandwich cake.'

. 'So I see,' Verity said, helping herself to a slice and taking a seat beside her aunt.

'Will you come back and live here, dear, if you get the Bournemouth job?'

It was something Verity hadn't thought about.

'I do hope so,' her aunt sighed. 'We'd *love* it, wouldn't we, Stanley?'

Uncle Stanley nodded. 'It would be like old times.'

But did she, Verity, want old times? Could one ever recapture the past and, if it came to that, did anyone really want to?

Verity had had an interview for the position of assistant matron in a small cottage hospital on the outskirts of Bournemouth. In a way she was too well qualified for it, and after the operating theatres and maternity unit of large London hospital it would seem very quiet. But she was anxious to be near her mother and away from Philip – she was not quite sure in what order – and if offered the post she would take it.

*   *   *

Old times. School in Bournemouth, a happy childhood wanting for nothing, except that the love of an aunt and uncle was not the same as that of a parent and siblings whom she saw all too rarely. She felt she had grown up without really knowing them and only in adulthood had she got close to Peg. Full of nostalgic memories, Verity made her way through the sanatorium to the balcony on which she usually found her mother's bed.

Only today it was not there. Her heart missed a beat as she looked frantically around for her and, seeing her expression, one of the patients called out: 'Your mum has been moved to a private room. She wasn't very well last night. I think they wanted to see you.'

'Thanks,' Verity said quickly, leaving the balcony and making her way to the ward sister's room. Just outside the door she bumped into the doctor emerging.

'Oops!' he cried.

'Sorry . . .'

'Oh, Miss Carter-Barnes. I was hoping for a word with you.'

'Is she worse?'

'She hasn't been very comfortable. We thought she would be better in a private room where we can keep an eye on her. I think the other patients are beginning to disturb her.'

'How long has she got?' Verity had a catch in her voice.

'Why don't you go and see her?' The kindly young doctor placed a reassuring hand on her arm. 'I think you'll be pleasantly surprised. And she had, after all, quite a good night. I think your other sister is with her at the moment, and a little girl.'

'Jenny.' Verity anxiously searched the doctor's eyes.

'She wanted to see her and we did think it was best. Don't read anything into it. Come, I'll show you where your mother is.'

Jenny was standing gaping at Cathy, her large, luminous eyes looking perplexed. Beside her, one arm protectively round her waist, sat Addie. She and Cathy appeared to be laughing and the doctor left Verity at the door, saying: 'I told you you'd be pleasantly surprised.'

195

Verity had a large bunch of flowers in her hand which she held out to show her mother, who murmured, 'Aren't they lovely.' She pointed to Jenny. 'Look who's here. I've missed her so much.'

'We're just about to go,' Addie said. 'We've been here ages. Frank is waiting outside. The doctor doesn't want too many people in the room at once so Frank left to smoke a cigarette.'

'He is so good, so thoughtful,' Cathy said wearily. 'I miss him. I missed you all, but above all' – she looked wistfully at the little girl at the bedside – 'I missed my Jenny.'

'Oh, *Mum*.' Jenny took a step towards the bed but Addie held her back.

'You know the doctor said not too near.'

'But I want to kiss Mummy.'

'The doctor said,' Addie began and then looked at Verity, who nodded her head. 'I think a quick kiss can't do any harm.'

Cathy held her granddaughter briefly in her arms, hugging her tight. Her lips lingered for a moment on the little girl's brow before she gently pushed her away.

The atmosphere had suddenly become emotional and as Jenny began to cry Verity took her gently by the arm and, producing a clean handkerchief, began to dab at her tears. 'It won't make Mum any better to see tears, will it?'

Cathy, seeming exhausted, lay back and closed her eyes.

'We'd better go.' Addie reached for Jenny's hand. 'We'll come again next week.'

'I want to stay with Mummy,' Jenny said defiantly. 'I want to stay here and look after her.'

Cathy opened her eyes and smiled. 'Don't worry about me. I'm being *very* well looked after here.' She raised her hand towards Jenny in a kind of benediction. 'Bless you, darling. You run along now and I'll see you again next week. I want to talk to Verity.'

But Jenny stubbornly remained where she was and in the end it took the gentle strength of the two sisters and much tender cajoling to persuade her to leave the room, which she did in tears.

When Verity returned, shaken, she was shocked by the sudden change in her mother, who had obviously tried to keep up appearances for Jenny's sake. Now she looked completely worn out, spent, two bright red patches on her cheeks, the rest of her face deathly pale. Her eyes glowed with fever and her forehead was bathed in sweat.

For a while Cathy remained silent and Verity sat on the side of her bed feeling her pulse and wondering whether she should summon the doctor. Then she gently began to wipe the sweat from her mother's brow and the pace of the pulse started to slow down.

'That visit upset you, didn't it, Mum?'

'I don't think I'll ever see her again.'

'Oh yes you will,' Verity said firmly, but Cathy shook her head.

'I'm not getting any better, Verity. I'm getting worse.'

'Oh Mum, you're *not*.'

'I am,' Cathy gasped. 'Why do you suppose they brought me here? So as not to distress the other patients. I think I'm dying.'

'Oh, *Mum*.' Verity squeezed her hand, too choked herself to reply.

'You must know, you're a nurse,' Cathy continued in a whisper. 'No use deceiving ourselves, is there?' She turned to her daughter with an expression of great serenity, which alarmed Verity more than ever because she thought her mother had lost the will to fight. Now she couldn't control her own tears and it was Cathy's turn to reach over to her and gently try to brush them away.

'I'm not afraid now, you know, darling Ver. I've known for some time it's hopeless. I can hardly get out of bed. They bring me a bedpan all the time. If I put a foot out I'm breathless. I spit blood.' She pointed to a handkerchief peeping out from her pillow. 'The vicar came to see me and somehow I think he helped, though I have never been much of a churchgoer. You are, though, aren't you, Verity? You believe?'

'Yes, I do, Mum.' Verity spoke through stifled tears. 'But I don't want you to go. I can't bear it, Mum. You have always been there. I'll miss you so.'

Cathy's grip on her hand tightened. 'You must look after the family, Ver. You're in charge. You're the eldest.' Her expression changed to one of anxiety. 'You didn't mind me letting you live with Maude and Stanley when you were small, did you, Ver? Giving you away, for that's what it was, and I always felt guilty about it.'

'Oh no, Mum, no. I know you had no option and I was very happy with them. They were very good to me. Still are.'

'I'm glad of that, because it's preyed on my mind these last few days. One does look back on one's life, you know, and I made so many mistakes. Now you have to take on my role. You have to guide Ed and Stella, who are very young, though Ed has always been a very practical, sensible boy. He came to see me the other day and he has a wisdom beyond his years. Ed will be all right. It is little Jenny I worry about so much.'

'Addie will look after her,' Verity said reassuringly. 'You know that, Mum.'

'But what will happen when she goes back to Harold? Will he take her?'

'She'll never go back to Harold. She won't leave Jenny now.'

'Then I worry about Peg. Is she going to marry that young man?'

'I don't know. Sometimes I can't fathom them out.'

'You like him, don't you?'

Verity nodded.

'So did I. I think he is very suitable.' Cathy made an effort to pull herself up on her pillow and gazed intently at Verity, feverishly clutching her hand again. 'Ver, if for any reason I don't see Peg again, tell her I want her to marry Alan. I know he's asked her. He loves her. He's strong and good and he will look after her.'

'I'll tell her, Mum.' Verity smiled, determined to try and be as brave as her mother.

'That's a good girl.' Cathy sank back on the bed again, her face once more as white as the pillow. 'You've always been so good, so responsible . . .'

'Oh Mum.' There was a catch in Verity's voice. 'I have *not* been so responsible or so good. I feel I must tell you: I had an affair with a married man. It lasted six months. It's finished now, but it began in the summer in Florence, a moment of madness . . .'

'Did he go back to his wife?' Cathy asked gently.

'He never left her and she was my friend. That was the trouble. He was a doctor at the hospital. He's left now and so soon shall I.'

'I'm glad you had the experience.' Cathy reached up and touched her face. 'I often wondered about you. Every woman must know a little about love, and you were so disappointed about Rex. I hope this man . . . what was his name?'

'Philip.'

'I hope Philip made you happy, if only for a short time.'

'He did.' Verity blew her nose hard.

'That's good, then. Darling –' Cathy momentarily closed her eyes, her hand loosely hanging on to Verity's. 'I *am* very tired. I have had a lot of visitors. Frank is waiting with Addie in the car. Would you go and tell him I would like a little time with him? Fetch him, there's a dear.'

Verity stooped and kissed her mother's brow, her lips lingering, and then made her way towards the door, pausing to look back one more time.

Cathy was laid to rest in the churchyard, within sight of the castle where she'd lived for over twenty years.

She was just fifty-one years old. Cathy Carpenter had led a full and not always happy life; she had had three husbands, five children, had worked hard all her life and had, by any standards, been a good woman. She could have hoped to have enjoyed a fruitful, contented and mellow old age with her beloved Frank. As it was she left a host of memories which would remain in the minds and hearts of all who had known and loved her for the rest of their lives.

As well as her granddaughter, her husband, children and numerous relations and friends, her sister and mother both attended her funeral. Sarah Swayle, who had always been rather critical of her daughter during her lifetime, and not helped her when she could, was scarcely able to contain her grief, which raised some eyebrows among her family.

She had been driven up by her elder daughter and son-in-law. Maude was still in shock at the premature death of a younger sister with whom she had had little in common, but to whom she had been greatly attached, especially towards the end when she had visited her often in hospital. They had made up then for what had been missing in their youth.

It was a fine, solemn funeral service. The coffin was borne into the church, decorated with white lilies, by six pallbearers, among them Frank and Ed. Ed was at Durham University studying for the ministry and he read the lesson from Proverbs, verses 10–31, in a deep sonorous voice which augured well for his future calling and left many in tears.

'Her children rise up and call her blessed;
Her husband also and he praises her;
"Many women have done excellently,
But you surpass them all." '

Ed was a tall, angular, rather solemn young man, a little eclipsed by his sisters, a boy and now a man of few words: bookish, pious but also keen on sports. He had been very attached to his mother, who had understood his wish to be different, to stand apart, and had encouraged him to enter the ministry

Listening to him, Verity felt a choking sensation in her throat, a deep longing for her mother and a sense of how little she really knew Ed, whom she had seen less of than any of her sisters. Not understanding his much older sister, she thought that in many ways he had taken care to avoid her, and was always out, or out of the way, when she came to visit.

In future, and keeping her word to her mother, she intended to remedy that. She could see her way ahead now quite clearly and knew what she must do. Because she was the eldest, and in many ways the strongest, she must take Mother's place and be there for them all, including the grieving widower, Frank.

After the last blessing, the procession re-formed, wending its way out of the church, past the packed ranks of the mourners into the graveyard where a grave had been prepared. There the last rites were enacted, the coffin lowered. The family, led by Frank who supported Cathy's mother, cast handfuls of earth upon it, while a melancholy crowd of onlookers, keeping a respectful distance, looked on.

Ashes to ashes. Dust to dust.

CATHLEEN CARPENTER 1874–1925.

The wake was held at the castle and, rather as they did at the annual staff party, Lord and Lady Ryland and their family looked in to offer condolences. Peg had not seen Hubert Ryland since he had rescued her from the unwelcome attentions of her cousin Arthur on the night of her twenty-first birthday party.

Their eyes met across the room and he made his way across to her and clasped her hands.

'My deepest condolences on the loss of your mother.'

'Thank you, Mr Hubert.'

'How you've changed!' he said.

Peg smiled sweetly. 'May I introduce Alan?' She brought him forward.

'Oh!' Hubert looked surprised. 'Are you married?'

'He's just a friend,' Peg said.

'How do you do?'

'How do you do, Lord Ryland?' Alan said coldly.

'Oh, I'm not Lord Ryland. That's my father.'

'I'm sorry,' Alan said dismissively. 'I know nothing about the aristocracy.'

Hubert turned to Peg again. 'Are you still in London?'

'Oh yes.'

'You must come and have a drink.'

'Thank you, Mr Hubert.'

'Hubert, please.'

'Thank you, Hubert.'

'I'll get your address from Frank. I must go and talk to him now. It's so tragic for him. They were so happy together.'

'Yes.' Peg nodded and smiled again as he walked away after a curt nod to Alan.

'I don't think he liked me much,' Alan said with satisfaction. 'Thanks for describing me as a "friend".'

'Well, you are. What else could I say?'

'I hate these people.' Alan's tone was rancorous as Hubert joined his family and they moved away towards the exit.

'There's nothing to hate. They are very nice. Just different.'

'Insufferable,' he insisted. 'So patronising. Look how Frank is fawning upon them.' Alan's lip curled in disgust.

'Oh, Alan.' Peg looked at him in exasperation. 'You'll never change, will you?'

'I hope not. And if I could get rid of these people I would.'

'By revolution?'

'If necessary. I'd chop their heads off.'

As often happens at funerals the occasion turned into a bit of a party. There was tea, sandwiches and cakes as well as sherry and beer, and some of the mourners who had arrived with sombre faces left with more cheerful expressions.

It went on quite late, until Maude and Stanley took Granny

Swayle back to Bournemouth and the rest of the guests began to drift away.

After saying goodbye to the last one, Verity walked down the hill with Ed and Stella, the youngest siblings, who she felt in many ways needed her most, while the others went on ahead. Jenny had her real mother, who in time would have publicly to acknowledge her.

'You read that passage beautifully, Ed.'

'Thank you, Ver.'

'Are you enjoying your studies?'

'Very much.'

'And ordination will be when?'

'After my degree I have to go to theological college.'

'Mum would be very proud.' Verity put her arm round his shoulders. 'I do want you, both of you, to know that if there is ever anything either of you want you must come to me. I promised Mum I would look after you.'

Stella, who had been very quiet all afternoon, suddenly stopped, got her handkerchief from her pocket and buried her face in it.

'Stella, darling.' Verity removed her arm from Ed and put it round her youngest sister's shoulders.

'I shall miss Mum so much,' she sobbed.

'We all will. We must be strong as Mum wanted us to be.'

'I think it's so unfair. She was so young. Look at Gran, strong and hearty and she's so *old*. Why Mum?' Stella, wide-eyed, stared angrily at Verity. 'Why Mum?'

'God moves in mysterious ways,' Ed said quietly.

'Oh, I don't want any of your preaching, thank you, Ed,' Stella stormed at him.

'I'm not preaching,' Ed said gently. 'It's true, isn't it, Ver? We never do understand the ways of God.'

'It doesn't make it any easier,' Verity said and pressed Stella's head comfortingly to her breast.

'I wish you could stay,' Stella mumbled. 'You never stay.'

'I *shall* stay,' Verity said firmly. 'I shall stay for as long as you want me to.'

It was true, now, that after Mum's death life could never be the same again.

Fifteen

May 1925

There was a slight chill in the air but the sun shone brightly on the waters of the lake and the yellow daffodils that filled the borders in the park. At the water's edge a host of ducks and other aquatic birds dived for bread being thrown to them from a small crowd gathered on the bank.

Couples sauntered arm in arm, children ran ahead with their balls or hoops, dogs barked or chased the birds and the brass band belted out a stirring march, its members in their uniforms with tight collars and stiff peaked caps perspiring with the effort.

Peg and Alan slumped in chairs in front of the bandstand, the remnants of their picnic in a basket on the ground in front of them.

Peg had been trying to read, but her attention kept wandering. She liked observing people and on this early spring day there was much to look at, as diverse and motley a collection as London had to offer. At its heart Regent's Park always had happy associations for Peg. It was where she and Alan had their picnics before Promenade concerts down the road at the Queen's Hall. Sometimes they would walk through it afterwards to get the bus in Camden Town or, occasionally, on a Sunday like today, they would meet up and, if the weather was suitable, take a packed lunch. After that they might go to an art gallery, a concert or the cinema to see a new film, maybe with Jackie Coogan or Rudolf

Valentino. Though with their highly developed social con-
sciences they both preferred something more stirring and serious
such as Griffith's *Birth of a Nation*, or a film of social realism
directed by the disillusioned Germans, or the Russian Sergei
Eisenstein's epic film *Battleship Potemkin*, which was being much
talked about.

Peg glanced sideways at Alan, lying back with his eyes closed,
his spectacles halfway down his nose, fast asleep. She thought
what a dear, kind, sweet fellow he was and how happy and
relaxed she was with him. He had been a tower of strength since
her mother's death, which had made her realise how isolated she
was, despite her brother and sisters.

You only discovered after a parent had gone how important
that person was. She could not remember her father, so there had
been no sense of desolation then. But now she realised there was
no one like Mum for reassurance, words of encouragement or
comfort, just knowing she was there.

In a way Peg felt she would be quite happy if this relationship
with Alan could continue in this way for ever. But it wouldn't be
enough for him. Would it, ultimately, for her? She knew that
Alan was just biding his time, hoping desperately that one day
she would say yes.

As if aware of her scrutiny Alan suddenly came to, opened his
eyes wide, pushed his glasses back up his nose and gazed at her,
blinking.

'I think I dropped off,' he said.

'I think you did.' She smiled affectionately at him, wondering
if he could read her thoughts. His expression suddenly became
serious, he linked his hands in front of him and looked gravely at
her.

'Peg, I've got something to say to you.'

'Uh-uh,' she murmured, leaning back, folding her arms behind
her head in an attitude of resignation.

'No, it's not *that*,' he said, as if he knew what she meant. 'The
truth is, I don't really know how to begin. I feel awkward about it

and maybe now is not the time, but I have to give an answer and I wanted to talk to you.'

Peg began to feel alarmed: 'An answer about what?'

'Oliver Moodie has asked me to go abroad for your paper as foreign correspondent.'

'He *what?*'

Patiently Alan repeated himself.

'When did this happen?' Peg sat bolt upright in her chair, leaning forward, taut with anticipation.

'This week. He rang the paper and asked me to go and see him. Naturally I was mystified. He said he'd remembered our conversation that night at dinner at his place, was impressed by my knowledge of foreign affairs and my newspaper experience and wants to try me out on a six-month assignment. If it doesn't work out he says he will offer me something home-based.' Alan's face glowed with excitement. 'But I think it will. I'll make it work.' He paused and his expression grew more contrite. 'He said the idea had first come from you that the foreign coverage of his paper wasn't good, relying too much on agencies. He knew you would be upset about it because you would have liked the job yourself.'

'And what did you say?'

'I said I'd prefer to tell you myself.'

'Well, that was quite brave.' Peg's tone was sarcastic. 'So what are you going to do? Accept, I suppose.'

'Naturally I'd like to accept.'

'He's given you the foreign job and wants me to write about cooking and knitting.' Peg's voice grew bitter. 'You should hear his views on women! Why isn't a pretty girl like me married? That sort of thing. Frankly it makes me absolutely sick.'

Alan put a hand placatingly on her arm. 'It's a big chance for me, Peg. He would never have given it to you. He says you're too young, and it's true you are a woman. He does think very highly of you and I'm sure you'll progress to important features. He knows you have a good brain. But he thinks Europe is a dangerous place, and I agree.'

'Then I don't want *you* to go!' Peg burst out, suddenly aware of the implications of what he was saying. 'I don't want you to be in danger, Alan. I really can't bear the thought of losing you.'

Suddenly she leaned forward and kissed him quite passionately full on the lips.

Alan clung to her as if he couldn't bear to let go.

'Then come with me,' he said as she pulled away, his face tense with excitement.

'As your assistant?'

'As my wife. What do you say?'

Her arm round Verity's waist, Geraldine ushered her into the drawing room, seated her on the sofa and then sat down next to her, still clasping her hand.

'I was terribly sorry to hear about your mother,' she said, her eyes brimming with sympathy.

'Thank you.' Verity, who had arrived unannounced, felt a sudden resurgence of affection for Geraldine and pressed her hand.

'I have so missed you.' Geraldine looked steadily into her eyes.

'And I've missed you.'

'Honestly?'

'Oh yes.' Verity smiled reassuringly. 'Honestly.' Now she and Philip were no longer lovers, it was easier to look Geraldine in the eyes. One day it might be possible to expunge the memory altogether, but not yet.

She had once enjoyed the short excursions to the Lakes or Cornwall, the dinners, outings to concerts, and of course Venice and Florence. Maybe it would once again be possible without the feelings of guilt that had kept her away?

Geraldine got up and pressed the bell for tea, then rejoined Verity on the sofa.

'Tell me, darling, how are all the family taking your mother's death?'

'In different ways. But on the whole I think bearing up well.

Frank seems the most affected and it's for that reason that I have decided to take a post where I can be nearer the family. I am going to be superintendent midwife at a small hospital in Bristol.'

'Oh – leaving London!' Geraldine looked dejected. 'I did so hope you would stay.'

'No, no. I must be nearer home.'

'I thought we could pick up where we left off, that we would see more of you, the days away, Florence – remember Florence?'

'Oh, I remember Florence,' Verity said with feeling. 'That was a wonderful holiday.'

Geraldine put her head on one side. 'Yet things never quite seemed the same after Florence. I never knew why. I thought in some way maybe I had offended you.'

'Oh no!' Verity clutched her hand. 'Not at all. You never offended me. You did nothing wrong. I became at that time very worried about Mother. Shortly after that her TB was first diagnosed.'

'Of course.' Geraldine nodded understandingly. 'But holidays, the days away, that sort of thing. Maybe again some time?'

'Oh, I'm sure,' Verity said, though she knew in her heart that such a thing would surely be unlikely.

'Not this year, unfortunately.' Geraldine gave a bashful smile followed by a meaningful pause. 'You see, I am going to have a baby.'

'Oh!' Then: 'What a lovely surprise!'

Verity thought Geraldine would understand, because she would misinterpret, her sense of shock.

'Isn't it marvellous news?'

'Marvellous. Of course.'

'We have been so dying for a son, but had practically given up hope after so long. Nothing ever happened.'

Geraldine bowed her head as if guilty of an indiscretion. Verity, fully conscious of the meaning of what her friend had told her, swallowed hard, determined to maintain her composure.

'I do hope your wish will be granted. Philip must be very happy.'

'He's ecstatic.'

'And his new work?'

Geraldine nodded. 'He's enjoying it very much.' She looked up at the clock. 'I hope he'll be in before you go. I know he would want to say hello to you.'

Alarmed, Verity stood up. 'I really should be going. I just popped in—'

Geraldine firmly pulled her down upon the sofa again. 'And I'm glad you did. You must stay for tea. I insist.'

'Very well.' Verity sank back on the sofa. Something in her rather did want to see Philip and have the chance to look into his eyes, as if that could tell him what a lying swine she thought he was.

'Ah, here is the tea.' Geraldine looked up with a smile as the maid came in carrying a laden tea-tray.

'How long have you known about the baby?' Verity tried to divert her glance from Geraldine's stomach, but to a trained midwife it was very difficult.

'Not very long. It is due at the end of the year. My doctor thinks I'm about four months pregnant.'

Verity thought that the cake, of which she had been given a very large slice, would turn to sawdust in her mouth. She knew that this was an emotional reaction and not the fault of the cook. She was literally choked, full of bile at the news Geraldine had given her.

The visit was turning into a considerable ordeal, but somehow she had felt it was something she must do. It was only polite to say goodbye. To have gone away without doing so might have given Geraldine food for thought.

'I really must go,' she said, swallowing her tea. 'I have some business to attend to.'

Geraldine looked at the clock with dismay. 'What shall I tell Philip?'

'Do give him my warmest congratulations.'

'I expect you'll meet at some medical conference.'

'I expect so.'

'Something obstetric.'

Both women laughed. As they rose Geraldine again took Verity's arm. 'I do miss you. I shall miss you, so much. Keep in touch, won't you?'

'You can be sure I will.'

They strolled into the hall and the maid appeared with Verity's coat and hat as the outer door opened and Philip walked in. He seemed at first quite shocked to see her, but rapidly composed his features into a welcoming smile.

'Verity. What a surprise. How good to see you.'

'And you, Philip.' Verity was aware that her response did not sound, could not sound, as warm as his. But it was essential to be as normal as possible for both their sakes.

'Come and have a glass of sherry.' Philip pointed to the drawing-room door but Verity shook her head.

'I can't. I have an appointment. Another time.'

Philip looked regretful. 'I hope so,' he said, handing his coat and case to the maid.

Geraldine pulled a face. 'Verity is leaving London, Philip. Isn't that awful?'

Her husband stuck his thumbs into the pockets of his waistcoat, which was threaded with a splendid gold watch chain.

'Oh dear. That is a pity. I was very sorry to hear about your mother, Verity. I suppose your departure is connected with that?'

'Yes, it is. The family need me.' Verity smiled at him sweetly. 'By the way, I was delighted to hear *your* news.'

'News?' Philip looked momentarily mystified.

'About the baby.'

'Oh yes. We're very pleased.' Philip studied the tips of his shiny black shoes. Then: 'Are you *sure* I can't offer you a sherry before you go?'

'Quite sure, thank you, Philip.' She turned and embraced

211

Geraldine, and the two women hugged each other for a few moments then kissed on both cheeks.

'Keep in touch,' Geraldine said.

'Oh, I shall, and give me news when the baby is born.'

'You will be among the first to know.'

Philip escorted her to the door. 'Come and see the baby.'

'Most certainly.'

Philip opened the door and gave a little bow. It was then that, temporarily out of sight of his wife, Verity turned and looked at him with the sort of contemptuous expression that only someone with whom one had once been intimate would be able to understand.

'Goodbye, Verity.' Philip lowered his eyes from that accusatory stare.

'Goodbye, Philip,' Verity replied and, turning, walked in an upright, dignified manner down the path towards the gate, confident that her erstwhile lover knew now exactly how she felt about him, and why.

'He said they didn't sleep together! That she had refused him marital relations for years. That seemed to me, in my folly, to make it all right. It was all lies. Now it's much, much worse. They're going to have a baby!'

Peg had never seen her sister, that elder sister she admired and looked up to, so distraught, and the sight was infinitely distressing. She had come home seeking counsel and advice from Verity, and now the positions were reversed and Verity was unburdening herself to her.

'You're the only one I can talk to' – Verity rubbed her fists into her eyes like a small child – 'now that Mum's no longer here.'

Peg put her hand on her sister's shoulder, feeling that it was a feeble, inadequate gesture in her attempt to comfort her.

'I'm sure Mum would understand,' she said. 'Mum would know what to do, what to say much better than me. I don't, Ver, except' – she paused – 'that I am *very*, very sorry.'

'You're a darling,' Verity murmured, pressing her hand.

They were sitting on the side of the hill overlooking the lake, and beyond that the church where their mother had so recently been laid to rest. Below them was the lodge, and slightly above them the castle.

This was home, Peg thought, looking around; dear familiar territory. She had spent most of her life here, a happy life, unaffected largely by the traumas that had afflicted her mother, who had always protected them and kept them safe, whatever happened to her.

In a way she wished that she could leave London, like Verity, and come back here; but maybe to cross the Channel and face what was happening on the continent, be in the thick of things, was a more adult thing to do than seek the security of home again. Maybe that also meant marriage, which was a risky and dangerous thing to contemplate too.

Verity had been forced to the countryside to get away from Philip, who had humiliated her, and also to fulfil the function she had promised Mother: as protector of the family.

'I feel such a *fool*.' Verity blew her nose hard. 'Being taken in by him. He *used* me.'

'You're not the one to blame.' Peg went on mechanically patting her shoulder. 'He is.'

Verity broke down again in a storm of tears, provoked by the extent of her indignation as well as by humiliation and remorse.

'I have always been religious,' she stammered, 'and this is what happens when you break the commands of God. We are given rules to follow and I failed to follow them and this is the consequence. I deserve my fate.'

'Nonsense,' Peg said robustly. 'You're being too hard on yourself.'

She broke off, not knowing exactly what to say, how to say it, what to do for the best, anxious not to exacerbate a difficult situation. She was deeply conscious of her youth, her woeful lack of experience. She may have covered riots and dangerous fires, excelled at political analysis of tortuous affairs at Westminster, impressed her superiors at work, but in matters of the heart she was a novice.

After a while Verity's storm of tears abated and she snivelled into her handkerchief: 'All men are liars. I shall never believe one again. Look at Rex. He deceived me too. He lied to me and told me he loved me. Philip told me he hadn't had relations with his wife for years yet all the time they were trying for a baby! How do you think that makes me feel?'

'Bad,' Peg went on, patting her back. 'But I don't think *all* men are liars. I don't think Alan would be, although' – a cloud briefly crossed her face – 'I'm not *absolutely* sure.'

'Alan is sweet.' Verity nodded, blowing her nose. Finally she tucked her handkerchief into her sleeve in what seemed like a final gesture and smiled. 'There. Better now. I'm sorry, Peg. I'm not going to break down again. I know I was a fool and I'm ashamed of myself. In a way I'm more fortunate than a lot of women disappointed in love. I have a job I like, a large and loving family. But I do so miss Mum,' she added soberly.

'We all do,' Peg said, then, hesitantly, as she was not sure whether Verity wanted to be bothered with somebody else's problems, which probably seemed trivial in comparison to hers: 'Alan is being sent abroad.'

'Oh dear.' Verity immediately looked concerned. 'Won't you miss him?'

'Terribly.' Peg leaned forward and, snapping off a blade of grass, stuck it between her teeth. 'But he wants me to go with him.' She looked gravely at her sister. 'He has asked me to marry him again.'

'And what did you say?' Now it was Verity's turn to put her arm round her sister. After all, hadn't Mum left her in charge? What right had she to behave like a snivelling schoolgirl, out of control, in front of a much younger woman who had problems of her own?

214

'I told him I'd think about it. I don't want to make a mistake. You see, I do like Alan very much. We do a lot together, all the time, and I would love to go abroad. It was my idea that the paper should have its own foreign correspondent, and I hoped Mr Moodie would send me.'

'Send *you*?' Verity looked aghast.

'Yes; it was a silly idea, wasn't it? Too young and, worse, he said, a woman!'

'Well, I'm glad he didn't send you. How did he know Alan?'

'He gave a dinner party in London to which I took Alan. Well, he asked me to.' She didn't add that Geraldine and Philip had been there, thinking that would add salt to the wound that already afflicted Verity so deeply.

'Last week Alan told me he'd been offered the job for a six-month trial.'

'Can't you go without being married?'

Peg shook her head. 'I couldn't leave the paper. Besides, I don't think Alan would consider it.'

'Alan has wanted to marry you for a long time. He's seizing his chance because he knows you want to go abroad.'

Peg nodded.

'And how do you feel?'

'Well, you know I don't love him. Or I don't *think* I do.'

'What *is* love?' Verity mused. 'That's what I can't fathom.'

'I imagine it's being swept off one's feet, as Addie was with Lydney Ryland and certainly was not with Harold. Perhaps we should take a lesson from that. Were you swept off your feet by Rex?' She looked curiously at her sister.

Verity shook her head. 'But I did know I loved Rex, deeply, and I wanted to marry him and have children and settle in a nice house in the Yorkshire Dales. I could see our lives as a long continuous thread, and it all seemed ideal. I was shattered when it broke down.'

She grew tremulous again as though that disaster reminded her

215

of her present misfortune. 'But it was not to be. You know' – she reached for Peg's hand – 'before she died Mum said that she wanted you and Alan to marry.'

'Mum said that?' Peg looked incredulous.

'She said she liked him very much, that he certainly loved you and would look after you. Mum wanted us all to be taken care of as she wouldn't be there to do it herself. She wanted me to tell you this if she didn't see you again, and she didn't. She died so suddenly. And you know Mum was very, very wise and far-seeing. Perhaps she was right.'

The two sisters fell silent, each buried in her own thoughts, and sat there for some time before walking down the hill to tea.

'I *like* having Aunt Peg and Aunt Verity here,' Jenny said, looking across the table at the two women. 'I like it with Daddy and Aunt Addie, and when Ed comes and Stella is back from school. I like us all as one happy family.'

'And we *are* a happy family, precious.' Addie leaned over and wiped some crumbs from her daughter's mouth, while the others looked on approvingly.

Indeed, Verity thought, it was a happy family and a united one, and for this they were most fortunate. Addie was proving a wonderful housekeeper and looked much happier in herself, and there was talk of a divorce from Harold. Mum had left a great gap, but she had also left a legacy behind her of love and mutual comfort. She had trained her daughters well. They were in a sense interdependent.

Even dear, grief-stricken Frank had perked up with all this loving care and attention, and was almost back to being his old cheerful self.

'When are you starting your job at the hospital?' Frank asked Verity.

'The week after next.'

'Looking forward to it?'

'Very much. I shall be able to see a lot more of you all. I shall try and come on all my days off. Take a lot more of the burden off Addie.'

'It will be like having you home again,' Addie said happily and Verity nodded.

'At last.'

Addie had always missed her elder sister, to whom she was closest when they were small, and the prospect of sharing much of Jenny's upbringing with her was so comforting.

As the three sisters washed up after tea Verity thought how quickly normality seemed to have returned, so that it was much as it had been when Mum was alive.

After tea and washing-up Addie took Jenny off to bed, following a protracted series of kisses and goodnights to each of the family in turn, including Stella, who had returned from choir practice and was having her tea.

Addie helped wash and undress Jenny and then sat on the bed as she said her prayers, hands clasped, eyes tightly shut. Since Cathy's death she always finished with: 'Please God, bring Mummy back.' She did so again tonight and as usual Addie said: 'Amen.' She then turned back the bedclothes and tucked Jenny up in bed with her teddy.

As she leaned over to kiss her, Jenny looked up at her with her large round blue eyes and said: 'Mummy isn't coming back, is she, Aunt Addie?'

'No, darling.' Addie smoothed her brow. 'She has gone to heaven.'

Jenny then pulled Addie towards her.

'Will *you* be my mummy, Aunt Addie?'

'Yes, Jenny,' Addie said gravely. 'I will.'

'For ever and ever?'

'For ever and ever!'

'You won't go to heaven like Mummy?'

'I hope not for a very long time.'

The little girl closed her eyes, her face lit by a contented smile, and Addie stood there for some time watching over her until she was fast asleep.

Downstairs she joined the little group by the fire. Frank was nodding over his newspaper; Verity, who always had to do something useful, was knitting, and Peg was chatting to Stella who was finishing her late tea.

Addie's face was flushed and Verity looked up from her knitting.

'Is anything wrong? Did something happen?'

'Something has happened,' Addie said with a smile. 'Jenny told me she wanted me to be her mother. Isn't that the nicest thing that could possibly happen?'

'Soon you will have to tell her the truth,' Verity said.

'I will.' Addie sank back in her chair. 'I'm going to tell her soon, but not too soon because I never want her to forget Mum and what we both owe her.'

Peg woke up before dawn when everything was still, the time of day she loved. Stella still slept quietly in the bed beside her and she thought first about the night before, the feeling of love and togetherness she'd had sitting round the table with Frank, Jenny and her sisters. It *was* a lovely and loving family.

The conversation with Verity also seemed to revolve round and round in her head. Mum had wanted her to marry Alan. Mum had always been so wise. Should she do what Mum wanted?

Maybe she did love Alan. She remembered her feelings when she had spontaneously kissed him in the park. She was horrified at the thought that he might go away. What would she do without him? Wasn't that feeling of dependence a kind of love? If you needed somebody so much?

Besides, it would be a chance for her to go abroad, to be, as his wife, an unofficial foreign correspondent. It would be so exciting to be there as events unfolded on a troubled continent.

It would be a completely new life, and yet . . .

The Blackbird's Song

Peg listened to the silence all around her with a feeling of tense anticipation, as if she was waiting for something: a message, a sign. And then it came, sweeping across from the hill on the other side of the valley: the sweet, piercing notes of the blackbird's song heralding a time of renewal and hope, of anticipation and fulfilment, now that the dark days of winter were over and the summer would soon be here.